Wayward
Saints

Wayward Saints

SUZZY ROCHE

voice

HYPERION • NEW YORK

"An Astronomical Question" by Hafiz, from *The Gift* © 1999 by Daniel Ladinsky.

Library of Congress Cataloging-in-Publication Data

Roche, Suzzy.
   Wayward saints / by Suzzy Roche. — 1st ed.
     p. cm.
   ISBN 978-1-4013-4177-0
   1. Women musicians—Fiction. 2. Mothers and daughters—Fiction. I. Title.
   PS3618.O3395W39 2011
   813'.6—dc23

                              2011022106

Hyperion books are available for special promotions and premiums. For details contact the HarperCollins Special Markets Department in the New York office at 212-207-7528, fax 212-207-7222, or email spsales@harpercollins.com.

Book design by Susan Walsh

FIRST EDITION

10 9 8 7 6 5 4 3 2 1

SUSTAINABLE FORESTRY INITIATIVE | Certified Fiber Sourcing
www.sfiprogram.org

THIS LABEL APPLIES TO TEXT STOCK

We try to produce the most beautiful books possible, and we are also extremely concerned about the impact of our manufacturing process on the forests of the world and the environment as a whole. Accordingly, we've made sure that all of the paper we use has been certified as coming from forests that are managed, to ensure the protection of the people and wildlife dependent upon them.

for Meg

Ma & Dad

Lucy & Stewart & Funque

What

Would

Happen if God leaned down

And gave you a full wet

Kiss . . .

. . . You would surely start

Reciting all day, inebriated,

Rogue-poems

Like

This

—Hafiz
from *The Gift*
by Daniel Ladinsky

PART

One

GLASGOW
1994

It was a Tuesday night at Crud, a club on the outskirts of the city, and the place was packed with skinheads and their girlfriends. Donal Hogan had said it was "a bit dungeonesque," but worse than that, it was a piss-hole toilet. Mary Saint stood behind the curtain by the side of the stage peeking out into the audience and cursed him. What was he thinking? This is a fucking shit sandwich——*Yer goona have ta troost me, Mary, next time you play in Glasgoo it'll be at Gustav's, fooking sold out.*

Sliced Ham had been all over England, blowing rooms away, mostly playing for college kids and hipsters, and Mary knew these weren't her people; they were savages——maybe even violent——they would eat the band alive. She noticed one goon in particular, his arms sticking out like legs of lamb, stained with tattoos. He was leaning on the edge of the stage with a whole line of other freaks, but he didn't seem to be hanging out with any of them. He scowled at the microphone where Mary was going to be standing, and every couple of minutes he'd say something to it. Christ, get me out of here, she thought. Who do these people think we are? Her legs were shaking with fear, and she was having trouble catching her breath. She held on to the red velvet curtain that was burned with cigarette holes and rubbed her lips up against it, trying to calm her nerves, as if it were a baby blanket.

If only she hadn't left the bottle of tequila in the dressing room. It was too close to showtime to run down to the basement and take another swig. She nervously checked her bra to see if her guitar picks were there and pulled up her indigo stockings, which were streaked with runs. Then, shaking her head back and forth, she bunched up her hair with her fingers, making sure not to disturb the bluebird feather she had pinned into a curl. It was a gift from the new bass player. He'd slipped it to her after the sound check, saying, "I'm an expat, too." What the hell, she'd wear it for the show.

Impatient, she spit on the floor, which was sticky from the fat-fuck-monitor-man's beef stew that he'd eaten half of—cold—out of the can. It had been knocked over in the sound check, and left there. She kicked at it with her high-heeled shoes like a wild horse, as if to say, Let's get this thing going before I bolt. Where the fuck was the band?

One by one they came up from the dressing room, heads drooping, shifting from foot to foot; the drummer flicked his cigarette down to the floor, and they all waited in a line in the tiny backstage area. The gray concrete wall by the stage was signed by some of the bands that had played there: the Four Broke Blokes, the Don't Ask Mes, Jed Syringe and the Shoot Ups. The Shoot Ups had left an illustration, somebody's idea of a masterpiece: an intricate pencil drawing of a couple of faceless vaginas with stick figure arms and legs that were dancing like chorus girls, in front of an audience of penises. The artist had given the penises eyes, noses, and in some cases beards. There were also assorted asses, tits, and guitars, scribbles and flowers, swastikas, hearts, and messages like BIG BARF BAG LOVES SHEENA and BOINK ME, BITCH. Mary leaned her head up against the wall, covered her face with her arm, and tried to breathe slowly to calm her heart. "I need help with this," she whispered to the wall.

The lights went down and the crowd raised its collective voice into a scream. Mary looked behind her to see if the band was ready.

"Go," she said as if she was the only soldier, leading unsuspecting farmers into a battle that she knew they couldn't win.

They stomped onto the stage and picked up their instruments. Mary's red electric guitar threw refracted light across the audience, which was packed into the dark cellar; she strummed down hard, and the crowd went dumb. Her voice was creamy and clear, spiked with agony, and like a hatchet it cut into their brains.

You wanna fuck, fuck, fuck, fuck, fuck, fuck, fuck me . . .

She couldn't hear herself. She turned to the monitor guy and yelled, "Turn it up, asshole!" The crowd screeched praise, and the magic of Mary Saint exploded over them.

Mary wasn't pretty; she was exotically beautiful, and she had no idea. She thought she was plain as a paper lunch bag. Her hair, a nest of black loose curls, flew around her wide face, her skin was pale and smooth, and her cheeks had a natural tint. She could have been a breakable china doll, except for her dark raccoon eyes, which marked her expression with perpetual melancholy, giving her the look of an abandoned child. Her eyelids were painted with too much sparkling raspberry goop, and her lips were wide and full, glistening with red. She'd glued a tiny silver star below her left eye.

The spotlight and the specials were on her, and they created a halo around her head in the smoky haze. She looked toward heaven, crazily, like a bird whose wing was hooked into a gate. Her breasts were large, too large for such a small-boned girl, and she offered them up to the room. She could have been a teenage hooker who was being forced to dance for old men. Standing tall on her skinny legs, her full hips swaying underneath satin boxer shorts, she let her hands explore her body; they went between her legs, they caressed her arms and face and breasts, and they danced in the sacred space around her, like everyone in the room wished they could do.

The skinheads and their girlfriends were hard to pull in; she had to work for it, and in the guitar break during the second song, "I Pee Like a Girl," she knelt down in front of the guy with the leg of lamb arms, and spoke to him, nothing he could possibly hear, but she touched her wet lips to the rim of his ear, and the crowd went nuts. It turned out that they were her people after all, they already knew her songs, and had memorized them. They wanted to be loved, and once they saw her look upon them with desire, they surrendered like kids lost in a fairy tale, swaying back and forth, their porcupine hairdos, skull rings, and pierced lips fluttered in the shadowy shift of red and blue lights. They might have even sucked their thumbs if they'd been alone. Careful not to make noise until a song was done, many of them mouthed her words, and then, at the close of every tune, they rose together in a collective moan to ask for more; raising their fists into the air, they chanted, "Ma-ry! Ma-ry!" She led them through the wilderness of her songs, allowing the lines of the lead guitar to carry her deep into the obliteration of her self. At one point, she looked out into the crowd and said, "Oh, there you are," and everybody thought she was their new best friend. But good-bye was what she was thinking. Good-bye. She opened her mouth and sang with the shattered heart she knew she had, its splinters flew from the stage. *I sing for you, I sing for you* . . .

Later, she remembered the vague feeling of surprise—*they're actually letting me fly*—she could pinpoint the exact instant when she dove into the void, a place that she had visited many times in her mind, in her dreams, in her moments of clear sadness, a pool where angels swam without their wings, where devils were free to stab and boil children. It all happened in a flash of stunned silence, after the last chord came crashing down on "The Back of My Ass," when nobody clapped and nobody screamed. It passed quickly, but for Mary, it was the heart of her triumph. I'm home, she thought. The fans followed her as far as they could, their eyes teary and stoned with reverence, but she went beyond, leaving them aching, their hearts melted and their brains branded. She'd had to pay a price, something private, unknown to them, so lonely, and yet she drove herself—on their backs—into her own oblivion.

When Sliced Ham finished their last song they left the stage but were called back four times, and when Mary Saint had had enough, she stormed off abruptly, turning once to blow a kiss to someone; but no one could figure out to whom.

After the show, in the bowels of Crud, thousands of miles

from home, she sat slumped in the ratty armchair in the dressing room, licking the rim of the bottle of tequila the band had passed around, and thought hard about short, bald Donal Hogan, the serious Irish guy with the bow tie, whom she'd met in the pub in London the Saturday night she'd arrived in England, ten months before. The place was wall to wall with kids who were drinking warm beer and smoking joints. After she'd downed her first few glasses of ale, she'd stood on her barstool and sang "Man in the Airplane Bathroom." The room had quieted, and Donal had elbowed through the crowd and slipped her his card.

"How the fook old are yeh? Sixteen?" he'd said.

"I'm twenty, darling," she'd said.

"Where'd yeh coom froom?"

"Made in the USA."

"Yer fooking brilliant, yer holy," he'd whispered into her ear, and his breath was so repulsive, she'd backed away. But he'd smiled at her in the most genuine way, and she'd gone right for his mouth, sticking her tongue deep inside.

"Put yer hoort in my hand," he'd said, lifting his delicate palm up to her breast. "You're goon a be a staar." She realized, now, that he was right. Up till now, it had been a gas, a good old time, but something had snapped tonight, and the power of it was coming back at her hard. She was transfixed in front of a cosmic mirror, looking at herself, but she was somebody even more ferocious than she'd thought she was.

Later, on the all-night trek back to London, in the van that Donal's friend Ricky Boyle was driving, when the rest of the band had fallen off to sleep, with their heads bent sideways and vibrating against the windows, Mary was wide awake. She peered out at the sky and saw the billions of stars. Big fucking deal. Each one was just a ball of burning fire. And then she saw the sliver of the moon, and there was someone swinging from its point. *I sing for you.*

Two
....

SWALLOW, NEW YORK
June 2010

*At the crack of dawn, when the streetlamps were still glow-*ing and the day was already warm, Jean Saint drove down Swal-low's empty gray roads, past the duck pond and the elementary school, where the passerine birds that gave the town its name were perched in a long line, high up on a telephone wire, wait-ing to greet the sun. Weary with age, Swallow—population five thousand—sat nestled in a valley between Ingleton Mountain and Spider Lake. To a stranger passing through, it might appear that nothing had changed in this town for fifty years, and yet, that was an illusion. The citizens of Swallow struggled to keep abreast, like the rest of America, propelled by prescription drugs, overburdened by gadgetry and technology, grappling with the word *global,* and coping with a broken economy (which, for Swallow, seemed to be a perpetual condition). Still, the people preferred to live modestly; a five-and-ten thrived on Main Street, and you could still get an old-fashioned jelly doughnut at the bakery.

Jean turned left at the Presbyterian church and passed the bike shop, slowly creeping down Main, where parking spots were plentiful at this hour. She was the first one into Fred's Papers and Mags.

Fred had only just switched on the lights and was bent down on one knee cutting the strings off the morning paper when the bells jingled on the door.

"You scared the bejesus out of me, Jean. What brings you out so early?" he said, breathing hard.

"Well, I'll be needing a couple extra copies of the paper today, Fred," she said importantly. "There's an article about my daughter in the 'What's On' section. She's doing a concert over at the high school next week."

"Of course she is, the whole damn town's talking about it. My granddaughter has been tweeting about it. Don't you think I won't be there, hearing aid and all. You must be proud."

Not realizing what *tweeting* was, Jean had a brief moment of feeling sorry for Fred, assuming that he must be getting a little mixed up with his words. "Well, I don't like to brag, but just between us two, I am a little bit proud. I'll take five copies."

"Huh?" said Fred.

"Five," said Jean, a little louder.

Fred looked up at her. "Why, Jean, that's quite a hairdo you've got."

Jean took a deep inhale. She'd mistakenly asked her neighbor, Celeste, a retired stylist, to cut her hair, just to save herself the trouble and expense of going down to Nadine, at Hair on Mane. It had been a mistake. Her bangs were crooked, as if they'd been chewed, not trimmed. She'd have to go to Nadine after all.

"Honestly, Fred, I didn't have a chance to fix myself up this morning," said Jean, annoyed, and she quickly checked her reflection in the window of the store. She was dismayed by what she saw and couldn't help thinking she looked like an old lady wearing a silver cereal bowl on her head. Haircuts had long been a source of frustration for her, but what business was it of his?

"I think you look swell," said Fred as he handed her the stack of papers. Jean embraced them as if they were a bunch of roses that she'd just been given after winning first prize in a beauty contest, and was so flustered that she rushed out of the store, forgetting to pay. Fred figured he'd catch her the next time she came in.

When Jean finally got her Chrysler safely back into the garage and carried the papers to the kitchen, she used all her restraint to put up the coffee before she would allow herself to flip through looking for the article. She carefully measured four heaping spoonfuls of Chock Full O'Nuts into the percolator and plugged it in, then pulled her favorite mug out of the cupboard, the one with the thin rim and handle, which had YOU CAN'T SCARE ME, I HAVE KIDS painted on the face of it. Jean popped two slices of Arnold bread into the toaster. She lifted the top off the butter dish, which she had taken out of the fridge as soon as she woke up, so the butter would be perfectly soft for toast. Though she was about to bust, she slowed yet again and set out her china plate, which she had glued together after dropping it last year (its edge was still chipped), and placed the napkin and knife in perfect alignment, even taking a moment to further adjust them. Only then did she allow herself to be seated and pick up the paper.

To her surprise, right there on the bottom of the front page was a small picture of her daughter and a caption that read, "Mary Saint of Sliced Ham—see 'What's On.'" She felt her heart pump. It was odd to see Mary's face on the front page of *The*

Woodside. Jean quickly turned the pages, skipping past the headline about the plane crash in India—*Good God*—past the traffic violations section; they'd nabbed another unsuspecting out-of-towner who was passing through at the stop sign at Main and Cherry—*what a racket*—the fire at the hardware store; John Stokes had tossed a cigarette butt in the garbage pail—*dope*—past the editorial on the mayor's outburst at the last council meeting—*what else is new?*—until she saw the familiar "What's On" logo, and there was Mary's face, consuming half the page. The photo was almost too big, embarrassingly big, and it had been taken at least ten years earlier. There was Mary in a pout, with a ring through her nose and her eyes heavily lined. The caption read, "Hometown Girl, Mary Saint from Sliced Ham, comes to Swallow High for a Solo Concert." Anyone could see that she was a pretty girl under all the makeup, but Jean was sorry they didn't have a better picture, perhaps one where she was smiling. It occurred to Jean that her daughter looked *poor*, and she hoped no one else would think that.

Jean took a moment to rub her eyes, and then she looked around her kitchen, trying to reassure herself, but for all its gleaming red tiles and imitation Kohler faucets, her dream kitchen was highly imperfect, the counters and cabinets cheap, reminding her of the poverty that shaped her childhood. The workmanship at East Swallow Meadows was of the cut-corners variety, and it pained her to admit it was made only to *look* expensive. For some reason, whenever she was the slightest bit agitated, her mind seized on the imperfections in her home, a nervous habit, she supposed, and she could not stop herself. Jean returned to the paper, her stomach swarming.

The article talked about the success of Sliced Ham, with Mary as the pivotal member, primary songwriter, and lead singer. It told the story of how Mary had left Swallow in the early 1990s at the ripe old age of eighteen to find her heart's desire, and within two years had made her way across the Atlantic, only to fall in with a scene of young musicians in London and form a band. Sliced Ham had "burned through the United Kingdom like a California wildfire," according to *The Woodside,* and by the time the band came to perform in America, Sliced Ham was already a "hit with the hip," and Mary Saint was "the fearless Goddess of Guts." Now, at age thirty-six, "Ms. Saint will be heading back to her hometown to strut her stuff alone." The article went on to describe the breakup of the group in 2003, shortly after the demise of the bass player, Garbagio, "whose tragic death was the result of a fall from a hotel balcony."

Damn it all, thought Jean, why did they have to go and mention that? What will people think? She remembered what she had thought when she first heard about it; for a moment she had wondered who Garbagio could possibly be. Who would name a boy Garbagio? He was probably someone dirty with a name like that. What else could it be? What foolishness. How horrible that his mother had had to hear her son was dead: the sobbing, the rage, and on top of it, that name. For what? He wasn't even a soldier, he was just a—who knows? Jean couldn't have even imagined who or what he was back then. *Garbagio,* obviously a stage name. Now that the article was out, she was sure that the great tongues of Swallow were flapping about all this nonsense. She wished the article had not delved into the past.

Jean guessed it was possible that people assumed Mary had a

stage name, too, and she hoped that wasn't true. There was just something about *Mary Saint*—she had to admit it could seem fake, showy. In reality, when Mary was barely eight years old, she used to entertain her mother, pretending to be a famous actress. It was the first time Jean had had any idea Mary was interested in being on a stage, for she had always been so shy. *Mommy, VaVaVa is my first name, Voom is my last name. Get it? VaVaVa Voom.* Jean used to laugh out loud.

It didn't say in the article, but Jean knew the private, tragic story of Garbagio's death, for Mary had kept in touch with her mother over the years through a stream of letters, which was like a string that Jean held on to, having lost sight of the kite it was attached to, in the endless blue of the sky. Jean knew about much of what had happened: the drugs, the shame of it. She wished that none of it had to be dredged up, printed in the paper for all to see. After all, the whole thing had been an accident, and so much time had passed. Why couldn't they just talk about the upcoming concert? She was beginning to dread the idea all over again.

The bread popped up out of the toaster, and Jean poured herself a coffee and scraped the butter across her toast. She looked out the window at the overgrown field behind her house; those weeds, the ones with the small white flowers, were still climbing through the lattice fence, and she remembered that Mr. Thoreau, the gardener, had told her they were called hairy bittercress. The thought crossed her mind that Hairy Bittercress could be a stage name, too, and she smiled at her own joke. Mary might find that funny; she must remember to mention it to her.

The truth was it could easily have been Mary who fell off the balcony. Throughout her childhood, even though Mary was fiercely obedient, she had been drawn to the bad seeds in the classroom and had continued following lowlifes every step of the way. I'm not perfect, either, thought Jean, fingering the medal of Our Lady of Lourdes that hung around her neck, before returning to the article.

Plenty of things weren't mentioned in the paper—thank God—the breakdown, the three months at the rehab hospital, the one particular *letter,* and the lingering heartache. Mary's and Jean's. No one wrote about the brutality at home under the heavy hand of Bub, husband and father, now in Three Forks Home, impaired from a stroke. No one seemed to know or wonder about that. Good. It was over now.

Jean had started a new life, leaving the memories of the west side of Swallow behind, and it was no one's business. When she moved into East Swallow Meadows, the upscale new housing community with the sweet movie-set streets, her life had improved. Except for the fact that she was told what flowers she was allowed to plant, what color her house had to be, and whether or not she could tie a ribbon on the wreath of her front door.

She picked up the napkin, wiped the crumbs from her mouth, and took another sip of coffee, looking once more to the open field. There was that damn hairy bittercress again. She decided that on Monday she'd really have to get after Mr. Thoreau to make sure he poisoned the heck out of it. She had to admit in some ways it was pretty, but a weed like that would grow all over the yard and ruin the grass.

Jean sat for a long time at the table, her eyes wandering way past the field to where she could see the faint outline of Ingleton Mountain. Mary had been her miracle child; at thirty-seven, after years of disappointment—month after month—Jean had finally conceived, even when Dr. Stevens said it was probably not going to happen and had made the suggestion that she look into adopting, which was totally out of the question. Jean had endured sex with Bub for years in the darkness of their bed with the hope of having a child. But the day that she learned the news, she felt it had all been worth it. She was released from her barrenness like a butterfly that had been set free after being held under a paper cup by a cruel child.

The pregnancy was easy—Jean hadn't been plagued by morning sickness or swelling legs—and when it turned out that Mary was a girl, Jean couldn't have been happier. Bub, however, couldn't hide his disappointment that the baby wasn't a boy, and though throughout the pregnancy it had seemed as if they might be able to make a fresh start, the euphoria didn't last. He tried to love his little girl, he just didn't know how, and in fact, Jean suspected that for Bub having a *female child*—as she'd heard him refer to Mary—reflected poorly on his masculinity.

But Jean adored her daughter. Mary was a quiet, sleepy baby and a somber child, sensitive to a fault; she'd cry at the drop of a hat and was so shy that she spent much of her time clinging to the hem of Jean's dress, and hiding behind her knees. Once in school, Mary proved to be smart and conscientious, but all her teachers delicately remarked that she seemed melancholy and had trouble making friends. There was the time Mary was sent home for wetting her pants. She must have been about seven years old. The awful old nun, Mother Superior they called her (what a perfect name), had forced Mary to take off her soaked underpants right there in the principal's office, and then she had Mary get down on her knees and search, bare-assed, through a plastic bag of spare ones that she kept in her closet, apparently collected from other children. Once home, Mary was wild with tears and could not be consoled. Bub, in an effort to stop the crying, slapped her across the face and sent her to her room without supper. Jean didn't dare intercede on her daughter's behalf, careful not to set him off further, since the slapping had recently progressed into paddle whipping, a step that seemed dangerous to Jean, though she had no idea how to stop it. During dinner, Bub sat sober-sided, chewing his pork chops in silence, with that horribly ashamed look on his face, his eyes misted with tears. That was always the problem; he suffered just as much as they did.

Later, Jean heard Mary whimpering long into the night. As usual, the three of them got up the next morning, never acknowledging that anything had happened. Bub cracked a few jokes, called Mary a coo-coo head at breakfast, and that was the end of it. But it was around that time that Mary started praying, incessantly. She'd sit in the wooden rocking chair in the corner of the living room with her blue plastic rosary beads entwined in her hands and rock back and forth, sometimes softly singing the Hail Marys to the tune of "Go Tell Aunt Rhody." She rocked so much that there were marks on the rug. Bub thought it was wonderful. But Jean thought it was, well, *ugly*, like a retarded person she had seen on the sidewalk outside a dress shop, several towns over.

Why bother thinking about any of this? None of it mattered anymore, although this week, with Mary coming . . . Jean wished it could be nice. Nice was all she had ever wanted, and nice was what she finally had on the east side of Swallow. The two sides of town were like different worlds to Jean, so much so that she rarely went across Main Street anymore.

She did have her crosses to bear, though, and getting irritated was one of Jean's greatest faults. People could drive her crazy; for instance, that pain in the neck Adele Graham, who worked at the bakery and also sat on the board of the Owners Association for East Swallow Meadows, was just the sort that could really irk Jean. But everyone agreed on Adele, she was nobody's idea of a good time, and Jean would be damned if Adele, or anyone else, was going to nip her excitement. Mary Saint was her daughter, she was coming back home to do a concert in town, there was a big article in the paper, and Jean was thrilled. Let the past be in the past.

But around noon on that same June day, a week before the concert, Jean came face-to-face with Adele, who was behind the counter at the Silver Tray. She was the one who had snickered when Jean first told her about the concert. Everyone in town had heard earfuls about how Adele's son played a tuba in the St. Louis Philharmonic Orchestra, and apparently Adele and her son held the opinion that if it isn't classical, it isn't music. Maybe someone had finally told Adele that Jean's daughter was on *The Tonight Show* once, because she was whistling a different tune now.

"Oh, hi, Jean," said Adele, her hair in a net. "Are there any tickets left?" she asked, peering over the slits of her turquoise glasses, pretending that she didn't really care.

"You'll have to check at the high school" was all that Jean would say. After all, why should she facilitate the tickets? Sure, now Adele wants to go, now that there's an article in *The Woodside*. Get your own damn tickets, thought Jean.

"I can't imagine it's all sold out," said Adele as she handed over the mini cherry pie that Jean had ordered.

"Well, I don't know, there was quite a lengthy article in the paper today, didn't you see it?"

"No, I must have missed it," said Adele. She looked beyond to the next customer.

Missed it, thought Jean, it was big as an elephant. As she pushed the screen door to leave the shop, she vowed to go to the Bread Bin from now on, even though it was a town away.

Three

WILLOW CEMETERY
October 2009

Nine months before the article in The Woodside, *and* before Mary Saint's concert at the high school, in the village of Crest Falls, thirty miles northwest of Swallow, an elderly couple made their way to Willow Cemetery. It was a brilliant autumn day. Once they'd pulled into the parking lot, Vincent Calabrese got out of his car and went around to lift his wife's wheelchair from the trunk. He was built like an ox; his broad round shoulders gave way to strong hairy arms, and his muscular legs were like a set of parentheses, causing his knees to stick out sideways. He paused for a moment to look at the gold and red leaves on the maple trees that lined the iron fence around the cemetery. After he lugged the chair out and opened it up, he went to help his wife.

"What a gorgeous day, Mrs. Calabrese," he said as he pulled the handle on the car door. "Look at those fine leafy trees blowing against the sky—what brilliant colors—and how about those big white clouds. It's magic, Mrs. C. I must say, I think you've got a best friend up in heaven. You're one lucky lady."

Vivian Calabrese stared blankly at her husband as he buttoned up her sweater and prepared to help her out of the car. These days he could never tell what she understood.

"Let's go visit Anthony," said Vincent. Vivian gave a vague smile, the kind that had become more and more frequent since she'd been diagnosed. He rearranged the yellowed pillow, which was flattened against the back of the wheelchair, just to make sure she'd be comfortable. He put her arms around his neck, pausing to kiss her on the lips and hold her face between his palms. Her hair was wispy white and her face was as smooth as a pearl, and through her skin, just beneath the surface of her face, little blue veins were showing like roads on a map. He hoisted her up and set her into the chair with a thump, then took out the red and white carnations, which were wrapped in brown paper in the backseat of the car, and placed them on her lap, folding her hands around them.

"Now, you hold on tight to these, Mrs. C."

He steered her up the familiar path, past the flower beds and the grand mausoleums, until they arrived at what the cemetery called the affordable mausoleums, which were smaller but, to Vincent's mind, still vulgar. It was here that they turned left to where the simple gravestones were lined up with only several feet to separate them. They passed a newly dug grave, with dirt piled to its side; the flowers had already been brought from the funeral home, and across one of the arrangements was a silver sash that said TIMMY. None of the mourners were there yet, so Vincent stopped for a moment. No man is named Timmy, he thought, it must be a boy. Vincent paused further and bowed his head. He pulled one of the carnations from the bundle on his wife's lap and set it over the mound of dirt.

They made their way to Anthony. They had felt lucky to get this particular plot, for it had a small cherry tree next to it. Years ago, in the spring, when Anthony had died, the day they placed him in the ground, the pink blossoms from the tree blew across his grave, and Vivian had loved that. They were both broken with grief that day, but Vincent would always remember the moment when Vivian had put her arm around him as he wept and blew his nose.

She'd said, "Look there, Mr. Calabrese. The tree, it's a gift from God, to you and me and Anthony." He had marveled at her faith, for he had nothing to rely on, even after all those years of going to church, in the face of Anthony's death, he felt utterly abandoned—to hell with church, to hell with God; he was done. He had wondered what kind of a cruel God would let such a thing occur, and he had no use for a world that could continue on without his son; he didn't know how he was going to live another day.

At the time, Mr. and Mrs. Calabrese didn't realize that no one else wanted the plot for precisely the reason that the tree was there. It was bigger now after all these years; today its arms were reaching to the sky, and especially on such an autumn day, even without the blossoms, it was still a sight to see. Vincent rolled his wife up to the stone. For a moment they remained silent, and then Vincent closed his eyes and sang:

> *Feet and knuckles*
> *In the garbage*
> *Don't suck on the bones*
> *Animals should not be eaten*
> *Stick to greens and ice cream cones*

Vivian smiled until her teeth showed, and she threw the carnations up in the air, watching them fall out of their paper wrapper and scatter over Anthony's grave. She clapped her hands as well as she could, and Vincent sang some more:

Feet and knuckles
Piles of bullshit
Don't believe the lies
Living things belong to nature
Can't you hear the piggy's cries?

"I like that song!" cried Vivian, as if waking from a deep sleep.

"I knew you would, Mrs. C; it's Anthony's song. Remember how funny it is? Now look what you did, the flowers are everywhere," said Vincent, and he laughed into the fresh air, raised his arms, and shouted, "This is my son!" proclaiming it to the other graves, to the cherry tree, and to the carnations, which were lying this way and that. "Anthony, my boy!"

"Anthony," said Vivian, clapping her hands.

Vincent took her left hand and kissed it, then bent over his son's grave and set about wiping the dirt off the letters on the stone. This was where they all would sleep together someday, it wasn't supposed to be Anthony first, but that was what it was.

He bent down on his knees and with his forefinger traced the words, making sure that no dirt was stuck in any of the letters. He wanted the whole world to see:

ANTHONY CALABRESE, BELOVED SON, MUSICIAN
"GARBAGIO"

Four
· ·

SWALLOW, NEW YORK
June 2010

After the incident with Adele at the Silver Tray, Jean called Betty Dunster, her best friend, who worked at the rectory as the house secretary and personal assistant to St. Clare's beloved pastor, Father Benedict.

"Hello, Rectory," said Betty.

"Hi, Betty, it's me," said Jean.

"Oh, Jean! Did you see the paper? That was some spread they gave Mary. Father Ben was so impressed. He's going to come to the concert next week!"

"How nice," Jean said, but she felt a spike of panic down both her arms.

"I was thinking," said Betty, "how about if I had a little gathering at my place afterward? I could invite a bunch of us from the choir, Father Ben, some of the gang from East Swallow Meadows, and anyone else you could think of."

Jean doubted that her daughter would ever agree to such a get-together, and anyway, it might not be such a good idea. The thought of Mary standing in Betty's spotless living room, on Betty's white rugs—*what if somebody spilled something?*—with members of the choir and—God forbid—Father Ben, did not seem plausible, and yet she didn't want to be rude.

"Betty, that's so kind of you. I don't know, it's such a lot of fuss. I'll run the idea by Mary, but she's never been one for parties. I'll tell you one person I wouldn't invite, though. Adele Graham. Can you believe that she actually asked for a free ticket?" Jean lied.

"Oh, Jean, she's a pill, just ignore her. Nobody likes her. As for a gathering, it would be my pleasure. How often does something like this happen? I don't think I've ever known a celebrity before. Why didn't you tell me that Mary was famous?"

"I'm not sure she's *famous,* Betty," Jean said. But she had the thought, for the first time, that maybe Mary was.

Mary's success in Sliced Ham had come and gone in the space of about seven or eight years and had been a bewildering surprise to Jean. As a girl, Mary always wrote what she referred to as *praying songs,* though Jean thought of them as nothing more than a child's simple musings. They seemed to grow out of her obsession with saying the rosary. But as Mary turned the corner into puberty, the songs took on a different quality; they became ominous and sorrowful. Jean had made the mistake of giving Mary a guitar for her thirteenth birthday, she'd found it in a lawn sale and wrapped it in newspaper. It came with a flimsy cardboard case and a simple instructional book, and when Mary tore the paper off and saw what it was, she embraced it and told her mother it was an angel. She went about teaching herself to play, and her devotion to the instrument seemed to replace her compulsion to say the rosary. She carried the guitar around the house like a suitcase.

For the first few years of high school, Mary was a sad-eyed teenager strumming songs in her room with the door locked, but then all hell broke loose. In the fall of her junior year, she announced that she was joining a band with some kids from another town. Bub finger-wagged, mocked her for thinking she could sing, and warned that he would take an ax to her guitar, but Mary did not back down like she usually did, and one night when she came home late, Bub belted Mary in the face, giving her a black eye. That time, Jean tried to get between them, so he grabbed her by the shoulders and shook her hard enough to pull a muscle in her neck. In the heat of his rage, he threatened to choke his wife to death.

It was then, as if cracking out of an egg, that a new Mary emerged; she became downright vicious, and it just kept getting worse. There were nights she didn't even come home. By the beginning of her senior year, within months of her eighteenth birthday, she was mouthing off to Bub regularly, giving back whatever he gave, grabbing at umbrellas, coat hangers, spatulas, brooms, or—most frightening—kitchen knives, whenever he got near her, which only further ignited his fury. And the fighting escalated until she left home one Saturday in September with a car full of boys.

Jean had watched from the living room window as Mary threw her guitar and pillowcase, stuffed with clothes, into the trunk of the car and screamed "Burn in hell!" to her father.

Bub was standing on the front steps in his slippers, his hairy stomach hanging over his boxer shorts, warning her that she would never amount to anything but a slut. Jean hadn't seen any of those boys before. The car they were in was spray-painted with every color imaginable. The Kelseys and the Yarmacs were in their yards gardening, and they stood clutching their rakes and shovels, watching the whole display as if they didn't have their own problems. Everyone knew that Pat Kelsey was a drunk, and forget about the Yarmacs, each of the four of them went to their own psychiatrist.

Still, it was not okay, none of it. One of the most stinging discoveries came weeks later, when Jean was looking through her file cabinet for an old credit card bill and happened to notice that the file labeled MARY was sticking up. When she examined the folder, though the old report cards and school pictures were in there, Mary's birth certificate was missing. Jean realized her daughter had known what she was doing. It wasn't the spur-of-the-moment escape that it had seemed to be; there had been a plan.

The very day that Mary ran off, Jean moved herself into the small guest room in the basement of the house. She made meatballs and spaghetti for dinner and put a plate in front of Bub in silence, taking her own plate down to her room, where she sat in peace and ate, looking out the half window, which was about six inches above the grass. And that was how it continued on. Bub grew colder, Jean remained aloof, and they spoke only when it was necessary. He couldn't scare her anymore; whatever he dished out, she took, stone-faced. She had her job at Carlyle and Benson, the household appliance company, while Bub, who had always had trouble keeping a job, remained unemployed and pretty much sat in a chair all day as far as Jean could tell. In spite of herself, she felt sorry for him; he suffered tremendously during those years after Mary left, before he was struck down by the stroke. He had few friends and not much of a life.

There was the one priest who came to visit him periodically; Father Aloysius, a benevolent beanpole of a man and a childhood acquaintance of Bub's, was in charge of a convent of nuns somewhere farther upstate. He and Bub would sit together stirring their instant coffees and discuss what was happening in the church. It irritated Jean, all the talk about religion and not one word about what mattered in this world, like how about being civil to your wife, for example. But what would Father Al know about that? Once Jean had pulled Father Al aside and asked him to intercede, to talk to Bub about his problems, but Father Al's eyes glazed over, he smiled, took Jean's hand, and limply shook it, as if he had the starring role in a play called *Priest*.

Bub had one other friend, the strange, troubled boy in his early twenties, Larry Ferguson, who lived a block away, on Tuttle Court. It had started as one of those parish "big brother" type things; Larry's parents were divorced, and the kid was straying into trouble when Bub volunteered, much to Jean's surprise, to *mentor* him. Perhaps Bub was fueled by guilt or even loneliness, Jean had no idea, but it was the first time he'd ever stepped up to do anything at the church.

When the doorbell rang, Jean would lead the boy, whose face was littered with whiteheads, swollen pimples, and razor nicks, down to the den, and he and Bub would spend an hour or so talking in low tones. From what Jean could tell, the boy would confide in him, and she could hear Bub's calm, gentle, encouraging tone; he was probably giving advice, which Jean thought was laughable. He was never able to be generous or patient with Mary, and Jean couldn't tell if it enraged her or broke her heart to hear him be kind to the boy.

Later, after the stroke, Larry came to the door one day, back from the service, spruced up in his uniform, and Jean brought him down to see Bub, who was sitting with his head cocked to the left, unable to speak. She regretted that. The kid stood, his lower lip trembling, and said, "Mr. Saint, it's me, Larry." But after a few minutes of watching Bub drool, he turned to Jean and said a polite good-bye, ran up the stairs and out the door, never to return.

It was awful because the boy hanged himself in his mother's closet six months later, and Jean wondered if the two incidents were connected. She wasn't sure that she hadn't been punishing the young man by letting him see Bub like that; he'd been the sole recipient of Bub's decency, maybe even love, and Jean resented it. Larry only reminded Jean that Bub had wanted a son instead of a daughter, and whatever else he wanted, she could not provide that, either, though for years she had tried every which way to please him. She had made his meals, washed and folded his clothes with care, and aside from being slapped around and sitting by while her daughter was slapped around as well, she'd even succumbed to what seemed to her his barbaric sexual appetite, not to mention his cruel words.

Through it all, though, she knew that, without him, there would be no Mary. In spite of everything, whenever she prayed, she thanked God for giving her a daughter, and she remained dutiful to Bub, no matter what, because a wife is a wife.

How many years ago had Jean fallen in love with him? When

she was eighteen, she had gotten a job at the steel factory, sign-
ing up men for hire. Bub (his name on the application read Bixby
Saint) had come in with a group of his buddies to apply for a job;
he was a ball of energy, cracking jokes and slapping guys on the
back. Big and burly, with a bushy head of black curls, Bub had
made her laugh until she cried. Within a week, he'd asked her
out, but he didn't take her to the movies, or even for an ice cream
soda; he took her down by the dock to see the sunset, and they
sat on a log, watching the garbage barges and the fishing boats go
by, and she'd fallen for him by the time the moon rose. She had
loved his touch, found his jokes funny, and believed in his goodness, but that was a lifetime ago. It was only a few months after
they were married that the raging outbursts began, and Jean
started to suspect that not only was her husband troubled but he
was dumb.

But the day in September when Bub drove Mary from home,
Jean's iron gate came down. She could not forgive him; though
she continued to tend to his daily needs, her compassion for her
husband shriveled like an untied balloon. Bub made several attempts to reconcile with Jean; he'd try to joke with her, or else
he'd stay in bed all day, as if he were sick, but she remained un-
moved. Once he knocked lightly at her basement door. When
she opened the door, he stood before her with his hands in his
pockets.

"Jean, when will you come back to me?" he said, pleading.
"I need your love." She'd never heard him say *love* before. She
found it striking, his choice of words, as if she didn't have needs
of her own. She realized, by then, that he really didn't know
much about love, had probably never truly been loved until she

had fallen so deeply for him. He'd been ruined before she ever said hello to him, and though she felt a tug at her heart and thought, for a moment, of putting her arms around him, it was too little, too late, and she turned him away, closing the door. After that, she often wondered how much she herself knew about love.

But so they lived, speaking only when necessary, pretending to be married, becoming strangers. Jean went about her life, feeling a bit like a ghost—half alive and half invisible—privately mourning. It was tending to the little things that held her to-gether: the outfits she wore to work and how they matched the shoes, the slightly varying shades of pink fingernail polish she bought, the slow practice of penmanship she applied to her boss's notes, the new exotic bird that opened on the calendar page as each month would change. And church.

One day, shortly before Christmas in 1998, she received a mysterious package in the mail with the return address "Planet of the Stars," from Greene Street in New York City, and though she'd been to New York City, she had no idea where Greene Street was. Inside the package were record albums (stamped RETRO VINYL RELEASE) and CDs with photos of Mary and some boys on the covers, and this was the first she knew about her daughter's success. The pictures on the covers were disturbing; on one of them Mary had her finger up her nose, and they had unhappy titles like *You're a Pig* and *I Can't Stop Eating*. There was a stack of clippings from various papers about Sliced Ham. One of the headlines said MARY FUCKIN' SAINT! and Jean wondered what kind of a paper would allow such language. Enclosed in the envelope was a typed letter from Janet, an "assistant manager," that said, "Mary asked me to send you these things." There were some letters, too, addressed to Jean, and she recognized Mary's handwriting, though she was afraid to open them and had to brace herself before reading them.

Jean was suspicious of the hoopla and feared not only the letters but also the music. She tried to listen to one of the CDs; there was a song called "Sewer Flower," which she selected because at least it had the word *flower* in the title. But when she put it in the CD player, it erupted into an awful collision of noisy guitars and drums, and then Mary's voice came screaming out of the speakers, as if she were being scraped in the face by a garden claw. Jean pressed Stop and never listened to another song. She put the collection of LPs and CDs, articles, letters, and newspaper clippings in a box in the closet, which she hid behind her skirts and dresses; it was a kind of secret shrine, shrouded in a mixture of pride and shame. Though Mary kept having the packages sent to Jean over the next five years, she never actually came home, and Jean had to admit that that was probably for the best. She loved her daughter, but she'd grown to be afraid of her and couldn't bear the thought of any more fighting in the house.

Apparently Sliced Ham had had a fringe hit with a song called "Feet and Knuckles," which had hurled them into the outer edges of the mainstream. Back then, college kids returning to Swallow for Thanksgiving weekend or winter break seemed to know the band, and when she'd run into acquaintances at Shop-Rite, they'd often refer to some piece of news about Mary that they'd read somewhere. The band was on TV, and of course, there was that time on *The Tonight Show* when Jean had stayed up to watch, hoping that maybe Mary's band had improved since the recording of "Sewer Flower," but she was so dismayed at how ridiculous her daughter looked, and how awful the music sounded, that she didn't sit through any more of the show to hear the second song.

She couldn't imagine why Jay Leno would want such a thing on his show. Through the years, she'd seen top-notch acts on his program, but she guessed the quality of everything was sliding downhill. What else could it be?

Mostly, Sliced Ham was popular on college campuses; there were write-ups in odd magazines. Not the kinds of magazines that anyone would actually read, but people in town were impressed, and though no one said a word, they were all very well aware of the troubles at home, and somehow Mary's success put a different slant on things.

Through the years, though Mary phoned only sporadically, she wrote to Jean about everything; it was an unusual kind of writing, and sometimes the sentences were hard to understand. Mary had her own way of putting her thoughts together, but several things were clear as day: the struggle with drugs and drink, the sagging morals, the sold-out shows, and the sleeping pills. Sometimes, when reading the letters, Jean felt as if she were privy to a dream sequence in a soap opera, but one too risqué to ever be shown on television. She marveled at the wildness of it all and couldn't help wondering, *How did this happen? Or even, Did this happen?*

In one of the letters, dated July 2001, Mary described a scene in a hotel outside of Cleveland. It was after a show, and her band and some of the hangers-on from the concert they had just done were lounging around drinking, sitting on conference chairs, which they had wheeled out of the hotel's business center and onto the patio by the pool. Apparently they were blowing up balloons and taking pictures of each other, using the balloons as *tits and dicks,* Mary had written. At one point someone dared a teenager to roll his chair into the pool, but the kid was too *chicken-shit.*

—Ma, it was a riot. Finally the kid rolled himself into the pool, fully dressed, with his sneakers on, still holding his Budweiser, and his cigarette was hanging out of his mouth. It was cartoon funny! But the bozo at the hotel called the cops, and the kid—who was dripping like a wet squirrel—was hauled off in handcuffs. I know it was a little bit mean, but . . .

Jean didn't recognize her daughter in these letters and didn't exactly know how to answer them, but she always wrote something—words of encouragement—back to Planet of the Stars Management on Greene Street in New York City, and sometimes she'd include an inspirational prayer card from Sunday Mass. She never referred to the horrors at home, Bub's continuing violent eruptions or the loneliness that lurked around the house. Sometimes Jean just sat on the edge of her bed and wept without making any noise, and the years went by.

In truth, Jean had actually laid eyes on Mary only a few times since the day her daughter had left home. About ten years to the day after she had hightailed it out of Swallow, Mary and Jean had an encounter at a Holiday Inn outside of Albany, where Mary chain-smoked and drank rum and Cokes at four-thirty in the afternoon. There had been a message on Jean's answering machine from a man who did not say his name.

"Uh, Mrs. Saint, your daughter is, well, a little outta control, and it might be a good idea if somebody showed up."

Jean had gotten in the car and ventured up the thruway, and when she arrived at the hotel, she found Mary at the bar, her face tearstained, with eyeliner running down her cheeks.

"Mommy, get the fuck out of here," she'd said, leaning into her drink in the darkened lounge, slurring her words.

"Oh, honey, please don't——"

"Hey! Where's good old Dad? I wish you'd brought him with you to kick my ass around the block . . ."

Jean had been distraught and horrified, but she couldn't do a thing about it and she'd wound up leaving Mary there, unable to coax her off the barstool. In a month's time, Mary had landed in the rehab hospital, and coincidentally Bub had had the stroke two days after that.

Everything changed. During the months that followed, Jean felt her life unravel to the very end of the yarn ball. She was completely alone, and when she spoke to Mary in the hospital, Mary showed no mercy for Bub. Upon leaving the rehab, Mary called Jean and told her she was going to *rethink her life* and move to San Francisco, and although Mary said she couldn't quite face seeing her mother yet——she needed some *space*——she promised Jean that she was all straightened up, and she would keep in touch.

"Why San Francisco?" Jean asked.

"It's pretty, but gritty. The buildings are the colors of Easter eggs, and I like the way they think out there," Mary answered.

Jean did not know what she meant, but she was too worn down to question it.

"Please don't let Daddy ruin your life anymore, Ma. There *are* such things as nursing homes," Mary said, which made Jean realize that her daughter wanted nothing more to do with her father. Meanwhile, Jean cared for Bub until she was spent. Only after hiring and firing endless aides did she arrange for him to be placed in Three Forks Home, at which point Jean took her retirement, packed up the house, and moved to the east side of Swallow. She'd gotten a smaller place, all on one floor, in the spanking new, la-di-da East Swallow Meadows, and she realized that no one really knew her there; none of them had even met Bub, and all they had was compassion for her husband, the poor man who had had a stroke.

To her surprise, her life began to blossom. She became more active in the church, did a bit of volunteer work at the hospital, and she didn't dread running into people in town anymore. She'd stroll down Main saying her good mornings, waving at that one, smiling at this one, and if the question "How's your daughter?" came up, Jean would say, "Oh, she's doing just fine," like any ordinary person might.

But something still nagged at Jean, something worse than any of the incidents that Mary had been involved with. It was a thing that stood out as the most disturbing of all; Jean felt so ashamed of it that she didn't know what to do, and it haunted her to this day.

It came in the form of a letter.

Several weeks after Mary's admission to the rehab, in the fall of 2003, Jean had written to her daughter care of Planet of the

Stars, begging her to stick with the program and expressing her deep concern. The letter that she received back came directly from the rehab hospital, a place called Mornings of Dawning Hope.

It was unlike any of the other letters Mary had written, which were shorter and disjointed. This one was levelheaded in its way, though it was written with a combination of crayons, pencils, and pens on the backs of some paper place mats. Mary had drawn little pictures on the borders of the pages; there were dogs and cats and bunnies; crucifixes and horned devils with daggers in their hands. And there were sketches of a lady, the same lady that she described in the letter, Jean supposed. There were whole sections that were crossed out and some that were underlined. The letter had the feel of a living thing to Jean, and it frightened her. There was something serenely clear about it, and perhaps that disturbed her the most.

Five

MORNINGS OF DAWNING HOPE REHAB
Fall 2003

Dear Ma,

First of all, I'm sorry for whatever happened at the Holiday Inn, I can't remember, I was zonkered. I'm going to straighten up, I promise. It's time for me to grow up, I know. I'm almost thirty years old! Can you believe it? But you have to, have to, have to stop worrying. I love the letters you send, and I keep the holy cards in my journal (you know I love pictures of saints), but I'm going to tell you about something that happened to me when I was seven years old, and when I do, you'll never worry about me again.

Are you ready? You better sit down.

Remember the woods down at the end of Trudy Lane where the abandoned Boy Scout camp was? Did you ever go in there? I can still smell the pine trees and the slippery needles that blanketed the ground. (I used to stuff fistfuls of those needles in my pockets, bring them home, hide them in my drawers, and sometimes in my pillowcase.) Under the tall, damp trees was a stream that trickled through the woods, it was lined with lily pads, skunk cabbage, and broken branches. Frogs and chipmunks jumped across moss-covered rocks like in a scene from a fairy tale, and sunlight fell down in slanted beams through the trees. I always thought that they were God's beams, but they weren't, and I'll tell you how I know.

Far into the woods, back behind the camp, stood a circle of evergreen trees and most days I wound up there. Now I know that those trees were actually a family, and I'll tell you how I know that, too. I must have sensed it because I liked to sit right in the middle of their circle and sing. You remember how much I longed for brothers and sisters. Maybe they were my brothers and sisters. Didn't you ever wish for other children, Ma?

One day, the day before Halloween, I was kneeling in the circle singing and rocking. The leaves were beginning to change, it was chilly, the sky was blue and cool, and big puff clouds were floating by high above the woods. I was wearing that yellow sweater with the zebras on it and those blue corduroy pants. They were the same pants that I peed on in school. Remember when they sent me home and Daddy got mad?

Suddenly I felt the wind pick up, but it was warm, not chilly at all, and as it grew stronger the wind became even warmer, almost hot. The leaves flew around like startled birds and the sky went dark as if a storm was coming. Worried, I stood to leave, expecting it to pour rain, and there on the path before me was a lady I had never seen before. At first I thought I'd conjured a ghost, but then I sensed that she was real. Her hair was long and brown and it blew around her face, but her eyes were still. Though serious and deep, they looked at me with kindness, and I had the feeling that she knew me. Her dress, made out of rags, was dirty, or dusty, like she'd been traveling for years on the open road, but she wasn't wearing shoes. Honestly, I wondered if she was a crazy person, but then I saw that she was clutching a rosary in her right hand.

We stayed with each other in silence for a long time. I was terrified, but for some reason I trusted her. I studied her face and she allowed me to stare; she was exquisite, weary and full of sadness. Oh, Ma, how beautiful she was. Her skin seemed smooth as a gingerbread cookie, and I wished that I could touch her. As we stood there, sunlight came back down through the trees even though the sky stayed dark, and the air wonderfully warm. I was drawn to her, and for some reason I untied my saddle shoes and took them off. Then I pulled my socks off, and waited to see if she would scold me, but nope, nothing. I wanted to take everything off but couldn't imagine doing it. Still, I unbuttoned my zebra sweater and let it slip to the ground, never taking my eyes off of her. So fierce was the impulse to undress that I was almost mad at her. (Can you imagine little old me wanting to take my clothes off in front of somebody?) She smiled at me, saying nothing, and I couldn't resist pulling off my shirt as well, and so I stood bare-chested in the warmth of her glow, a little unsure. My thumb went to the button on my pants, and I unzipped them, letting them fall to my ankles. Calmly, I stepped aside, and voilà! There I was in my Carter's in the middle of the woods. (Remember those underpants with the tiny raised polka dots?) Ma, you won't believe it, but I took them off, too. I thought I would feel ashamed, standing naked in the middle of the woods, but with the warm wind swirling around me, I felt pretty, especially as she looked at my body, and she did, she looked at all of me.

"I know who you are," I said, surprising myself. I was so brave; you would have been amazed.

The lady smiled but said nothing.

I had an overwhelming desire to touch her. I stared directly into her eyes, and I approached her very slowly, because even though I was brave, I was scared s*%#less. (pardon my French!) She knelt down and held out her hand, which I took, raising it to my cheek. I had to feel if she was real. Her hand was warm and weathered, but soft to the touch. I reached up and kissed her on the lips, and then I said, "I love you." I don't know what came over me; I kissed her again and again. I can still remember the feeling of her lips, smooth and moist.

THIS IS ALL TRUE! But, please, Ma, don't freak out.

She asked me if I knew who she was, and I said something like, "Yes, you're the same one who visited Saint Bernadette in Lourdes; my mother told me all about you. You're the Blessed Mother. Mary."

She broke into the most genuine smile. And then she said, "No, you're Mary and I'm Other *Mary." She laughed at that.*

She was the most beautiful person I'd ever seen; just thinking about it now gives me goose bumps. I continued to kiss her again and again until she took my face in her hands and gently moved her lips around my face. She had the most amazing smell. Her breath reminded me of one of those sweet watermelon candies that you used to carry in your purse, remember those?

She pulled me into her embrace and cradled me, caressing every inch of my body, and I curled up like a puppy in her arms. It was the best I've ever felt in my life.

"You and me," she whispered. "We're a lot alike."

I told her that couldn't be because I was bad and she was good, but she told me I was not so bad. She also said that I was going to go on a strange journey but I shouldn't be afraid.

She told me to look around and see everything exactly the way it was—the sky, the trees—and we stayed that way for what seemed like a year. To this day, I still remember how the wild-flowers and the weeds were leaning in. Weird. It was as if they were listening to her.

We watched the blue jays and the crows crisscross in the air, and we named the animal shapes in some of the ominous clouds. She said she never understood why the sky was blue and the leaves of the trees were green. "What a color combination," she whispered, and her lips touched the rim of my ear. "I prefer the sky when it is gray, the way it is right now," she said. She told me that all the slanted beams of light belonged to her, and not to God, and she also let me in on the secret about the trees being a family. The world looked different to me, I could see colors that I never saw before, and it seemed like every bird in the woods had flown to the nearby trees just to be close to her. I don't know how long we were together. Much of the time we didn't speak, but the noise of the silence was like a symphony. Music of birds, of wind, of leaves, music of sticks and rocks, music of smelling and seeing and touching; the music of kindness, Ma. Music everywhere!

But then, and this just killed me, she said, "I have to go. Now, wasn't this fun?" She actually used that word. (I wouldn't have exactly called it fun.)

I cried out loud and begged her to stay. You should have heard me wail. She said, "It's okay to cry, I know how sad you feel, I've been watching you. But guess what, I feel sad sometimes, too. Don't worry, this is how it goes. Just promise to remember me, will you promise?"

I said something like "But if you leave, I might die."

"Oh, come on now, I don't think you will," she said, teasing me.

I could barely speak; my lips were quivering, and as she rose I stood before her, pleading, trying to memorize her face. "I'm lonesome," I begged. "Please don't leave me here, take me with you, please."

And then, listen to this, she said, "Every time you sing, I'll be listening. So sing for me. And don't worry about being lonesome, but always be true. Sing, and I'll sing with you." *I'll never forget it, Mommy.*

She vanished as quickly as she had appeared. I don't know how, one moment she stood before me, and then, poof!

So there I was, standing in the woods, naked. I started shivering, because as soon as she left, it got cold again, even though the sun had pushed back through the clouds. I hurried to put on my clothes in case anyone might, you know, see me. When I reached for my shirt and pants, I saw a family of deer; they must have been watching the whole scene. They were as wary of me as I was of them, and they ran off into the bushes once they realized that she was gone. I turned and ran home, Ma. But I couldn't tell you, even though I wanted to. I was afraid. Isn't it all so odd?

So you see, you have nothing to worry about. THE BLESSED MOTHER IS LOOKING AFTER ME! And she was right about the journey, wasn't she? I know I've made some mistakes, but I'm getting better now. I know you won't worry about me anymore.

I'm sorry I never told you about this before, but you understand why. I didn't want to burden you. Oh, and it might be a good idea to keep this to yourself, or else people might think I'm nuts!

Love,

Mary

Six

SWALLOW, NEW YORK
October 2009

Several days after Vincent Calabrese took his wife to visit
his son's grave at Willow Cemetery over in Crest Falls, Bill De
Sockie stood under the fluorescent lights of his classroom in the
heart of Swallow High School. He stared at his fifth-period
sophomore English students with heavy eyelids. The class, com-
fortably stuporous, was for the moment quiet, except for the
intermittent buzzing and dinging of the students' cell phones,
which were supposed to be on *off* but somehow always remained
in some semblance of *on*. A fierce hip-hop-infused rendering of
the Brandenburg Concerto No. 3 burst forth out of a student's
phone, temporarily jolting the class into communal attention.
For a moment Bill De Sockie had forgotten where he was; the
dreary autumn rain was proving to be more potent than a sleeping pill, and he couldn't pinpoint the culprit. "Cell phones off,"
he said, wearily. "Come on, people."

De Sockie was a tallish guy who looked younger than his
forty years, with a brown mop of uncombed hair, sweet blue
eyes, and a chubby-cheeked face. His red short-sleeved shirt was

untucked, hanging sloppily over his khaki pants, and one of his Hush Puppies was untied.

"Mr. De Sockie! Earth to Mr. De Sockie!" said Hazel Froelich, twirling her dirty-blond ponytail as it fell over her shoulder. "You were daydreaming again," she delivered in a little song. "And . . . ahem . . . your shoelace is loose, and we'd hate to see you trip, Mr. De Sockie."

The class erupted in laughter, and even Michael Ping, who was deep into his own dream, woke up and lifted his sleepy head off his arms, which he was using as a pillow, only to set his head back down a moment later. Bill De Sockie despised Hazel Froelich. Pretty blond Hazel, with the Gucci knockoff blue-rimmed glasses, was one of the few in the class who paid attention to his every move. She was the daughter of the school board president and a suck-up. She was on him like a sniper, hoping to catch him in a flub, even if it was a wrong answer of hers that he may have overlooked on a weekly test, or a slight suggestion that he might have scribbled on her perfectly dull poems. She wanted him to be *wrong*—it didn't matter about what—even if her own grade was going to suffer.

"Hazel," said De Sockie, collecting his wits, "actually, I was not daydreaming at all. I was thinking. T-H-I-N-K-I-N-G. It's a thing I do from time to time. A thing I'm trying to get you all to do. And by the way, guys, no gum in class, I'm sick of peeling it off the floor." He ripped a page from his pink pass pad and sauntered down the aisle to Hazel's desk. Without looking at her, he held out the paper for her to drop her gum into. "Thank you, Hazel," he said flatly. "Now, let's get back to business. What does the poet mean when she says"—and he read the words slowly, feeling the weight of each one:

> . . . *Howling with mournful laughter*
> *We gasped at the stars as they fell*
> *And toasted all the outer spaces*
> *Please remember us*
> *Because before it had been lonely*
> *We had been forsaken*
> *Our little hearts were drab until*
> *We fired like two red-tipped matches*
> *On the rock of our own lives*
> *And one wonders at the accident*
> *It's possible we never would have met . . .*

Bill De Sockie felt a lump in his throat, and before he could stop them, a tear bubbled in each of his eyes.

"Mr. De Sockie!" cried Hazel. "Now you're crying?"

"Duh!" piped in Jason Miller, who was sick of Hazel's monopoly on the class. "It's a sad poem, stupid. Can't you just shut up for once?"

"What a pansy," spit Bruce Fulton under his breath, and Penny Summers threw Bruce a sly smile.

They all thought Mr. De Sockie was gay, except for the girl who met him most afternoons in the ShopRite parking lot, which was down the street from the school. That was Sarah Spalding, a gorgeous bookworm who hung out in the cubbyhole named the Word Room, which was in the new wing of the high school.

It was supposed to be a place where kids could go to *discuss books* with the English teachers in their free periods in a casual, relaxed way. Sarah was a serious student, but she also had a *rack* that the English teachers regularly joked about in their lounge and thick, perfectly formed lips, which kept all of them rapt whenever she talked about anything. Sarah had originally approached De Sockie on a matter of poetry. She wanted him to sponsor an independent project of hers: a collection of poems about Iranian women. De Sockie had been flattered that Sarah wanted to work with him, but he spent a fair amount of time trying to convince her that she might want to start with a subject she knew more about.

"What is it about Iranian women?" he asked her.

She paused for a few seconds before she reluctantly confessed that Mrs. Perble, the guidance counselor, had suggested a project like that might look good on a college application.

"Horse balls," he said. "You gotta get deep into yourself, Sarah." When he asked her what she felt she knew about most, she admitted that she'd barely traveled more than fifty miles out of the town of Swallow. "That's okay!" he said. "Swallow is a world, a universe, a galaxy! There's plenty here to write about." That's how they'd gotten involved in "off campus" research, which eventually led them to the woods. The beauty of Galaxy Swallow ultimately wound up exploding between them, as Sarah's poems started to sound a lot like love poems to an older man, and Bill De Sockie found himself thinking about his very special student late at night, in the privacy of his bed.

One day, after a couple of hours of awkward groping among the rocks and roots, where the old Boy Scout camp used to be,

Bill De Sockie and Sarah were sitting in his car, which he'd parked discreetly on Trudy Lane, the dead end a block away from Sarah's house. It was their habit to linger in the car for a few more minutes with their fingers intertwined, until he'd snap back into being Mr. De Sockie and tell her it was time to go home. He'd watch her run through the bushes to her house, her miniskirt swishing, and wonder what the hell he was doing, who the hell he thought he was. The girl was sixteen years old, and yet he couldn't stop.

This particular day he'd brought some music to play for her. Besides getting into Sarah's pants, he'd convinced himself he was also trying to educate her—no, to inspire her about alternative music; how poetry could really be used in songs in new and provocative ways. He had been telling her for weeks about Sliced Ham ("the best band of the nineties," he'd said), that she had to hear their *stuff,* as he referred it. "So, dig this, Sliced Ham was un-fuckin'-believable. It was a real tragedy when they disappeared from the scene." Sarah glanced up at him, and he was afraid by the look in her eyes that she was tiring of his little lessons and wanted to get on with the kissing.

"Nobody understands," he said, lifting his hands to heaven, faking exasperation, clearly performing for her. "You don't always have to be pretty in a poem!" he went on, as if he were on a one-man crusade to present this concept to the world. He figured he'd play her a couple of cuts from *You're a Pig.* "Listen to this shit," he said, flipping for the track on his iPod. "This was their big album," De Sockie explained as the electric guitar kicked in and he pulled her close to lean against his chest. "It has the song 'Feet and Knuckles' on it, which was the hit, but Mary Saint

didn't write the words. The bass player, Garbagio, who actually
died by falling off a hotel balcony—if you can believe that—
wrote them; the thing is, he was a vegetarian, that's basically
what the song is all about. . . . It's a catchy tune, but light-
weight writing. Still, she sings the shit out of it, in her own way,
you know?"

"Yeah," said Sarah, but De Sockie was worried that he was
losing her now.

Halfway through "Feet and Knuckles" he stopped the music.
"I mean, this is just commercial bullshit, really," he said. "Mary
Saint was the heart of the band, the real genius of Sliced Ham."
He flipped through his iPod again and found one of Mary's songs,
"The Penis of a Married Man," and as Mary Saint's voice crept
over the track of electric guitars and drums, singing *Hey, mister,
undo your zipster,* De Sockie reached over to Sarah's open lips
and they kissed while he slipped his hand down into her panties
and then up into her shirt, unclasping her bra and setting her
breasts free.

"I love this song," she murmured, coming up for air. "I love
that line, *like a baby on a bottle.*"

"So do I," he said, as his unmarried penis throbbed.

But Sarah broke away suddenly and said, "You know what?
I've heard this before."

"Really?" said De Sockie.

"Yeah, you're not going to believe this. My stepfather's son from
his first marriage has this CD, and he told me that the lead singer's
mother lives here in town. He said there was a song called 'I Can't
Swallow You No More,' and it's all about Swallow."

"Are you shitting me?"

"I swear to God, Mr. De Sockie! This is the same band."

He cringed whenever she called him Mr. De Sockie. "I know that song," he said. "It never occurred to me . . . I mean, I thought it was about, you know, a blow job or something . . . I never made the connection."

"Not only that, she grew up here, I swear he said that her mother still lives here. I mean, I could ask my half brother about it."

"Oh, come on, Sarah," he said, looking into her eyes to see if she could possibly be pulling a fast one on him.

"I'm almost certain, really. I'm not kidding."

"How could I not know that? Duh, duh, duh."

That night as Bill De Sockie padded around his condo in his stocking feet and red boxer shorts, waiting for his meat loaf with mashed potatoes and peas to sizzle in the microwave, he couldn't stop thinking about Mary Saint. The thought skittered across his mind that he could track down Mary Saint's mother and inquire about the possibility of having her daughter come home to Swallow to do a solo concert at the high school. *Holy shit.* He couldn't believe the ingenuity of his own idea. How was he going to pull this off? He sprang into genius mode, the opposite of dork mode (he felt he lived his whole life vacillating between the two extremes). He hunted down the new Swallow phone book, which, when it arrived in the mail the other day, had seemed like a piece of garbage and, in fact, was somewhere in the middle of his pile of newspapers, waiting to be carried down to the recycling room. When he located it, he flipped quickly to the S page and found two Saints. Fyodor Saint and J. Saint. Fyodor didn't sound right (Could anyone in Swallow be called Fyodor?); it must be J. Well, I'll be, he thought. This is actually a possibility. The next day Bill De Sockie sprang out of bed and called Jean Saint, even though it was only eight o'clock in the morning.

"Mrs. J. Saint?"

"Who's this?" asked Jean, about to hang up, suspecting he was selling something.

De Sockie quickly explained that he was an English teacher at the high school and a fan of Mary's, and was wondering if Mary might be interested in coming to do a concert at Swallow High. He asked if he could meet her for coffee at the Silver Tray to discuss the idea.

Jean hesitated, thoughts rushing through her head—the pros and cons—but she couldn't quite think of a reason not to meet him, except that she didn't care for Adele, which of course she couldn't admit. There was also no other place in town to have coffee, and she certainly wasn't going to have him over to her house, because she hadn't any idea who he was. She told De Sockie that she'd think about it and call him back.

Jean immediately called Betty to see if she had any info on him, but Betty said that since her daughter Pauline had graduated from Swallow High ten years ago, she had lost track of all the teachers there. It sounded to Betty like he was a new guy.

Jean had to admit the idea of discussing Mary with a fan was unsettling. It was as if her daughter existed in her mind only. Jean didn't want her life to be disturbed, simple as that. She'd had enough trouble, and she couldn't quite bring herself to pick up the phone and call him back, but the next day De Sockie rang again, asking once more. He was polite and respectful, and after some hemming and hawing, she agreed to meet him the following day.

It was another rainy October morning when Jean bundled up in her raincoat and bonnet, and held her umbrella against the wind down the sidewalk to the Silver Tray. When she opened the door of the bakery, the smell of freshly made pastries and bread made her realize that she was hungry. The Silver Tray was packed; most of the tables were filled, and she looked around the shop, dismayed to see that no one seemed to be waiting for anyone. She had deliberately tried to be late, but it was something she just couldn't do. Luckily, there was a free table back in the corner, away from the counter, where Adele was placing the fresh chocolate cream puffs on a sheet in order to slide them into the refrigerated display case.

"Hello, Jean," said Adele, as she tried to slip by unnoticed.

"Oh, Adele, good morning! I didn't see you there. What are those, chocolate puffs?" said Jean, without waiting for an answer. She made her way to the back of the store and took off her raincoat and bonnet, shook out her umbrella, and sat down at the far table, making puddles everywhere. She was irritated because there were crumbs on the table and the seat, which were now soggy; obviously a child had been sitting there. On the small round table was a foam cup of milk with a chunk of doughnut floating in it; some of the milk had been spilled, and wads of wet napkins were plopped here and there. She went to the sideboard, where the creams and sugars were, and grabbed a handful of napkins, all the while thinking that Adele should really be told to keep the tables clean.

Jean was busy wiping up the table when Bill De Sockie walked in. He looked around the place and spotted her silver hair from across the room. She could have been any old lady, with her cardigan sweater, white blouse, and loose blue slacks tucked into rubber rain boots. He walked up behind her and tapped her on the shoulder, introducing himself.

"You must be Mrs. Saint. I'm Bill De Sockie." Jean was flustered and knocked the half-drunk cup of milk on its side, and it spilled all over the floor.

"Oh, Mary and Joseph!" she said. "Damn!"

"No worries," he said, hurrying to help. "Let me get that."

They bumbled around the table, and De Sockie pulled out the chair, bending down underneath it, trying to clean up the mess, until Adele came over with a wet rag and snapped, "I'll get it, just move to the side."

Jean stepped away, humiliated and annoyed that Adele had had the chance to push her around and was now involved, somehow.

"Hello, Bill," said Adele. "What brings you here? Shouldn't you be in school?"

"Free period, Ms. Graham."

"Oh, I thought maybe you were giving Mrs. Saint a private tutorial," she said, meaning to make a joke. But it fell flat. Jean found it offensive but couldn't figure out why; Adele just had a way of rubbing people the wrong way.

After Adele tidied up, Jean and De Sockie sat down across from each other at the tiny round table.

"Well," she said. "It's probably not hard to tell that she's a little harsh for me."

De Sockie laughed. "Takes all kinds, right?"

"I guess that's true. Can I call you Bill?"

"Sure, if I can call you Mrs. Saint."

How polite, thought Jean.

"I have to tell you, Mrs. Saint, I'm thrilled to meet you. You must be a very special person to have raised Mary." Jean was worried that he was talking too loud. "She is the real thing, as we say in the literary world. You know, I'm a writer myself, and believe me, I know good writing when I see it. She may be primitive, but I think Mary is right up there with some of the greatest songwriters of all time. She might not get the attention she deserves because, well, people are jerks——"

"Bill," said Jean, who was beginning to wish she had a remote volume control for De Sockie's voice. "Shouldn't we get something to eat and then we can talk? It's just that I worry about hogging the table."

De Sockie looked around, confused. "Oh . . . I never meant to hog. I'm sorry. I'm just excited. Of course, what can I get for you?"

"I'll take a chocolate puff and a coffee, with cream," she said, reaching for her purse.

"No, no, I insist, my treat," he said, and off he went to place the order with Adele. Jean didn't like it already; the young man was nice enough, but there was just something silly about him. As he walked up to the counter, she noticed that he also seemed a bit messy for a teacher. Why was his shirt sticking out of his pants? What was with the hair hanging in his eyes? He looked like a teenager. I must be getting old, she thought, but she also didn't like the way he was gushing about Mary; it seemed a bit like flattery, and Jean was no fool for flattery.

De Sockie made his way through the tables and set Jean's

coffee and chocolate puff down in front of her. Suddenly the pastry seemed grotesque, with its big bulbous top dripping with chocolate sauce.

"What do you have there?" asked Jean.

"Peach peppermint tea," he said.

"Fancy," said Jean, trying to be playful.

"A chocolate puff is pretty fancy, if you ask me," said De Sockie, dismayed by his own sarcasm. He felt like one of his students.

Jean wondered what his point was but let it go. She wished she'd stuck to coffee. The puff *was* too fancy, and she left it on the plate, instead taking small sips of coffee; she'd wait and eat at home.

"Mrs. Saint, as I was saying, I think it would be so exciting to have Mary come to do a concert. The kids would learn a lot from her. Would you consider asking her?"

Jean had no idea how to respond, and for a moment the two of them sat in silence. "I have a date picked out in early June; exams will be over, it would be kind of an end-of-the-year cele-bratory extravaganza . . . ," he said, trying the hard sell.

Jean surprised herself by being frank. "Bill, my daughter's wild and crazy days are in the past. If you're looking for some kind of a freak show, it's not going to happen."

"What?" said De Sockie. "Look, I've even talked to the prin-cipal, Dick Dworkin. He was thrilled. They're always looking to bring culture into the school."

"Really?" said Jean, and she took a moment to consider that, if the principal was all for it, how bad could it be? "Well, Bill, what I mean is, Mary has been through a lot." Jean immediately regretted saying anything at all.

"Mrs. Saint, your daughter is a highly gifted artist. Her songs are truly poetic; she has a lot to offer," he said.

Jean took a napkin and patted her face. She had to get out of there.

"I can pay her eight hundred and fifty dollars, plus airfare."

Jean had no idea if this was a good price, but it made her pay attention and she managed to crack a joke. "Heck, I'll do it for that," she said, deadpan.

"Hey, that's pretty funny, Mrs. Saint." He laughed. "I see where Mary gets her sharp mind."

Jean slid her chair back from the table, indicating it was time to go. Oddly, though, De Sockie's comment pleased her.

"I'll call her, Bill, but I can't promise you anything. All I ask is that you respect her."

"Mrs. Saint, I have nothing but respect for her," said De Sockie solemnly.

For some reason, what popped into her head at that moment was the letter that Mary had written from the rehab, six years ago; the business about the Blessed Mother. The thought of it now made her stomach tighten, and she wished that Bill De Sockie would disappear. Something was wrong with this whole idea; something was *off*. She wanted to be protective of Mary, but part of her felt trapped into De Sockie's plan, and she left the Silver Tray feeling duped into making the call to her daughter.

The next morning Jean woke late, after having been up half the night with worry. First of all, she couldn't even remember the last time she had picked up the phone to call her daughter.

Usually, Mary was the one to call, on Mother's Day or Christmas, and the experience was always like walking on china cups. Although it seemed that Mary had straightened herself up and settled down, Jean worried, for she had heard that it was easy for a person to relapse, and Mary had been a difficult case. But if Jean was going to be honest, it wasn't just that. She was worried about what people in Swallow might think of a concert of Mary's. Mary was *different*. Jean was ordinary, like most everyone else, and Mary's difference embarrassed her.

There was also the matter of the letter about the Blessed Mother, it had to be dealt with. Jean felt that the shameful description of being fondled by the Holy Virgin in the woods must somehow be explained or expunged from existence, like a bomb blown up in a safe room. She had to clean it up somehow. Jean's faith hung on her belief in the goodness of the Blessed Mother; secretly she could never quite relate to her own concept of God, a powerful old man in flowing robes, who yelled at everybody, and scared people half to death. The Holy Mother was gentle and kind, and she would never touch an innocent child. Or would she? And if so, what could it possibly mean? Everyone knew *that* kind of touching was wrong. In the middle of the night, as she tossed and turned, Jean had thought that perhaps Father Ben, with his big heart and modern perspective, could put her mind at ease and maybe even absolve Mary of her unholy fantasy, and although it would be excruciating to reveal the letter to the priest, doing so might be her only hope. After all, it was Jean who had first told her daughter that the Blessed Mother does make visitations, and perhaps that had been a mistake. Wasn't confession the key to forgiveness?

At 9:00 A.M., with great trepidation, she phoned Betty at the rectory.

"Hello, St. Clare's."

"Hi, Betty, it's me."

"Mercy, Jean, you're up and at 'em this morning," said Betty.

"Listen, I have to ask you a favor. I have a . . . matter . . . a private matter . . . that I need to discuss with Father Ben, and I don't feel that it's something I can do in confession, since it's not really a confession. It's a . . . *theological* issue about the sinfulness of something. Oh, Betty, it's hard to describe, but I was wondering if you might be able to see if Father Ben would talk to me about it. What I mean is, I'd like to come down to the rectory and have a private meeting with him."

"Honey, I'm so sorry, what's wrong?"

"Betty, I'm going to have to ask you to trust me that this is something I can't really discuss with anyone but a priest."

Betty was careful to say that Father Ben only rarely met with people privately, for she didn't want to make it seem as if she had any pull with the priest just because she was his secretary, but she did say she'd try to set something up.

"You're a doll, Betty," Jean said, hanging up the phone and feeling relieved that she would finally be able to unburden herself. *It's going to be okay.*

Since Mary lived in San Francisco and it was three hours earlier there, Jean would have to wait until noon to make the call, so she busied herself by dusting her collection of figurines. She wiped each little piece carefully, then sprayed Pledge on the cloth and ran it over the shelves before she rearranged the whole collection in a slightly different configuration. She fussed over each statuette, making sure to catch the dirt in the crevices under their big eyes and bulging bellies, the humans as well as the animals. She particularly loved the one little guy with the big black boots. His slacks were bunched up over his boots and his hands were in his pockets; she'd had to glue his head on a few years ago, after she dropped him while dusting in a hurry. She'd been careful with them all ever since.

As she worked, her mind wandered, and she considered that the idea of the concert had its upside, for not everyone had a daughter in show business. Maybe it wouldn't be so bad.

At noon, Jean took out her address book and flipped through to the M section until she found Mary's numbers. One after another had been crossed out, and two entire pages were a mess, filled with now defunct numbers, like wreckage from a plane crash strewn across a field.

Jean dialed the 415 area code and punched the rest of the numbers into the phone until it rang and rang. Finally a man's voice said, "Mary's magic castle."

Startled, she said nothing.

"Hello?" said the voice.

Right away, Jean regretted making the call, but she spoke up, saying, "Is Mary there, please?"

"And who might you be?" he said.

Jean wondered if he was a boyfriend. His voice was raspy and strange. "It's . . . her mother," said Jean, as if she were apologizing.

"Oh! You must be Ma. I see," said the man.

"Yes." Jean tried to hide her irritation and disappointment.

"It's your mama!" Jean heard him say. And then she could hear Mary's voice muffled in the background; she was saying something, but Jean couldn't tell what; there was some rustling and knocking, and Jean thought that Mary took the phone, but no one said anything until Jean, in a panic, said, "Hello, hello?"

"Ma, are you okay?" asked Mary.

The sound of her daughter's voice was a relief. "Of course, yes, I'm fine. I just have . . . I hope I'm not disturbing you."

"Not at all, it's early in the morning here is all," Mary replied, which Jean took to mean that Mary and her friend were just rolling out of bed. She pushed away visions of pipes, needles, and empty whiskey bottles scattered around a dirty room.

After a few long seconds, Mary said, "I'm glad to hear from you. Happy shedding moon."

Whatever that meant, Jean didn't want to know. "How are you, Mary?"

"Well, I'm really good, really, really, really good."

Jean was not so sure, but she decided to take her daughter at her word and jumped in with her business, not being able to think of anything else to say. "Honey, I have a question. It's somewhat odd. . . . There's an English teacher at the high school here. He's a . . . well . . . a fan of yours. He approached me. . . . He wants to have a concert with you . . . and honestly, I don't know a thing about him . . . but . . . I promised I'd . . ."

"Really. That is very strange," said Mary.

"Strange? Well, that's what happened," said Jean.

"Wow, I get that," said Mary with wonder, as if she were

contemplating a complex phenomenon. "I find it, well, extremely synchronistic."

Jean let that pass.

There was another silence. Mary said, dreamily, "To tell you the truth, you're blowing my mind, Ma—wow, this is—whooosh. Just a few minutes before you called, I read my horoscope, and it said that I was going to be asked to do something that would lead to great personal revelations. Maybe this is the thing I'm being asked to do, can you believe it?" Then she added, "Of course, sure, I have to do it. . . . Super . . . I mean, is there a payment involved?"

"Eight hundred and fifty dollars," said Jean, careful not to give an opinion on the sum. "Plus airfare. . . ."

"Gee, that's not so much. I guess I'm a has-been." She laughed. "Oh, who cares about the money? We can take long walks in the woods—imagine us both in Swallow again looking straight into each other's eyes! All expenses paid. I like this. I do."

Jean couldn't really see herself walking in the woods or looking straight into anybody's eyes, but she said, "Eight hundred and fifty dollars is not exactly nothing. I could probably buy seven dresses for that."

"Seven dresses! You have a good point. You're right, nothing is exactly nothing; everything is something."

"What?" said Jean. She wanted to say *stop that,* but thought better of it.

"I said 'nothing is nothing.' . . . You know what I mean, don't you? Look, I will come for the concert, I really will. Who is this fan of mine? Is he a coo-coo head?"

Jean laughed out loud. "Oh, Mary, how could you say that word!"

"I say it all the time. Probably every single day," she said. "Daddy had some funny lines." She chuckled. "How is he?"

Jean was happy to be laughing with her daughter and wanted to end the conversation there before the tide turned. "Daddy is growing older," she said, "and one day you might come and see him."

"I see him every day. He haunts me like a goblin. Boo!"

"Oh, Mary, don't say that. It's all changed now."

"Is it, Ma? I hope it is for you. Me, I'm still running around in circles. You were always stronger."

"Let's not dwell on the past."

"Mommy, you're enlightened. I know you are."

"Mary, honey, are you okay?"

"Of course, of course. Nothing to worry about here. Thaddeus and I are having a ball. He's enlightened, too. I hope someday you'll meet."

Thaddeus? I doubt it, thought Jean. "Well, look, Mary, I'll get you the details about the concert, but you're sure, honey, you're up for this?" She knew she was walking on thin ice but couldn't stop herself from adding, hopefully, "And I guess it will just be you?"

"Yes, I'm *up* for it. And don't be alarmed. I won't bring Thaddeus with me. He's a, well, he calls himself a chocolate tranny. I don't think he would fit in. And by the way, he's from my church and I'm not sleeping with him. He's living here because he has no place else to go."

"That's . . . very nice of you, sweetie," Jean said, at a loss for words. *What kind of screwup has noplace else to go?* "So, good, I'm glad I called. I'll be in touch with more information soon, and . . . maybe think about this for a few days."

"No, Ma, my answer is yes. I just have a gut feeling about this; there's something in the atmosphere," said Mary. "But, jeez, I hope I can still sing."

"Well, then," said Jean, remembering the sound of Mary's "singing." "You have a good day now, dear, and stay well."

"I love you, Ma, good-bye!"

The phone went click, and Jean shook her head. *Chocolate? Tranny?* For the first time in her life, the word *church* sent shivers up her spine. What kind of a church could Mary be going to?

Jean searched her mind for someone to blame, and it didn't take but a moment to land on Bill De Sockie. There was just something about that guy that struck her as odd. And now look what he'd gotten her into.

Seven

....

SWALLOW, NEW YORK

October 2009

Father Benedict knelt on a cushion by the window in his bedroom, and leaning on the windowsill, he reached for his rosary beads, which lay like a small pile of espresso beans on the night table beside his bed. The window looked out onto the yard behind the rectory. The end of October seemed unusually cold this year, the ancient oak tree was ablaze with red leaves that would probably blow off within the week. He loved the tree; he called it his praying tree, and as his fingers traveled between the beads, from Hail Mary to Glory Be, and his mind wandered, he would pull it back by focusing on the oak tree, every time.

For the priest, it had been a lifetime of rearranging and fine-tuning his concept of God. Recently, he felt like a man who'd been whittling the same piece of wood down to a toothpick. The tree was as close to the Almighty as he could get. He arrived at a simple idea in the end. It was the way the tree stayed rooted there, no matter what; it withstood the autumn wind, the sheets of rain, and the burden of heavy snow upon its branches. Through sweltering summer days, or endless gray Januaries, through the slow dreariness of every soul's unending sadness, and the fleeting brilliant joys, the tree remained, loyal and dependable. For Father Ben, praying was the peephole to peace, and it required dedication to the practice of moving between wakefulness and dreaming. Sometimes he was able to hover there, on the edge of communion with God, and that was his greatest joy, but many times he failed, and fell back into frustration and blame, anger, or just plain boredom.

Everybody loved Father Ben, but often it was more than he could bear. He was forty-seven years old, and as far as he could tell, nobody really knew him or the grim outlook he had. How long could this go on? It wasn't that he didn't love his job or his parishioners; he tried to apply his heart to each one. He took his time with the children as they came one by one into the confessional on Saturday afternoons to tell him about their sins:

Bless me, Father, for I have sinned, I stole a Mars bar out of my sister's Halloween bag.

Father, I'm ashamed. On Monday I had the thought—which almost seemed like a wish—that Sister Lydia would choke on chalk and die. What does that mean?

Father Ben? I hate going to church, especially the part when you have to turn to the person next to you and say, "Peace be with you." I don't like shaking people's hands when I don't know who they are.

Father? I'm afraid of my family, what should I do?

Before he'd send them off with their penance, he'd speak gently to them, telling them not to worry; they were good and they only needed to do their best. But he didn't really think it was true; nothing could protect them, he knew. Their *badness* would rise up like the boogeyman, and scare them into lying or defending themselves, and they would wrestle forever with it, and only once in a while get a whiff of peace. If it weren't for his tree, Father Ben would wonder where God went. Even in this sleepy little town, far away from starvation and war, people suffered, and for all his priestliness, he was just one of the people, though he was always summoned for the most heart-draining occasions. Last weekend, in one day alone, he'd performed three baptisms, married two teenagers (the bride was pregnant, and the families were warring), given last rites to a young father who had come to the end of his battle with leukemia, and finished the day hearing the confession of a man who'd been cheating on his wife, trying to convince him not to kill himself.

This morning his secretary, Betty Dunster, had penciled in a private meeting with a parishioner, and he'd forgotten to ask her to push it back an hour, so he felt obliged to go through with it. He had to move quickly through his rosary, which meant he'd struggle all the way, not having the time it took to settle into the depth of prayer. These one-on-one meetings were always stressful for him, as he was more comfortable in the pulpit, or shaking hands at the bingo game, or after Mass, when the parishioners filed out of the church. People had a way of disintegrating when they were alone in a room with a priest, and rarely was he able to fix their problems. The best he could do was to absorb their heartache, and that was a heavy load; sometimes he felt broken by the pain.

He walked out into the kitchen, where Betty had prepared his Earl Grey tea and Grape-Nuts with sliced banana. The bowl, spoon, and cup sat lifeless on the table, perfectly arranged on the same brown place mat as usual. Sometimes he felt as if Betty, in her buttoned-up cardigans and her endless wardrobe of formless, calf-length frocks, was a scientist and he was her rare captured monkey. He imagined that she might have secret cameras hiding around the rectory in order to study him, so that she might please him better. Her dedication was quiet, patient, and relentless, and he knew that among all the ladies of the parish, her job was coveted and respected; to be the priest's secretary was the middle-aged woman's equivalent of dating the captain of the football team.

Grape-Nuts—every single day—the morning ritual of chewing gravel. No doubt she would make him bacon and eggs if he asked, but that would be too extravagant, yet he sometimes imagined he could smell bacon or even ham as he crunched the cereal around with his teeth, and washed it down with tea. He had appetites.

Within seconds of his finishing, there was the all-too-familiar knock on the kitchen door.

"Betty, is that you?" said the priest.

"Good morning, Father Ben," she said, holding the door open a smidge. "Not to disturb . . . but I did want to remind you that you have a nine-thirty with Jean Saint this morning."

"Thank you, Betty, I'll be out shortly," he said, wanting to kill her.

He ran through faces in his mind—Jean Saint, which one was she? He couldn't quite remember.

Jean rang the rectory bell at exactly 9:30, having waited in her car until 9:26 so as not to be early. Betty came quickly and gave her a nod and a wink. "Hi, dear, come right in," she whispered, showing her to the parlor outside Father Ben's office. Jean sat in one of the large brown leather chairs with the grand curved headrests. She put her purse beside her feet on the floor and ran her hands along the smooth arms of the chair, feeling proud just to be sitting in one of them. She glanced around at the holy pictures on the walls: the crimson-robed Jesus, kneeling in prayer, with his blue eyes looking toward heaven; the rather stodgy picture of Pope Benedict XVI, whom Jean had to admit she didn't particularly care for. Every item in the room, from the enormous table lamp, through the richly colored rug and velvety drapes, to the various golden picture frames, looked very expensive, and Jean wondered where all the money came from. Certainly, her weekly two dollars in the envelope didn't make a dent. The place was fit for a monarch; even the crucifix looked like a billionaire's. And there she was, surrounded by all this wealth, invited into its grandness, but it pained her deeply to think of what had brought her here to talk to Father Ben. Wouldn't it be interesting if she and Betty could trade places, even just for a day? She quickly pushed the thought out of her mind, sickened by her own covetousness.

After a few minutes, Father Ben came through the French doors with the pretty lace curtains and extended his hand, offering her a gentle greeting.

"Hello, Mrs. Saint, so lovely to have you here. You can come right into my office."

Jean was thrilled to see him, noticing again how handsome he was; his large dark eyes were like a puppy's, deep and inquisitive. "Oh, Father Ben, thank you for taking the time to meet with me today. I'm sure you must have better things to do."

"It's all my pleasure," he said, closing the door to his office and pointing toward the slat-back chair. "How can I help you, Jean?" He paused in front of his mahogany desk and then took a seat behind it.

Jean felt herself heat up and quickly unbuttoned her quilted jacket. She took it off and folded it in her lap, hoping that the dampness she felt on her neck and face would not progress into drops of sweat. There was a box of Kleenex on his desk, but she couldn't bring herself to reach for it; instead, she patted her forehead with the sleeve of her blouse, hoped for the best, and jumped right in.

"Father, I have a troubling matter to discuss with you. It's about my . . . daughter. I don't know if you are aware, but she is a somewhat well-known singer, and . . ."

"Really?" he said, leaning back in his chair and clasping his hands around the back of his head so his arms stuck out at the elbows like a pair of frog's legs. (It was one of those chairs that had wheels and a lever to adjust its angle for comfort, Jean noted.) "I had no idea! Is she a folksinger? I used to have a guitar. But I sang like a toad, I'm afraid." He laughed.

"Mary's songs are, well . . ." She stopped here, realizing that she didn't really know what kinds of songs Mary sang, but she knew about the titles, and judging from the one song, "Sewer

Flower," that she had heard, she had a feeling they weren't the kinds of songs that Father Ben would like. "It's a little different, but yes, probably similar to folksinging."

"Does she have recordings? You should have brought me one," he said. "My mother loves folk music."

Jean thought about the CDs that she had in her closet, those awful images on the covers, and the grimy titles; she would sooner put her hands in a box of worms than give any of Mary's CDs to Father Ben. She soldiered on. "The funny thing is that it looks like she'll be coming to sing at the high school in the spring. There's a teacher who wants to put on a concert, and that's what got me thinking about the matter I've come to see you about. It's not an easy . . . I mean . . . I'm not quite sure . . . my daughter is *different*. Oh dear, may I confide in you, Father?" asked Jean urgently.

Father Ben realized that he should skip the small talk. Mrs. Saint was on the verge of tears, he could see that her bottom lip was quivering, and it brought him to attention. *Stop fooling around, you dunce.* "What's wrong, Mrs. Saint? Nothing can be so bad. Of course you can confide in me," he said, getting up and moving around his desk to be nearer to her. He sat down on a small stool next to her chair and took her hand, holding it with both of his.

"Mrs. Saint, as I'm sure you know, sometimes things seem very bad until you get them out in the open," he said, trying not to condescend.

She was not used to being touched by a stranger, and it rattled her. She looked down at his hands and noticed how perfectly square and clean his fingernails were. Briefly she wondered if he went to Karen's Nails on Kennedy and Green, or if he did them himself, or if there was even a chance that Betty got involved in that. The thought of it filled her with envy. If only she could be so close to something so clean. But here she was, as close as she could get, with something so dirty to say.

Father Ben looked at Mrs. Saint, as if for the first time. Her face was soft and wrinkled, her thin lips painted unevenly with lipstick. She had a freckle just above her right cheek. *Breathe and listen to the woman.* He dropped down into himself and miraculously fell into being a priest.

Jean pulled her hand away to reach for her purse. She undid the golden clasp and took the letter out. She paused to take a breath. "My daughter sent me this letter some years ago, and I've never told a soul about it. I was wondering if you would read it and, well, forgive her," said Jean frankly, surprising herself. It was as if a person she had never met had suddenly spoken.

Father Ben took the envelope, and right there, sitting so close to Jean, he took out the pages and read them. Jean studied him, in silence, as he read. She could not believe what was happening; there they were, not a foot of space between them, and Mary's letter in Father Ben's hands. She sat still as a statue as he bent over the letter, using his two hands to hold it. She examined his eyes as he turned the pages and noticed he was concentrating hard, but she couldn't tell what he was thinking. When he finished the letter, he carefully folded it back up and paused for a moment, rubbing his forehead. He set the letter in his lap and looked out the window, concerned.

"Mrs. Saint, this is quite something," he said, turning back to her. "You say your daughter is *different*. What exactly do you mean? Do you think she made this up, or do you think it's true, or . . ."

"Well, Father, I don't really know. The problem is, how can one tell if it is true? It seems, frankly, disgusting to me, to be fondled naked by the Virgin Mother. Our Lady would never do such a thing, would she? But how could Mary have made it up?"

"This is a bit of a tricky situation—remarkable, actually. I have to admit, I don't know what to say. But, Mrs. Saint, technically . . . well . . . I should probably report this to the Church."

"What? Oh no, no . . . please, no," exclaimed Jean, raising her hands to her mouth. It never occurred to Jean that Father Ben would tell a soul. "I really wouldn't want you to. I only wished that you could forgive her. She's been troubled, Father. I'm sure that's all it is."

"Well, I see three distinct scenarios. One, it's possible that her story is true—and I wouldn't rule that out; we don't know the mysteries surrounding these kinds of visitations. The Virgin Mary can do whatever she pleases," said Father Ben, trying to be very careful. "On the other hand, if your daughter's disturbed, you might want to see about getting her to a therapist. Some-times people slip out of touch with reality, and counseling can really help; believe me, there's no shame in it. But, of course, there's always the possibility that she's somehow fooling around or making a joke, and in that case, perhaps you should just let it go. I can see why you are alarmed, Mrs. Saint, but we'll figure this thing out."

Jean was taken aback. "When I said Mary was different, I didn't mean disturbed. She's not mentally ill, Father. Perhaps

I've just overreacted. I beg you, please don't tell anyone about this. It was selfish of me to come; I wanted to confide in you is all, to lift my own burden. I've had a hard time forgiving her myself."

"Ah," said Father Ben.

"Like I said, she's going to be coming here, and I wanted to clean her slate, that's all."

"Mrs. Saint, you can't clean your daughter's slate; it's up to her," Father Ben said gently.

Jean was in too deep. She stared at the priest; he was still holding the letter in his hands, and she had the impulse to grab it from him. They both sat frozen for a moment until he turned away and moved back to the seat behind his desk. "Mrs. Saint, have you ever asked her about this?"

Jean's tears came freely now, and she reached for the box of tissues. "No," she sniffled. "No, I haven't." Jean wiped her eyes. "How could I, Father? Can you possibly understand the way I feel? It's *dirty*. Please don't tell. Please."

Father Ben thought for a moment about how he could solve this. "I'm sure we can get to the bottom of it. Come on now, don't cry, Mrs. Saint. The problem is, it's either a darkness or a light. Herein lies the mystery. You can't judge your daughter unless you know the truth. It's unfortunate, but as I'm sure you know, there is a trend these days to drag our holy icons through the pop culture. You say your daughter is a popular singer; she may be using this sort of imagery to shock her audience."

"She's a good person," Jean said as she looked at him, afraid. "She's my *daughter*."

"I know how hard this is for you," said Father Ben, aware that he was making a mess of things. He heard himself fumbling around for the right words, but the truth was, he didn't really know what to say. The letter was strange, but did it really matter in the big scheme of things? He was stumped. "Look, Mrs. Saint, I suggest you pray about this, and I wouldn't worry so much. Sometimes we lose members of our flock"—he cringed at his own use of the phrase—"but in time they come back home."

This was not the way that Jean had wanted it to be, she should have thought this through first. Coming here had only made the whole thing worse. She stood up to leave. He didn't understand that Mary would never *use* the Blessed Mother. He didn't know the Mary she knew, the little girl who rocked back and forth saying the rosary every day. Now Jean felt that she'd betrayed her daughter by coming to the priest, for as kind as he was, he was still a stranger, and he didn't understand about Mary. She got up to leave. "Father, thank you for your time. I know you're busy."

"Mrs. Saint, just remember, it's possible that your daughter's story is true," he said, finally returning the letter to her. "In which case, not only is she different but she has been *chosen* by Our Lady, and that . . . is a miracle."

"Yes," said Jean, not so sure, heading for the door. As she was about to leave, she turned once more and begged, humiliated, "Please don't tell anyone, Father Ben."

"I'll be praying on this as well. Don't worry. You did the right thing by bringing it to light. God bless you, Mrs. Saint," he said.

"Yes, God bless you, too, Father," said Jean quickly.

She hurried out the front door of the rectory, rushing right by Betty's desk without saying good-bye.

After Jean Saint left his office, Father Ben felt as though he'd been alone fishing in the ocean and had accidentally reeled in a giant dolphin. He had to decide whether to throw it back into the sea.

Eight
....

NASHVILLE, TENNESSEE
November 2009

Eliot Bemblatt had opened a small entertainment manage-
ment agency in Nashville in a strip mall not far from Dolly Par-
ton's compound. When he was in his twenties, he'd been a
damn good drummer in a rock band called the All American
Duck Farts (sometimes referred to as Duck Fart of America). In
the beginning, the band was called Pencil Prick, but they went
round and round about it and the Duck Fart contingent won,
especially since they were all privy to the same Chinese meal that
had inspired the name. They couldn't get a gig outside of lower
Manhattan, but they were serious about trying and were also
having a bit of fun, although it was rough going and tough to
be poor.

Bemblatt woke up one day, hungover and broke, and thought
about how his brother Mitchell had already gotten married and
built a sprawling house in the Long Island suburbs, all based on
his management job at Bed Bath & Beyond. As if he'd been
touched with a magic wand by a sparkling fairy princess, Bemblatt decided that very morning to look around for real work, and
in a couple of weeks was able to quit his bartending gig and land

an assistant's job at a midsize management agency in New York
called Ichabod Smythe.

Soon Bemblatt noticed that he was the one doing all the work,
while his boss Craig Lantervul was busy trying to get his nose
up the ass of any celebrity that walked through the door. Lantervul, who wore his hair in a mullet and fancied suede pants even
in the summer, turned out to be a shameless star-fucker. Bemblatt put up with it for a year and a half, worked his tail off, and
wound up stealing two up-and-coming acts from under Lantervul's nose. That wasn't all he stole, for he moved to Nashville
with Lantervul's wife, Belinda. He hadn't set out for it to happen
that way, but apparently she'd had enough of Lantervul, too.

One of the acts he absconded with was a blond countryish,
popish, hipsterish girl, who looked rather astonishingly like a
Barbie doll. She went by the name of Lula, but her real name
was Rose Peterson, and she was only eighteen. The other act was
a black hip-hop DJ, who pretended to be from the Bronx but
actually grew up in an upper-middle-class town in Connecti-
cut. He went by the name R.U. Nuts, but his real name was
Chester Alphonse, and he'd recently graduated magna cum laude
from Yale.

Eliot had a nice-sized office in Nashville, and it made him feel
good to be a bigger fish in a smaller pond. Real estate was so
much cheaper in Nashville, and since he'd always been a penny-
pincher, he had saved enough money to afford a down payment
on a house and still be able to hire a girl to help out in the office.
Since the birth of the Internet, it almost didn't matter where you
were situated. New York City seemed less and less like the center
of the world, especially if you'd gotten started late. Bemblatt

figured he could never afford the New York City office rents, or come close to buying a loft in Tribeca, or a railroad apartment with a backyard garden in Brooklyn Heights. Screw New York; he had no intention of living in a five-floor walkup for the rest of his life.

R. U. Nuts caught on rather well and was bringing in a nice pile of dough for Bemblatt, even though the kid was a pain in the ass. He had ballooned into a real monster, demanding that Eliot see to everything, including getting his laundry done and keeping his girlfriends in line. It was tolerable for Eliot as long as the checks kept coming in, and besides, R. U. Nuts was a *cool* client, which Eliot felt might attract other hip acts.

Lula, or Rose Peterson, on the other hand, was not working out; there was just something about her. All the parts were there; she looked great, sounded great, even wrote some decent songs, but nothing ever clicked. She was almost too perfect— although it turned out she had a bit of a problem with bulimia, which wasn't necessarily a bad thing, for at least she wasn't fat. She also had a brother, Ned, who fancied himself a poet and who'd followed her down to Nashville after Eliot convinced her that that was where she needed to be if she was serious about her career. Ned was a sweet guy, and Eliot was intrigued by how close the siblings were. He eventually went about convincing Lula to change her name back to Rose Peterson and to team up with Ned to be a brother and sister act. It was really an ultimatum.

Bemblatt came up with the name the Tennessee Twinsters and a backstory to go along with it. They were to say they were twins, and they looked so much alike that people sometimes thought they were. In truth, Ned was three years Rose's senior, but he was one of those guys who would forever seem boyish. Eliot picked a small town off a map of Tennessee by the name of Michie, and they agreed to say they were from there, even cultivating a bit of a southern twang, though they were originally from Delmont, South Dakota.

"Who cares?" Eliot said. "A small town is a small town. Do you want to make it or not?"

Rose and Ned went about creating their act. They wrote a set of songs and sent it in to Eliot, but he wrote them an e-mail with the heading "Back to the Drawing Board—Guidelines":

All songs must be somewhat uplifting and inspirational except for the occasional . . . and I mean OCCASIONAL . . . sad ballad. FORGET ABOUT BEING A POET, NED, drop the obscure lyrics. It's not bad to seem Christian; as a matter of fact you might want to work that in more. Here's advance money (to be recouped from record one, as discussed). Now, go get some southern-style clothes. Cowboy hats and boots for both of you, square dance dresses for Rose . . . NO PANTS. And Ned, be careful not to look or seem GAY! Make a day trip to Michie, Tennessee, and see if you can write a song about being from there. Believe me, this plan will work, we're about ready to blast off . . .

Within a few months, they had written a repertoire, and much to Eliot's surprise, the songs were just what he had envisioned, and the two of them sounded super singing together.

The Tennessee Twinsters were developing a strong following in and around Nashville. Eliot was even able to send them up to

Asheville and some of the surrounding towns, and they were a big hit there as well. It was proving harder to get them a national audience, though. The record business was crumbling, and even though the Twinsters had made two CDs on a small label called Fudge Records, Fudge didn't have powerful distribution, so Eliot was frustrated. He really felt he had something with the Tennessee Twinsters, and besides, he'd *invented* them.

It was getting to be Christmastime, and he was thinking about the new year, trying to come up with a plan, tapping his pen on his desk and staring out the window, when the phone rang. His girl, Stacey, was out to lunch, so he picked it up. "Bemblatt," he said.

"Yes, I'm interested in booking Duck Fart of America," said the voice on the other end of the phone.

Eliot was caught off guard. He paused for a moment but then jumped right in. "That's interesting, what dates are you looking at?" His mind was racing through the possibility of reassembling his old band when the voice on the other end of the phone busted out laughing.

"Bemblatt! It's De Sockie!"

"You asshole!" said Eliot. "What the . . . hey, man . . . how the hell are you?"

"What's goin' on down there, Bemblatt?"

"Busy. Super happening here. It's been a while, you turd."

"What, you thought somebody was actually interested in Duck Fart? Man, I haven't picked up a guitar in over ten years."

"Well, you know . . . always thinking . . ."

"So how's life in the South? How's Belinda? How's R.U.?"

"Everything's hunky-dory, on to some big shit. What's going

on at the high school? All those adolescent girls! Are you getting
any action, my man?"

"What, are you fucking kidding me?" said De Sockie, embarrassed. "Listen, I'm just about to blow your mind, Bemblatt. You're
not going to believe who I got to come and do a concert at the
high school. I had to call you with this one."

"Uh, Eminem? How the hell do I know?"

"Somebody you used to wake up wet from, dude . . . Mary
Saint."

"What? You're full of shit. I thought she might be dead by now.
How did you pull that off?"

"The weird thing is, Mary Saint actually used to live here in
good old Nowheresville. Can you believe it? Her mother is still
here. I had no idea. She's this little old church lady, straight as a
pin. I actually contacted her. It's all set up for June."

"That's pretty good, De Sockie. Pretty fuckin' good," said
Eliot, thinking about how he could get in on it. "Hey, listen, do
you have an opener?"

"What? I was thinking it would be an *evening with*," said De
Sockie.

"No, it's just that I have this really amazing act, it's a duo,
brother and sister, they'd probably be perfect. They're blowing
everybody away down here, and I've been trying to get them up
north. If I could tack them on to your show, it'd be a good an-
chor for a little tour in the Northeast."

"The only thing is, I don't really have any money to pay them.
This is a really small-potatoes thing."

"It won't cost much, no sweat. Could you swing three hundred bucks?" asked Bemblatt.

"Oh, Christ, you really are slick. I'm on the phone for five minutes and already it's costing me money!" De Sockie laughed.

"Come on, De Sockie, I'm tellin' you, it'll be a good show. Maybe I'll even fly up for it. Couldn't you squeeze the school for a few hundred?"

"Well, truth is, Mary Saint just took what I offered, kind of pathetic, actually."

"Really? What did you quote her?"

"Eight fifty plus a cheap ticket."

"Jeez, she must be desperate. That's sad. It's a long slide down from the big time, isn't it?"

"Yeah, well, it could be she's not a money-grubbing pig like the rest of us. I always thought she was the real deal. Anyway, it would be a hoot to see you, man. Sounds like a plan. I guess I could scrape together a couple of hundred."

"I said three hundred, De Sockie!"

"You are a weasel, Bemblatt, some things never change," said De Sockie, disappointed by how much of a weasel Bemblatt had actually turned out to be. "Send me some of their albums when you get a chance."

"You can get them on iTunes, De Sockie, just fucking download the stuff."

"Like I need to spend ten dollars? Come on."

"All right, I'll e-mail some MP3s. You kill me. So we have a deal?" said Bemblatt.

"Okay, okay. Look, it's great to talk to you. Best to Belinda and—love ya, man."

"Yeah, right, take it slow, De Sockie. I'll send you a contract," said Bemblatt, before he hung up the phone. He sat at his desk for a second, thinking about what a sentimental guy his old friend De Sockie was. Bemblatt could picture De Sockie going home to his little rented condo in Swallow, New York, making his pitiful little dinner while he downed a few brewskis and grooved to one of Mary Saint's CDs. Even after all these years, the poor guy was a sap, a bighearted sap, and for some sad reason, he couldn't even get a wife.

Nine

CREST FALLS, NEW YORK
December 2009

The sun slipped down in splendor, and now it was as if mischievous angels had thrown buckets of red wine at the sky. Mr. and Mrs. Calabrese sat on their glassed-in porch. He was stretched back in his easy chair, and she leaned to the side in one of the wicker chairs, with her head against a pillow. An hour had gone by while they watched the sunset as if it were a TV show. It seemed to Vincent Calabrese that the show had slowed to an end, and so he stood up and stretched his arms, took his wife's shawl off the small round table that was wedged between the wicker chairs, and put it around her shoulders.

"Well, sweetheart, that was a good one, wasn't it? It's getting downright cold out here; I think we ought to go inside. Tomorrow's another day, and Donna will be coming by to sit with you. Donna, Donna, Donna, you remember Donna, don't you?" He turned to look at her, and she looked back as if she didn't even know who he was. "You are one pretty lady," he said, staring deep into her eyes. He loved the grayness of her eyes, their soft, vague gaze. It seemed to him that she saw beyond what he could see, as if she had a glimpse into the next world and was too distracted by its wonder to acknowledge him.

"Are you Daddy?" she asked, out of the blue, looking up at him with hope.

He paused to sigh. "Yes, Mrs. Calabrese, I am whatever you say I am. And Donna is your sister; don't you remember her? She's going to take care of you while I'm away. I have to go out on a long chore tomorrow, and I won't be able to take you with me. But I'll be back by nightfall, so don't you worry."

"I want meat," she said, near tears, reaching her hands up toward him.

"What did you say?" he asked, bending in to hear her better.

"I want meat," said Vivian.

"Meat!" he said with a little laugh. "Okay, dear, let's see what we can find inside." But first he turned and stood with his big hands against the cold glass window that enclosed the porch. He looked both ways down the street where they lived; the houses were lined up in either direction, one almost exactly the same as another. The Jeffersons' had the pink front door, and the Heffrons hung the American flag; everybody had a different color car parked in the driveway, but lately, all of it appeared to be unusually dull and vacant. What was the use of having sidewalks when they were broken and overgrown with grass? It seemed that people didn't take walks anymore, and it used to be that families were in their yards at sundown. No one seemed to be anywhere, and Vincent wondered, Where are all the people?

He helped his wife into the house and sat her down on the couch in the living room while he went to the kitchen to see what he could find. In the refrigerator were some cold cuts, smoked turkey and ham, with a couple of slices of Swiss cheese left over from a few days ago, when he'd made a picnic for her. It was one of the last warm days before the winter air blew in. They'd gone to Spider Lake, a few miles out of town, and had sat on a blanket, buttoned into their sweaters and tied into their scarves, watching the gentle whitecaps roll over the water. It was a windy day, and Vivian's white hair had blown around until she looked like an old dandelion ready to seed. He'd laughed at her, and she'd laughed back. She'd seemed to enjoy the wind and water, and they'd eaten the sandwiches and sipped lemonade from little cartons, which came with their own tiny straws. A young couple had successfully launched a red kite that was flying grandly, and the Calabreses were mesmerized, sipping and pointing like two kindergartners, as the kite got smaller and smaller.

Now Vincent unwrapped the pumpernickel bread and fixed up a few sandwiches, but by the time he brought them into the living room, Vivian had dozed off, so he placed the tray on the coffee table, slipped off her shoes, and lifted her legs and feet up onto the couch. He took her shawl and the crocheted blanket that Donna had made for them years ago, and placed them over his wife, just in case she got a chill. Settling into his chair, he flicked on the TV, making sure to keep the volume down, and found a program about migrating birds. He sat engrossed, marveling at how many miles birds can fly before they rest.

Donna showed up bright and early the next morning with a bag of Dunkin' Donuts and said, "Put the coffee on, Vinnie!"

Vincent had grown to appreciate his sister-in-law over the years; he always thought it was funny how the sisters were opposites. While Vivian was shy and soft-spoken, Donna was a babbler, and bossy. But she'd always been there for them. Back when Anthony died, she'd been the first one over to the house, she'd handled everything, and it was a good thing, too, because both Vincent and Vivian fell apart and didn't seem to know what to do. Donna got right on the phone to the funeral home and called all the necessary friends, and she took Vincent and Vivian to the cemetery to pick the plot. She was a godsend, as Vivian used to say.

The morning they got the phone call about Anthony, on that hot August day in 2002, Vivian and Vincent had just finished painting the living room. They had worked on it together over one weekend, and they were putting the furniture back against the walls before Vincent went to work when the phone rang. Vivian answered the call; the voice on the other end was faint, and Vivian thought perhaps it was a child.

"Hello, my name is Mary Saint. Is there a Mr. Vincent Calabrese?"

"Mary Saint, aren't you the singer in Anthony's band?" asked Vivian.

The girl said, "Yes, I am."

"I'm Vivian, Anthony's mother."

"I . . . is your husband there? They told me to speak to your husband."

"Who told you? What's wrong, dear? Where are you?"

Vincent came over to the phone, sensing the worry in Vivian's voice.

"Is your husband— Can I please talk to Mr. Vincent Calabrese? I think I ought to speak to him," the caller repeated.

When Vincent took the phone, Mary said, "Mr. Calabrese, I'm so sorry to have to tell you that Anthony has had a terrible accident. I . . . don't know what one says . . ."

Vincent said nothing.

"He's dead, Mr. Calabrese. It was an accident . . . he fell . . . out of the twenty-second floor of a hotel in Los Angeles last night. I loved him," she said. "He was my dearest friend. He adored you, he always . . ." She broke away, crying.

Vincent could feel that his arms were shaking, and he looked up at Vivian, whose hand was over her mouth; she knew that something was terribly wrong. Her gray-green eyes were pleading, and she shook her head, over and over. She kept saying "No." That was all Vincent could remember about the call. He somehow got off the phone with the girl's room number and the name of the Japanese hotel, Pinku Ishi.

Donna stepped in right away and called Mary Saint back to find out the details. Mary said they'd had a bad show, opening for a big band whose name Donna had never heard, something like Snarkle Rot. Sliced Ham had gotten terrible reviews in the two major Los Angeles papers. One of the reviews described the band as a collection of frauds and said that their songs were *stoopid*—Mary had spelled it out for Donna—and not only was the band sloppy but Mary Saint was too fat to wear a tight-fitting dress. According to Mary, the picture of her printed in the paper had obviously been snapped from the front row, right below the stage, and it was all *thighs, boobs, and nostrils.*

Mary told Donna in painstaking detail, "There was a pool

party at Snarkle Rot's drummer's house the night after the concert, and there were a couple of copies of the reviews floating around the party. Snarkle Rot got a rave, but we were creamed. When we got back to the hotel, I was stomping around like a baby. I got out of control, ma'am, telling Anthony that the picture of me looked like a farm animal going to slaughter—which was, you know, a passionate issue for him. I was trying to make him realize how I felt. I just kept saying, 'Garbagio! Can't you understand? I didn't used to care about this crap, I used to let it all roll off me, no matter what they said, but I'm poisoned, and now I'm just part of the consumer pop culture, I've let myself be ruined.' You know, Garbagio—that was his nickname."

But Donna already knew that, because it had been his nickname since he was a little boy, when he had been given the chore of emptying the garbage and they all used to tease him about his many attempts to avoid actually doing it.

Mary said she'd been in a rage about the review and that was why she had gotten smashed. She wandered out onto the balcony of their hotel room, which had a floor of Japanese stones. She began picking up the stones and hurling them at cars down below, screaming at the cars, telling them what a big fatso she was, when Anthony came out and tried to calm her down, convince her to stop throwing stones and come back inside. When he tried to pull her away from the lowest part of the railing on the balcony, he slipped and fell over the edge. It happened so fast, according to Mary, that she didn't even know how it was possible. She tried to tell the police that it was all her fault, but after she had explained the story to them, they told her it was an accident.

Donna didn't say it, but since Mary Saint was all messed up on drink and drugs, how could she know what was possible or not? At the same time, Donna was struck by how candid the girl was; it seemed to her that someone else might have lied, or at least tried to paint a more flattering picture of herself, but Mary Saint had spewed the information into the phone unabridged, and ended up begging for permission to come to the funeral.

Donna tried to convince Vincent to keep Mary away, for Vivian's sake, but he insisted that if Anthony had loved the girl, she had a right to be there, and Donna backed down when she otherwise might have pushed because she realized that Vincent could not take another ounce of pressure.

Vincent put the coffee on and showed Donna where all the meds were, and what he had planned for Vivian to eat that day. She said, "Don't worry about a thing, Vincent, I have it covered."

He knew that was true, and so he kissed his wife on the forehead and said, "I'll be home for dinner, Mrs. C." Then he turned to Donna and said, "Probably around six this evening, depending on traffic. Thank you for doing this, Donna."

His sister-in-law took hold of Vincent's arm and said, "It's going to be okay."

Vivian didn't seem to notice when her husband walked out the front door.

Ten
. . . .

THREE FORKS HOME
December 2009

Jean Saint knew the shortcut to Three Forks Home: up Eagle Valley Road, a sharp right onto Route 10, follow along the reservoir, look for the abandoned shack on the left, turn onto the tiny nameless road that can easily be missed, cross the rickety old bridge, and turn left again at Gazely Highway, which was hardly a highway at all. Three Forks Home was set back from the road, and a winding driveway led visitors to the parking lot. It was named for its three wings, A, B, and C, which were crookedly laid out, like a prehistoric bird's foot. It was unclear what the purpose of the crookedness was, perhaps an architect's creative urge. Years ago, when Jean first saw the place, she had thought it might as well be called Three Forks Prison.

As soon as Jean got out of the car, she noticed how the wind had picked up, and she pulled her coat collar tighter around her neck. The clouds were dark gray, moving fast across the sky, as if they were rushing to seal up earth from heaven for the winter months. A flock of geese honked overhead, and she took a moment to watch them flap across the sky in a V. There were always a few stragglers, so she waited for a moment. Sure enough a lone goose appeared, and she endured the wind for one more minute, just to watch it fly, and marvel at how it got to be so alone. When the bird was far off, nothing more than a speck in the sky, she took her shopping bag full of cookies from the backseat and headed for the entrance to the home.

To say that Three Forks was decorated for the holidays would have been an understatement; every inch of the place was flowing in gold and silver tinsel and Christmas ornaments, with balls of red, blue, and green hung haphazardly. A line of holiday cards dangled overhead across the reception desk; there were glittered snowmen, Marys and Josephs, baby Jesuses, Santas, bells and holly, angels and snow scenes, one or two Jewish stars, and a couple of pictures of families. A fake Christmas tree stood in the corner by the coffee machine with cheap strings of lights blinking rapidly and garishly. Thick strands of tinsel were thrown carelessly across the front of it, and on the counter by the coffee machine was a menorah, three of its lights lit in blue and two missing altogether. The coffee cups had Santa Claus faces on them, and the napkins had holly leaves and berries around their edges.

"Mrs. Saint, happy holidays to you!" said Delores.

"Delores, my dear, how are you?" said Jean.

Delores, a large black woman, probably close to Jean's age, came out from behind the reception desk to give Jean a hug. She walked with difficulty on weakened knees and pulled Jean into a tight embrace. Jean's face sank into her bosom like a baby kangaroo into its mother's pouch. Even though she was not the touchy-feely type, Jean had long ago surrendered to the hugs, because almost all of the people who worked at Three Forks were huggers, and they were all black as well. Jean figured it was just their way. The aides were the only black people Jean knew, and they all wore pink uniforms. It was as if the home were a planet all its own and Jean qualified as an illegal alien, a regular visitor for years.

Jean dug into her bag of goodies and pulled out a package for Delores. "Here, I've brought you a little something."

"Oh, Jean, you shouldn't have gone to the trouble."

"It's the least I could do. And it's really nothing, just some of my cookies, the usual, you know."

"Oh, honey, just what I need, another cookie! They are good, though. I'm going to hide these babies in my drawer." Delores laughed in her big loud way.

"How's he doing?" asked Jean.

"Well, you know, he's doing fine," said Delores. "You can go right on back and see him."

As Jean turned in to the hallway, out of the corner of her eye she saw Mrs. Hollingberry, the director of Three Forks, and her plump English assistant, Harris Wood. They marched into the lobby, and Mrs. Hollingberry let Delores have it, somehow unaware that Jean was there. "Delores, for God's sake, clean this up! We have visitors coming through this lobby. Don't you know how to trim a tree? Really, take some pride in your work. It looks like the patients decorated this place."

"Yes, Miz. Hollingberry, I'll see to it," said Delores, brushing off the harshness as if it were an annoying fly.

Jean winced. The sound of Mrs. Hollingberry's voice grated

on her, and the way she spoke to Delores and the other aides was unforgivable. Jean wondered how they put up with it, especially since Mrs. Hollingberry was all handshakes and blowy kisses with the clients; she came off transparent as cellophane. People whispered about Mrs. Hollingberry's troubles, of course. Her husband had been murdered in New York City, on their twentieth wedding anniversary (Jean could never understand why anyone would want to go to New York City, and this just proved her point). Mr. Hollingberry had made a sizable fortune in textiles, and apparently the couple was splurging with a stay at the Plaza hotel. On a whim, before the fancy tea that came with the weekend package, they'd gone for a stroll and were approached by two hoodlums on the way into Central Park. One of the men grabbed Mrs. Hollingberry's purse. Her husband bravely went after them, but one of the two turned and stabbed him. The thieves took off, disappearing into the crowd on Central Park South, and Mr. Hollingberry died right there on the sidewalk amid a circle of onlookers. It made Jean shiver, just to think of it.

Perhaps because of that, Mrs. Hollingberry had a *breakable* quality, or perhaps that was why she was mean, or perhaps it was just her nature. Generally, she seemed to be moments away from cracking into a thousand pieces, and it was widely known that she'd had a brief stint in a hospital (for *mental* reasons), but still, Jean thought the aides were easy targets, especially Delores, who was as kind and loving as anyone she'd ever met. Delores had an uncanny ability to absorb Mrs. Hollingberry's pain, which ironically seemed to unleash her boss's fury. Once, Jean had gathered the nerve to pull Delores aside and suggest to her that she shouldn't take the abuse, but Delores had said it didn't bother

her too much, and she'd discreetly shared about a time when Mrs. Hollingberry had broken down like a little child in a back office. "I rocked that lady in my arms. Believe me, I know something about trouble, and once you been struck down by violence, you never the same, you can see it in the eyes," she had said. Jean remembered faking a sneeze and looking away, later realizing she feared what Delores might see in her eyes. On subsequent visits, Jean had wondered about Delores's eyes, but she never inquired further about any of it and was careful not to study Delores too hard, thinking it might be rude.

Jean walked down the hallway, peeking into some of the rooms. There was Mrs. Glickman, in her frayed blue terry-cloth robe, sitting in the chair beside her bed, staring.

"Hello, Shirley," Jean said and waved, stopping for a moment. Shirley Glickman had come in around the same time as Bub; she'd had a broken hip back then, but she never recovered enough to go home. There was no one at home to take care of her, and she was able to pay, so she'd stayed at Three Forks, and now she seemed to have lost her mind. Jean walked into her room and was immediately repulsed by the smell of urine; there was a bedpan, not yet emptied, on the floor, and she saw that Shirley's feet were swollen and pink, sticking out of her slippers. Jean took one of the extra little bundles of cookies that she'd wrapped with napkins and tied up with snippets of red ribbon that she'd salvaged from the bottom of her arts and crafts bag, and set it on Shirley's night table. "This is a Hanukkah gift for you, Shirley." The woman said nothing, and Jean patted her hand, leaving as quickly as she could.

As she went farther down the hall, she saw that Lateisha,

Rowena, and Alvin were bathing Lucas Conrad, a nasty old crank. He was hollering and cursing at them as Alvin held his arms down and Rowena rubbed soapy water on his chest while Lateisha washed his feet. When they saw Jean, they left Mr. Conrad for a moment, first taking care to put a towel over him and then lifting the guardrails on his bed. Lucas Conrad yelled at Rowena, calling her a whore. But they only laughed and showered Jean with hugs. She gave each of them some cookies, and Lateisha said that her husband, Paul, ate last year's all in one sitting, and Jean was secretly pleased.

She wondered why she felt so close to all the aides. They were different; yes, they were *black,* but they were also *good.* Her relationship to them was simple but deep. She felt that they were doing God's work, as if they were really nuns and priests. The horrors of the home were clear enough to see, and Jean wouldn't have been able to endure a single day of it—the bedpans, the naked old bodies, the smell, the hopelessness; she couldn't even begin to dwell on it. She was humbled by the work they did and guilty, too, for she never could quite forgive herself for bringing Bub here. She knew there were much worse places; she'd heard gruesome stories about other homes where the staff were mean to the patients, letting them sit for hours in their own stink, and there'd been a story on the news a while back about one place, farther upstate, where they beat the patients. Three Forks was a good home. But still.

She turned in to Bub's room, the last door at the end of the hall in wing C. It was one of the best rooms because it looked out onto a small pond surrounded by birch trees, which were bare and chalky in the winter months, but it was much better than looking out at the brick wall of one of the other wings. Bub's room was nearly empty; the bed was freshly made, white sheets, clean and tight, with a gray wool blanket tucked tautly into the mattress. Beside the bed were a pitcher of water and a small white paper cup. Also on the table was a lamp that Jean had brought from home. It was the one that had always been beside his easy chair, and it had a sailboat on the shade. Not that Bub had any interest in sailboats, but secretly she hoped the aides would think it had some meaning. She wanted them to think she'd had a happy life and a lovely family, a family with tender memories of birthday cakes and anniversaries.

She'd also brought Bub's blue transistor radio, which he used to listen to his ball games on, but it was now collecting dust and looking like a relic from another time, although Alvin said Bub seemed to like the hip-hop music station. How he figured that, she couldn't tell, but she doubted it was true and shuddered at the thought that Bub would have to listen to that noise. She didn't say anything, though, for fear of getting on the wrong side of Alvin, who she sensed could turn on a dime.

Next to the radio was a picture of the family on vacation. Mary, as a girl, and Jean, with her arm around her, sober-faced. Bub's eyes were half-shut, and he was looking off to the side with his arms crossed. They were standing in front of Niagara Falls; they had asked a stranger to snap the photo. It was one of the few vacations they had ever taken. Mary's baby face was smiling, happy and proud.

In reality, the trip had been a disaster. Bub had sunk into a slump; he'd gotten mad when a restaurant hostess wouldn't seat them because Mary had culottes on instead of a skirt. Bub didn't even know what culottes were. The whole thing was absurd. The hostess had had the mistaken impression that she was running a high-stakes operation, which was perhaps understandable considering the popularity of the restaurant, and it might have been funny or manageable if Bub hadn't gotten so mad and abusive. But he'd called the woman a hippo, and she'd countered by calling him an ass. But he couldn't leave it there, and to Jean's embarrassment, he'd called her a baboon. Even more surprising was when the hostess had come back at him, yelling, *"Stick it up your ass, mister,"* at which point the manager, a skinny guy with big round glasses who couldn't have been more than twenty-five, had come and escorted the Saints out the front door. They'd had to walk through the line of people who were waiting for tables. Mary had been sniffling and ashamed, and Jean had just wanted to get out of there.

They spent the remaining three days of the vacation in the cloud of one of Bub's dreary silences, with Mary afraid and Jean pretending nothing was wrong. It occurred to Jean that these days no one knew what culottes were. Little girls wore shorts and skirts practically up to their waists, and what difference did any of it make? All the fighting and fussing for nothing.

Now Bub sat in his wheelchair, facing the window, unlikely to cause a fuss of any kind. Jean went around to see his face. It must have been hard to shave him; his whiskers were sticking out. Jean thought he looked a bit like a leprechaun. He stared up at her blankly; then he reached his bony fingers toward her face and she took them into her hands. "Hello, Bub," she said. Luckily, he didn't smell bad. He was mute, that was all . . . and gentle. Finally, gentle. His spindly legs were like an ostrich's, and he had on the silly bunny-eared slippers that Lateisha had given him last year, for whatever reason; it was possible they had belonged to a patient who had passed. He wore a faded blue hospital gown, and he was clean.

Jean was relieved to feel a spurt of tenderness rush through her. If only he could have been gentle all those years. Quiet. It seemed to her more and more that, if people couldn't talk, the world would be a better place.

She pulled up the chair from the corner of the room and placed it next to him.

"It's Christmas, Bub. Merry Christmas." The two of them sat side by side, looking out the window at the pond, holding hands, like best buddies. After a while, Jean went over to her bag of gifts and pulled out one of the smaller packages of cookies, wrapped in a napkin. She undid it and took out a Saint Nick cookie, breaking a piece of it off, and raised it to Bub's lips, and he let it enter his mouth. He had one good tooth on the upper right side, and she felt the tooth grab the cookie and start to break it down. She rewrapped the cookies and set them on the table beside his bed. When he had successfully swallowed the little piece of Saint Nick's head, she tried to give him another chunk, but his mouth, as if it were a thing of its own, wouldn't open, and so she threw the piece of cookie in the garbage pail.

Mrs. Hollingberry and Harris Wood were showing an elderly gentleman around the hallway. They stopped briefly at Bub's room, and Harris Wood said, "Merry, Merry!" Jean smiled stiffly, going along with the show. Mrs. Hollingberry stuck her coiffed head and painted face into the room, saying, "Hello, Jean. Happy holidays! So nice to see you here! How's . . . our friend?" She paused ever so slightly, blew a kiss to Bub, and Jean realized she had no idea what his name was. "How's he doing?"

Jean felt her lips purse, but she said, "Very well, thank you," as if reading from a script. She glanced past Mrs. Hollingberry at the man taking the tour. He had a round, kind face and a big hook nose, his shirt starched and sky blue; he held a suit coat over his arm. He seemed embarrassed at the intrusion by Mrs. Hollingberry, and Jean was grateful for that. She remembered what it was like when she'd come for the tour; she had dressed up, too. How terribly strange the home had seemed; how cold and dull the institutional rooms had looked to her. She couldn't have imagined getting used to such a place, and yet here she was, in her old slacks and a sweatshirt, as if she were in her living room.

On her way out of the home, Jean stopped in the chapel for a prayer, as she always did. The chapel was small and painted seashell white, not the harsh green that was on the walls of most of the rest of the home. An altar, which was covered with a plain lace cloth, held a single yellow rose in a thin glass vase. Above the altar was a simple chandelier made of wood. Flames from the pillar candles that were placed around the room gave a feeling of life. The pale winter light came down through the windows and cast changing patterns over the pews through a crystal that hung down from the chandelier.

The floor was made of textured stones, and ten dark brown

pews, roughly cut, with an aisle in the middle, made room for people to pray. As far as Jean knew, no one else used the chapel; it was as if she had her own private church. She wondered who had thought to build this room, and why it was given so much more care than the rest of the place.

Heading to her usual spot, at first she didn't see him. She heard the muffled cries, and then she realized that the man who had been walking around with Mrs. Hollingberry was hunched over, kneeling in the far left side of the first pew.

Jean's heart began to pound. She stayed put for a moment, trying not to make noise, and then slipped into the last pew, sitting down as quickly and quietly as she could.

The man's big round arms and bald head were resting on the railing in front of the pew. In her stillness, Jean thought the sound of his crying was more like that of an animal than that of a human, something like a dog whimpering in a trap. It was unbearably sad, and Jean wanted to do something. She thought about finding Mrs. Hollingberry or even Harris Wood.

The man let out a wail. It was loud and uncontrolled, like he was being punched or kicked, and Jean felt herself stand up and rush down the aisle. Before she knew it, she was by his side.

"Are you all right?" she asked, alarmed.

He looked up at her as if she were a ghost, his eyes wet with tears. He had a handkerchief in his hand, and he quickly wiped his eyes to see if she was really there. "Who are you?" he said.

"I'm the woman who was in the room that you passed by," she heard herself answer.

"Oh, yes, I'm sorry. My wife," he said in a whisper. "I have to bring her here."

"My husband is here."

"I can't do it," he said, staring at her.

She studied his face, his brown eyes and big old nose. His lips were full, and his bulky cheeks extended into jowls around his neck, which stuck out of his blue shirt like soft ice cream swirled from a machine. She felt herself take hold of his arm with both her hands. "I know the way you feel," she said. But in truth, Jean remembered the day she had brought Bub into this place; she had been at the end of her rope with him. Something had clicked, or a switch had turned off. She'd been relieved and had a sense of being set free.

"I love my wife, she's all I have, she's a beautiful soul," he said and then dissolved again into sobs.

"I'm sorry," said Jean, pinched with jealousy and awe.

"Vivian," he said out loud.

"No, my name is Jean," said Jean.

"Her name is Vivian," he said.

"My husband's name is Bub," said Jean.

"My name is Vincent," he said.

And something made them both laugh. As the sun went down and the chapel settled into darkness, dotted by the light of the candles, Jean and Vincent sat together talking in low tones about various things: first, their spouses; then they moved on to key lime pie and the wild weed called hairy bittercress. By the time they landed on their children, they were already friends.

"I had a son," said Vincent. "He died in a bad accident. What a character he was. A musician."

Jean hesitated, letting the word *musician* roll around her brain. She wondered if she could call Mary a musician, but she had to say something. "What a coincidence. My daughter, too, is some-thing like a musician, I suppose. Some people say she is a poet," she said, thinking of Bill De Sockie.

"Really," said Vincent. "You must be proud. A poet is a gift to the world."

"Well, she's not a Robert Frost type of poet. At least I don't think so. She was in a band for a while. A sort of rock and roll type thing, I guess. They were somehow successful. Honestly, Vincent, I've never really heard her music."

"Well, I can understand that," said Vincent. "My son was in a band, too. I know it was hard to understand his music at first. His band wrote a song called 'Feet and Knuckles,' a funny little song, and it was a hit, supposedly. Vivian loves the song, even still. He was a vegetarian, he always loved animals, and that's what the song is all about."

" 'Feet and Knuckles'?" Jean laughed, thinking those words rang a bell.

"My son, he was a good kid."

Jean was afraid he might cry again. "It seems you've had your share of trouble, Vincent. May I ask what happened to your son?"

"He fell from the balcony of a hotel room."

Jean sat up straight; she didn't know what to say. She grabbed his arm again.

"I know. It was a terrible, terrible tragedy," said Vincent.

"No . . . you don't understand," said Jean, uneasily. "I think I might know something about your son. . . . Do you know the name . . . Garbagio?"

"Jean, that's his name. I mean, his name is Anthony, but we

called him Garbagio. It was a childhood nickname. How do you know about him?"

"My daughter, well, her name is . . . Mary Saint. Sliced Ham? Is that the name of the band your son was in?"

He looked at her for a moment, and then he smiled as if she'd just said something wonderful, but his eyes were pained. "Oh boy, this is hard to believe," said Vincent, looking away but then quickly back at her. "I've met your daughter, Jean. She came to Anthony's funeral. She was his best friend, and she was there when he died. I think they were very much in love. She blamed herself, poor girl."

Jean was horrified. She could not hear another word. The pain of Mary's world came crashing back down on her. Everywhere she went, she was reminded. Was there no peace? They heard the click of the chapel door; Mrs. Hollingberry stuck her head in. "Anybody in here? Why, yes. Visiting hours are over now," she said, and the smiling cheerfulness turned off like a light in the hall.

Jean stood up abruptly. She didn't know how to end this, but that was all she wanted to do. "I've left my purse on the pew back there," she said, and turned to go, rushing down the aisle. She grabbed her coat and her purse, leaving the shopping bag with the extra bundles of cookies behind.

"Jean, what are you doing? Wait!" called Vincent. "It wasn't her fault! She's a darling girl, Jean!" he pleaded, but the chapel door had closed and Jean was gone.

In no time, she was down the hall, and there was Mrs. Hollingberry again, now standing over Delores, who was on her hands and knees, wiping something up off the floor by the front desk.

"No, the spot I'm talking about is right there. Don't skip it," said Mrs. Hollingberry.

"For the Lord's sake, would you stop abusing Delores. You're an absolute witch! It's Christmas. Shame on you!" cried Jean. In her seventy-two years, she had never spoken to anyone with such force.

Delores looked up from the floor, stunned. Mrs. Hollingberry whipped her head around and stood with her eyes wide and her hand on her heart as she watched Jean escape into the darkness, out into the chill of the night, without bothering to button up her coat.

Once outside, Jean hurried to her car, didn't even buckle herself in, and drove away. No more, she thought. Enough. She could not accept another morsel. What more had Mary done? Vincent had said it wasn't her fault. Why? Jean hadn't said it was.

As Jean pulled out of the driveway and down Gazely Highway, she wondered how it would be if she drove herself right off the lovely old bridge that had no name and into the stupid little stream. What if she were the one to cause trouble, to make a scene, to die, to love, to be rude, strange, and unruly? How would they all like that?

PART

Two

Eleven

SAN FRANCISCO, CALIFORNIA

January 2010

The mist blew in from the Pacific, crept across Golden Gate Park, and had already begun to erase the Panhandle when Mary Saint woke to the sound of beaded curtains knocking against the bay windows in her bedroom. She peeked through the curtains, and though it was still dark, she could see that the eucalyptus trees were threatening to disappear into the fog. Please don't, she thought. It was early, but Mary had the sinking feeling that she was up for the day, and from the moment she opened her eyes, the blues were there to greet her. She reached behind her to feel for the softness of her dog's paw. Two Toes was a brown rescue named for a birth defect on her front paw, and she lay across the sheets as if she were a movie star, leaving Mary to lie like a pencil on a sliver of the bed. The dog stretched her legs and rolled over, groaned and closed her eyes again, but one of her ears was up, waiting to hear what Mary would do. After staring at the ceiling for a good long while, Mary rose, closed the window, and reached for the nearest sweatshirt, as it had gotten chilly through the night.

Thaddeus, who had been Mary's roommate for the past six

months, was sleeping on the mattress in the living room, curled up like a baby under his green blanket riddled with holes. He carried it with him from one temporary dwelling to the next, and he'd agreed to let Mary wash it but not mend it, as if she even could. Mary tiptoed past Thaddeus into the kitchen, leaving Two Toes to resume her twitching and dreaming. She filled the teakettle with water, put it on the stove, and looked out the window again.

Daylight was coming slowly; on Oak Street a lone car passed, its headlights beaming in the haze. The gloom still hung in the air, and though Mary was glad to see that the fog was thinning, her ghosts were all around her. No one was out walking yet, and the Panhandle looked ominous and cold; it would be an hour or so before the old women gathered across the park for their morning practice of tai chi, and even longer until Thaddeus would rise with his good-morning songs and a recap of his dreams. Yesterday, he'd dreamed that he got chopped up into little squares and put into a plastic ice cube tray.

"That's not very funny, Thaddeus," Mary had said.

"I know, I know."

She shivered at the darkness and thought how lucky she was to have a place to live; that she'd had the money, years ago, to buy a flat was a miracle. A place to live—four drafty rooms with rattling windows, somewhere she could be. It had really gotten down to basics. How panicky she'd become after her early years of free-falling craziness.

Mary made herself a cup of lingonberry tea and sat at the small table in the kitchen, fingering the ceramic salt and pepper shakers. One of the shakers was a white dog with dots of black paint for eyes and a nose; the other one was a black dog with dots of white paint for its eyes and nose. Everything was a dog. She had pictures of dogs that she had drawn, painted, and sketched all over her flat; there were dog poems, dog cups and plates, postcards of dogs; even the sugar bowl had a top that was a dog's face, and the bowl itself had a small tail. She'd replaced all things musical with all things dog, but the music still haunted her, and now she'd flung herself, like a banana peel, right back into its path. When her mother had called her, back in October, about a teacher at her old high school who wanted her to do a concert there, of all places, she'd hastily agreed. The concert, scheduled for June, now hung over her like a sky full of knives. Why didn't someone—Thaddeus, anyone—tell her she was crazy to take the gig? Maybe it was not too late to cancel it. For the past few weeks, she'd had the old performing nightmares, and almost every night she'd wake up in a sweat, seeing herself naked on the stage, or peeing on the stage, or forgetting all the words, the audience rising up against her. Unlike Thaddeus, she didn't want to talk about her dreams; they made her feel ashamed.

She thought about what seemed to be the impossibility of forgetting. The memories of what her life once was were absurd, unreal. Life on that thing called the road, moments of incredible freedom, laughter, possibilities; as if a person could fly, these feelings were sewn into the agony of great humiliation, failures so extreme, so *public*—rave reviews and vicious dismissals—revolting, bone-chillingly cold dressing rooms; stained toilet bowls and sticky floors; dented aluminum ashtrays; cigarettes and joints; platters of curled-up pieces of roast beef and melted

American cheese left out in the heat for hours; *head cheese,* whatever the hell it was; precut carrot sticks and celery in supermarket bags; whiskey and bottles of tequila—with worms at the bottom that were supposed to be swallowed—posters of bands, mostly guys in leather pants, their crotches bulging, hairy arms inked with tattoos of girls and dragons; photographs of herself posing with electric guitars, in ridiculous outfits that she had thought she ought to wear, ripped stockings that made her legs look diseased, garter belts and makeup like war paint; attitudes, her own and everybody else's; songs that she wrote from her heart and what they actually turned out to be; who people said she was and who she really was; who *she* thought she was and who she turned out to be; thousands of people cheering for it, the noise of crowds yelling, *We love you, Mary Saint. Garbagio rules! Sliced Ham, Sliced Ham! Feet and Knuckles! You're a Pig!* It had been a long Tilt-A-Whirl ride, the predictable clichés—hotel lobbies, airport bars, and the exquisite uniqueness of those very same places—everywhere a carnival, the ghoulishness of it all; the costumes, the buffoons, the down-and-out drug-laden, liquor-soaked good old times; the goofiness, the innocence, the mistakes, cruelties, lies, and beauty; the mixture of fakery and truth; the sadness; the laughs. The commodity that was Mary Saint, the things that people used to say about her—to her—the things that she had said, shooting her mouth off about this and that, hurting herself and others, being cheered on like a pit bull in a ring. All of this led up to the death of Anthony, the event that had cut her life in half and ended his. This was what she remembered of herself. She'd wrestled with her lover until he fell to his death off the balcony of a hotel room. Why? Because in the end someone had said she was fat and *stoopid*. She had lost herself along the way. This was all she had to "go on."

When Donal Hogan, her longtime agent and manager, and what else could she call him but a friend, had taken her out to lunch and told her they were going to drop her from their roster, she had just turned thirty; it was after Anthony's death and her stint at the rehab. She'd thought her life was over. By then Donal had become hugely successful, a superstar himself—the creator of Planet of the Stars. Every major act was signed to him, and if not, they wanted to be. She had been his first major success, and it could be argued that she put him on the map, but it also could be argued that he put her on the map. In truth, they both had come to understand that the map was always being redrawn and empires came and went quickly. They had felt their footing shift, and talked about it many times, privately, in hotel bars and on tour buses, never really thinking it would end. It had been almost seven years since she'd seen him or spoken to him, but she remembered him, and the Irish accent that he'd tried so hard to lose when he moved his agency to New York City, fondly.

When the waiter had set down their salads, Donal had grabbed her hand and said softly, "Look, Mary, yeh had a good run. Yeh have a couple of *quid,* get a place to live and take it slow for a while. A lot of bands don't go as far as Sliced Ham. It was just never big *enoof.* Yeh took a hit, losing Garbagio. *Lookily,* you got a wee bit of change to live off of for a while. Whatever yeh do, my dear, don't go solo. Don't be one of those sad porky rock stars that starts playing rubbish gigs for no money, singing songs about how they feel." It was clear he'd had no intention of being in touch with her again.

Things changed quickly. If Planet of the Stars dropped her, then no one else would want to pick her up. It was the kiss of death. She went from being Mary Saint onstage, on the road, calling in to the office to complain that the windows in her hotel room wouldn't open, and singing herself ragged to crowds in darkened theaters and clubs, to being Mary Saint who instantly had nothing to do, nowhere to go. Aside from her loyal fans who to this day wrote her the sweetest letters and recognized her from time to time as she roamed the streets of San Francisco, she had not one friend left from the whole charade. Even Donal, after everything that had happened between them—poof, gone.

There had been that night in Pittsburgh, at a hotel bar after a show. He'd said, "I adore you, Mary dear, you know I've been in *loove* with you for years."

"Oh, Donal, come on, don't."

"Yeh owe it to me, Mary," he'd panted. "I mean, don't yeh even fancy me after all we've shared?"

That was when she gave in, went limp, and let him have her. On the elevator he started in with wet kisses on the neck; by the time they reached his room, it was sloppy and rough. Poor Donal, he was shaking with desire. And she did love him; maybe he was right that this was what she owed, she really didn't know. How many times had she cried on Donal's shoulder, called him at three in the morning? But she realized, now, with great embarrassment, that it had all been business and she was the one who'd been mistaken about it. Donal's conscience was clear, he was just doing his job and he was damn good at it. As for that one measly night? What the *fook*, it happens.

Within a year or so after Planet of the Stars dropped Mary, it was as if she'd turned radioactive or had contracted a highly contagious disease; she'd needed to be disposed of. No hard feelings. It was even odd the way the band had disintegrated so easily. Gabe Jones, the drummer, quickly got into another band, and she'd seen something recently about how he was replacing the drummer in Snarkle Rot, which was still going strong. The guitar player, Frooty Peterson, went back home to London and got a job at his father's ad agency; they'd barely said good-bye to each other, it was awkward and quick, as if they'd been strangers who had just had sex in the bathroom at a bus station.

Everyone knew that after Anthony died the whole thing was over. Whoever she had been, she wasn't anymore, but the band limped on for a while. She remembered how Donal used to joke with her: *Miss Mary, yer gettin' a wee too old.* None of them ever seriously considered that that was a remote possibility . . . she wasn't old, just old news. Either way, the band was dying. They'd gotten a replacement bass player, Joe Dixon, a brilliant studio musician who spent most of his time on the phone, securing sessions back in L.A. Nobody liked him, and he couldn't wait to get off the road.

Someone was bound to be a casualty, left hanging around in his or her own life, but seven years was a long time. What the hell had happened? *Ass kicked, ass kicked, ass kicked* . . . resounded in her brain like the ticking of a clock. Many slow weeks rolled by in the course of those years, as Mary trudged up and down the streets of San Francisco, spending entire days wandering around the city, sometimes with Two Toes and sometimes alone.

She'd visit the old buffaloes in Golden Gate Park, or wander through the Castro and the Mission, up into Potrero Hill for a cup of coffee at Farley's, or all the way to North Beach just to browse around City Lights bookstore again. She never tired of the cool air, the constant dance between sun and fog, the smell of the Pacific, the Victorian houses, and the sadness. Mary roamed the streets as if it were her job. She loved seeing the exotic words written in foreign alphabets on the Chinese, Turkish, and Japanese businesses. She imagined what San Francisco once was, a city built on dreams of elegance and beauty, but the way its lovely light-colored buildings had become grimy and battered gave the place a soulfulness that spoke to Mary's own sense of loss. Anyplace that allowed its citizens to paint elaborate, colorful pictures on the sides of buildings was okay with her. And though she'd meet people now and then, it was the city itself that had become her friend, and being alone became a way of life. She lurked around, in sunglasses, in backs of the rooms of AA, rarely accomplishing a connection. Only occasionally, like when she volunteered to walk the lonely dogs at the pound in the Mission, did she feel useful. She accepted her fate as penance for all she had done, but lately there were some points of light, and, at thirty-six, she was starting to feel alive again.

The sun began to creep into the kitchen, and Mary was relieved to feel its warmth. She heard Thaddeus stirring in the other room. It was a joy to make breakfast for Thaddeus, for he was so appreciative; he'd ask for pancakes with cinnamon butter, and omelets with goat cheese and olives, things she would never have dreamed of making. He'd sit and read to her from the cook-book, calling her Chef Mary, and even though she barely knew her way around the kitchen, he'd say she should have her own cooking show. Sometimes she felt easy around Thaddeus, the way she used to feel with Anthony.

She remembered that time in Glasgow, almost twenty years ago, Anthony's first gig with the band. What a cutie. He had seemed a little slow to her, but maybe it was just that he was shy. He'd shown up with a bandanna tied around his curly black hair, and somebody said his name was Garbagio. He was a big kid, soft-spoken and so ridiculously polite it was funny. Another American, that was interesting, too. She wondered what he was doing in the UK, for he seemed so utterly USA.

After the sound check he'd given her a bluebird feather, and she'd worn it in her hair for the show. The first time she ever heard the word *vegetarian* was when he approached her one night in the dressing room, asking about the deli platters.

"Do you think it would be possible to have a vegetarian plate? I don't eat meat," he said meekly, which for some reason caused her to laugh uncontrollably.

"What are you doing in England?"

"Seeing the world, I dunno," he said.

"Oh, yeah? What a world. Where are you from?"

"Just a little town in upstate New York nobody's ever heard of called Crest Falls."

"Oh, come on! No fucking way! I'm from Swallow! Holy crap!" she said.

"Are you kidding? Really, that's unbelievable!" he said.

"Hey, boys, listen to this, Garbagio and I are from the same pathetic patch of suburbia," she said, turning to the rest of the guys. "Do you realize how weird that is?"

But the boys had no idea what a bond it was. For Mary and Garbagio, who were far away from home, way off their own turf, it proved stronger than even they realized.

Within a week, they were sleeping together. Mary found him irresistible, and their lovemaking was tender; she'd never known such affection from a guy. Afterward, they sat naked on the bed at the Jurys Inn, outside of Manchester, and wrote "Feet and Knuckles" with her figuring out the melody on her guitar as Anthony fed her the words.

She'd also told him about *Other Mary* that night. She had never uttered a word about it to anyone before. She shivered as she described the scene in the woods to him, afraid that, if she spoke the story out loud, the lady would never be with her again.

"Do you know who the Blessed Virgin is?" she said.

"Uh, Mary, are you crazy? I was an altar boy. Of course I know who she is."

"Well, then, listen . . . the lady was *her*. It was *her*, Anthony," she said, studying his eyes to see what he might think.

"Holy Toledo," he said, holding her face in his hands. He kissed her eyes and lips. "You're amazing."

"I've never told a soul. Don't go weird on me."

"You are an exquisite goddess," he said.

"And you're a beautiful boy," she said.

"I'm not a boy."

"Okay, I just think you're sweet." She kissed him.

"You know, it seems to me that the same thing that happened to you happened to Paul McCartney—*Mother Mary comes to me*—

didn't you ever wonder about that? Do you think *Other Mary* and *Mother Mary* could be the same person? There's just a one-letter difference," he said. She wasn't sure if he was making fun of her, he was so bloody innocent. He could tell that she was suspicious of him, and he said, "What's wrong, Mary? You can trust me, I'm kind of a good person."

Mary got up from the bed and moved to the window, pleased that he was watching her every move. She was thinking about Paul McCartney, still worried that Anthony was kidding; he had a way of saying things so simply, you could think he was cracking a joke. But she considered for the first time that it was possible the *Mother Mary* that had come to Paul McCartney was the same as her own *Other Mary*.

"Maybe she really does visit people," he said.

She turned to him and said, "She told me that every time I sing, I should sing for her."

"Wow. Do you?"

"Yes, are you kidding? I could never do it otherwise. She's always with me when I sing. Sometimes I think I see her. I feel her love; I actually *feel* it. She is my reason for living; how embarrassing. I am devoted to her. I can't explain it, but I wouldn't know how to sing otherwise. Honestly, Anthony, I don't know how to do anything, I barely went to school."

Anthony was silent for a moment, and then he said, with complete seriousness, "It's weird that she goes to rock and roll shows."

"I know! I think about that all the time," she said.

"I mean, I'm not trying to be funny, but you say *fuck* more than anyone I know, and you're so sexy."

Mary laughed and said, "I might be wrong, but I don't think she minds that kind of stuff. I think she minds other things, like lying, and being mean. And I do those things sometimes."

"You're kind of mean, I've seen it."

"Look, I'm sort of in a weird position," she said.

"Mary, I think I'm a little bit over my head with you. I'm just a guy with a bass. I love music, and I'm not that smart, like God is not ever going to come my way . . . and say, 'Hey, Anthony'—"

But she cut him off. "Please don't make fun. I shouldn't have said anything."

"I'm not making fun. . . . I just know that something happened to you that probably won't happen to me. I'm only a bass player. I've never met anyone like you before."

"Do you believe me?"

"Yes, of course I do."

"Without her, this rock and roll thing is one big steaming pile of turds. It's meaningless to me," Mary said. She made Anthony promise that he would not tell a soul, for fear the whole thing would become a joke among the band or, worse, leak out to the press.

"Mary, I won't say anything to anyone . . . but . . . is that really true, you don't like rock and roll?" said Anthony.

"Duh, don't be stupid, Anthony," she said, turning her face away.

"You can be very cruel," he said. "Why be cruel to me? I thought you liked me."

He was right. Why was she so cruel sometimes? It was in her blood.

"I'm just like my father," she used to say, though she carried her warrior's flag against him. Back then, fueled by her vision of him as enemy and abuser, it was easy to feel righteous, but lately, at idle moments, she affectionately recalled his jokes, even laughed aloud, and when she looked into the mirror, she could see his face in hers; he was in her lips, the way they quivered nervously, defensively. What use was her case against him now? She wondered what she would say if they met for the first time. "Hello, Mr. Saint, who are you?" Blaming him was a curled old leaf on a tree. It would blow away soon, on one of these cool days.

Anthony had a great father; maybe that was why he was kind. She'd met both of his parents at Anthony's funeral, and she couldn't believe how generous they were to her, especially his father, Vincent. After the burial, there was a reception at the Calabreses' house; it was uncomfortable for everyone that Mary was there, but they'd welcomed her anyway. At the time, she was so screwed up and oblivious.

Mr. Calabrese took her out on the porch and said, "Mary, you must promise me that you'll take care of yourself."

"I have no reason to live, Mr. Calabrese," she said. The thought of her selfishness made her cringe now.

"Believe me, Mary, I know how you feel," Mr. Calabrese said. "But you can't blame yourself . . . It was not your fault; Anthony was drinking and taking drugs, too. He had a history of it; don't you think I know that? You can't carry this around with you, Mary. You have your life ahead of you."

"I am so sorry, Mr. Calabrese, it feels like my fault," she said.

"I forgive you," he said, "if that helps. But you must take care; Anthony would want that, you know."

After assuring Mr. Calabrese that she would take care of herself, though, she did not. Instead, she slowly disintegrated, until she hit the rock and roll home run and finally slid into home base—the rehab—and that was the end of Sliced Ham. It was after the months of serious AA meetings, the hard work of rehab—where she drank more coffee and smoked more cigarettes than she'd thought was humanly possible—when she could finally think straight, that Donal took her to lunch and cut her off, almost as if, sobered up, she just wasn't rock and roll enough anymore.

"I'm up!" said Thaddeus in his scratchy voice, which made it sound like he had laryngitis. He came into the kitchen in a nightgown, looking like an extremely tall eight-year-old girl with a five o'clock shadow. Two Toes followed him in, wagging her tail, sniffing for breakfast. "What's to eat and what are you doing up so early? Uh-oh, you look like you've seen a ghost, Mary."

"Me? What, are you kidding?"

Thaddeus was skinny, all muscle, wild and handsome, but he also would have been a gorgeous girl. He was the color of milk chocolate, his hair cropped short and his face spectacular. He had the cheekbones of a tiger, delicate and fierce at the same time, His eyes were always smiling, as if he were just about to tell a secret, and his two front teeth were the slightest bit crooked.

"Today's the big day, remember? After church, we're going over to the Bunny to see about your job," he said.

The Crumb Bunny was one of the last remaining hippie joints on Haight Street, and it had been taken over by an irritable old queen, Cooper. Thaddeus and a couple of other guys worked there, and Thaddeus had gotten it into his head that Mary should get a job there, too. Mary had pretty much run out of money and was going to have to do something. Her royalty checks were dwindling dramatically; the last one had been for twenty-one cents. The *cushion* had flattened, she was going to have to work, and she was nervous about how she would accomplish that. It wasn't going to be easy, as she was unskilled, had no résumé, and except for being a celebrity in a now defunct rock and roll band, she'd never held a job. No matter where she went, she was still apt to be recognized by someone, and she couldn't bear the thought of being behind the counter at the Crumb Bunny having to explain her new career to a fan. She figured she could coast along for a little while longer, but Thaddeus had insisted that having a job was about more than just the paycheck. "It's about being a member of the world," he'd said, and the other day he had come home with the news that one of the guys at the Bunny had been fired for throwing spitballs at the customers. Thaddeus was excited, sure that there would be an opening for her.

"You can wear a wig! Nobody will know who you are," he said.

She'd met Thaddeus last summer at an odd church, on the edge of the Tenderloin, a place that was barely affiliated with any religion as far as she could tell. Mary had wandered in when she'd heard strange music coming from a slightly opened door. She noticed the sign GOD's KINDNESS CHURCH and figured it was probably safe to enter. When she peeked inside she saw a band playing music in a simple, broom-clean room. A faded, stained-glass window was high up on one wall, a weak beam of light streamed through, and at the front of the room was an altar, adorned with candles, stuffed animals, and dying flowers. Hung behind the altar, a white bedsheet was draped, spread across the wall like a banner at a football game, with the phrase "All welcome" spray-painted in blue.

A tall, thin black woman danced in a blue silk pajama top that flowed to her knees. Her right hand hovered over her belly button as she swung her hips and held a toy microphone. The drummer, a young girl in her twenties, was heavy and had fuzzy sideburns, while the guitar player was older, with a shock of white hair. He played dramatic lead lines high on the neck of his Rickenbacker, and another man stood off to the side, blowing on a clarinet, with his eyes closed.

The woman began to sing in a falsetto, soulful and sexy:

> _People put a penny in the pot_
> _We know this is not the only thing what we got_
> _Pennies only will not help us through_
> _We know that what we gotta do_
> _Believe, Believe, Believe._

Mary stood in the shadows by the door, protected by the darkness of her sunglasses and the curtains of her hair. It would have been easy to think that the band was awful and the dancing woman laughable. She wondered what it was about them that touched her so deeply. She had the thought that she was jealous. On the rare occasions that she'd pull out her guitar and try to sing, her voice would tighten, and her brain filled up with fear and dread. The ragtag band was free to make its own music, something she desperately wanted to be able to do. But that wasn't all; the scene was *humble*. It was a word she'd looked up just the other day—"not arrogant; offered in a spirit of deference" was the definition she'd found. The word had been rolling around in her head, and here it was, personified. She felt as if she'd caught a glimpse of another planet that was farther out, way beyond the planet Earth. The band was waving, like a group of goofy neighbors, across a wide lawn, a galaxy, saying, *Come on over.*

When the song fizzled to an end, the tall black woman who was singing took off a curly red wig, and Mary realized *she* was a man. He turned out to be Thaddeus Ladue.

Before long, Mary became a regular at the church, she was able to slip right in, and it seemed to her that she was hardly noticed. Nobody asked her to do anything. It was okay if she sat on a chair. She had her eye on Thaddeus, the strange guy who liked to dress up like a woman and who ministered like a priest. She found herself confused by her attraction to him; he was irresistibly sexy, and yet maybe he was gay, or something else that she'd never run into before. He had an injured look in his eyes, but it wasn't stopping him from living, and she found herself wanting to be around him. Slowly, she began helping with the coffee and setting out pamphlets, and no one seemed to know or care who she was. One evening, when she went to put away some dishes after Sharing Our Food Night, Mary discovered

Thaddeus sleeping in the office, the place he called the Heart Room. He was curled up under his green blanket, all six feet of him, in the crummy old armchair by the bookcase. He looked like a pile of bones. She walked in on him, and he woke up, startled.

"I'm sorry," she said.

"No, it's okay," he said, holding his blanket with clenched fists.

"I didn't know you lived here," said Mary.

"No, I don't live here. Just a little down on my luck." He folded his long dark legs into himself so his knees were up against his chin and wrapped his arms around his shins, leaving his face, alone, exposed. She could not believe how handsome he was, and she became flustered. She felt herself flirt for the first time in years.

"Hey, if you're interested, you could stay with me. I've been looking for a roommate," she said, but it wasn't true.

"A roommate?" he said in his raspy voice. "Funny, you don't seem like the roommate type, and I don't exactly have rent money."

"No prob, I have a dog," said Mary, as if that made any sense. "No, look, I mean it, why not give it a whirl? It just occurred to me. . . . It's no big deal, man."

"Man?" he said and laughed. "You're funny."

"I didn't mean to say *man*," said Mary, cautiously. "Look, what pronoun do you prefer? You know, he or she?"

"Oh, I don't know, I like so many pronouns, it's hard to pick. I like *it, they, you, me, he, she, none, all*, and then, of course, they have that new one—*ze*—which is interesting, but my favorite is *we*. Any of them will do. But what I really prefer is the indefinite article, *a*; it leaves room for interpretation. And anyway, I think of everybody's life as a work of art, so *a* stands for Artist. Get it?"

Mary wasn't really sure what he meant, but she thought she might be on the way to finding out.

Mary and Thaddeus became unlikely friends. For one thing, where she'd come from, people made fun of guys like Thaddeus— guys who dressed like girls and wore flowers on their sleeves. Those guys were fodder for a good joke, and nobody would be surprised if they got knocked around the block.

For all of Thaddeus's sweet resplendence, he was no slouch. Though he referred to himself, cheerfully, as having "issues," he revealed to Mary how screwed up he'd been with drugs and alcohol. He'd spent time living on the street, sleeping in doorways, scrounging around. He had gotten himself sober in the hard-core rooms of AA and NA, found the church, and gotten involved there. He was an engine of hope for many of the people who came to God's Kindness, and it wasn't hard to see why. His energy was full of grace and compassion. He was good to everyone, no matter how down on their luck; but he didn't take shit, either.

Mary found him mesmerizing. Thaddeus slipped easily in and out of social situations, yet he remained outrageous, breaking rules, but always in the service of others. He was drawn to anything that was hurting. One day an old woman happened into the church; she smelled so bad, as if she hadn't bathed for weeks, and it was hard to be near her. She carried her possessions in a straw bag. Her hair was matted and her legs were cut and swollen. When she walked into the church she was on the verge of collapsing, and Thaddeus welcomed her, called her *Mama*. He kissed her on the cheek and offered her a cup of tea and her face broke open into a toothless smile, a sight so stunning and intimate that Mary had to look away.

Mary could not get enough of Thaddeus, and they fell right in with each other. He was actually fun. He cheered her up and inspired her to participate, even though she had largely forgotten how to be a member of anything, and at times would fall back into despair.

Thaddeus could tell that something was eating at her, but he kept at her to join in. "You think you're so special, my love, but you're just like me. There's nothing worse or better about you, so you better just drop it, because I won't be going away. And, by the way, do you think you could stop saying *fuck* all the time? You've outgrown that, no?"

"*Fuck* is the language of my blood, my songs, my poetry," she said, hurt.

"That's a good place for it, keep it there," he said. "You can write the word in every song and poem you want. Fuck, fuck, fuck! That's different. But there's no harm in being careful when you're being social. You don't have to be onstage. You're a civilian now, and you never know who you could wind up talking to." He blew her a kiss.

As hard as it was for Mary to hear these things, she got a big kick out of the messenger. There were so many ways of behaving that she didn't understand; it was as if she had been raised in the wild and had wandered out of the woods. Almost everything she said came back at her as self-centered and wrong. She needed a teacher, and he was the perfect one for her.

Twelve

SAN FRANCISCO, CALIFORNIA
January 2010

"Why do people have to wear clothes?" Mary said while rifling through her drawers, desperately searching for something to wear for her job interview at the Crumb Bunny. "It's stupid, who am I supposed to be? I hate clothes; if you think about it, they cause a lot of harm." Thaddeus searched through his own bag of clothes, which he kept in a duffel bag under the couch and referred to as his costume bag. "This is not a great time to have a fit, Mary. Did anyone ever tell you you're a pain in the ass? I look at it this way: all the world's a stage, and we have to play our parts. Besides, *nude* is a flamboyant outfit. We could try it, but you might not get the job," he said, pulling out a cornflower blue T-shirt with a lace ruffle around the bottom that he'd sewn on.

"You should wear blue more often; it suits you," said Thaddeus.

He found a pair of unripped jeans hanging on a nail in the back of her closet. They were a little loose on Mary, so he took one of his tie-dyed sashes and threaded it through the belt loops, tied it in a bow, and let it hang down her right leg.

Then he pulled out his wigs.

"Really, Thaddeus? You think I have to wear a wig?"

"I don't want to take any chances. I don't want anybody recognizing you and giving you an excuse to flee. Let's see," he said,
sifting through the pile that he'd strewn across the couch.

"You know what, Thaddeus? I'm not sure that's going to be a
problem, actually."

"How about this one?" he said, holding up a long blond wig
that had some pink streaks in it.

"Oh, Christ!" said Mary. But then she took another look at it,
grabbed it from him, and went to put it on. "Ta-da," she said as
she came out of the bathroom. "I love this thing."

"You look fantastic. Come here and let me see that. *Sista*, you
have a great face for wigs. You're stunning." And it was true,
Mary was a classic beauty, but she was unaware of it. Mostly, she
ignored the way she looked, but with Thaddeus around she was
beginning to peek into the mirror again.

They went back and forth about makeup. Now that she was
gung-ho about being in a costume, she lined her eyes with a
thick black pencil, but Thaddeus made her wash it off and
start over again. He said, "If you insist on makeup, can't it be
subtle?"

"Forget about the makeup, I don't care," Mary said. "I think
we're done."

"Thank God," said Thaddeus.

"I love myself with yellow hair," Mary said as they stood side
by side, studying their creation in the mirror.

"You just love anything that's not yourself."

"Right," she said, giving him the finger.

The boss, Cooper, whom Thaddeus had warned her about, was downing a salad when they arrived at the Crumb Bunny. Wooden tables and chairs were scattered about the café, and there wasn't a customer in sight. A bulletin board was tacked with ads for yoga classes, dog walkers, spiritual piano lessons, and corporate/networking guidance counselors. Below it, a stack of weekly hipster newspapers lay strewn across a table. The butcher-block counter held a cash register and a case for assorted baked goods, and off to the side was a sorry collection of toaster ovens and a beat-up refrigerator. Above the counter, on the back wall, were a mirror and a green chalkboard, where the various food and drink items were listed, and under the board were the coffeemakers and cups.

Cooper was a dyed blond, and his face was wrinkled with disappointment, giving him the perpetual scowl of someone who smelled garbage everywhere. He wore a loose-fitting blue Hawaiian shirt splashed with red palm trees, which barely covered his bulbous belly. He looked Mary up and down, and said, "So, you want to be a coffee maid? What's with the wig?"

Thaddeus could see Mary's eyes tighten, and he intervened quickly, whispering, "Cooper, it's not polite to criticize, she thinks it's pretty."

"I don't like to hire people's friends," he warned, stopping for a moment to check his teeth for lettuce in the mirror behind the counter. "This is not an easy job."

"She can see that," said Thaddeus, and he looked around at the empty shop. "With these crowds, you really have to be on your toes."

"Okay, smart-ass," said Cooper. "But you have to show up on time and shit like that; I can't endure one more slough-off." He never looked at Mary and began to push back his cuticles with the tines of a fork.

"No, I'll show up," she said.

"I've heard that before," he shot back. At last, bored with the whole subject, he said, "Okay, you lucked out, Miss Wiggy. We'll give it a test run, but no spitballs, promise?"

"Yep," said Mary, but she knew it was going to be tough for her to be a coffee maid.

By the time they'd walked back to Oak Street, Mary's spirits had taken a nosedive, and halfway home she'd pulled the wig off and was carrying it over her arm. "You don't understand; I haven't had a job, ever."

"You keep trying to tell me what your life was like before I met you," said Thaddeus. "But I'm in your life *now*. Forget what happened then, it's over. I don't keep dragging you into my old life."

"Actually, I don't mind hearing about your past," said Mary, stopping halfway up the street.

"It was a mess, enough said. If I thought about the bad mistakes I made all the time, like you do, I'd have to jump off the Golden Gate Bridge."

"But where did you get the *skills*?" she asked.

"Honey, have you ever watched the news after a huge disaster? Say homes have been wiped out, loved ones were lost; don't you ever wonder how those people carry on? This is life. It's what happens to people. Everybody falls apart. Sometimes it's obviously horrible, sometimes it's harder to detect. With a person like me . . . well . . . I'm not exactly . . . socially acceptable, so I had to find a road back, and in my case, it had to be a back road. Where I grew up, it was bad. People called me names. I was laughed at, thought of as disgusting. I had to fight for every ounce of self-respect . . . and there were other things, too. But look at me, now; I'm not so bad."

Mary had to admit that Thaddeus was not so bad at all. In fact, the sight of him, his skinny arms waving around, infused by his own urgency, touched her deeply. He seemed like the most respectable person she'd ever met.

When they were back home from the Crumb Bunny, Mary said, "Thaddeus, I'd like to tell you something. It's a kind of secret, I guess, hard for me to talk about."

"I suppose I had a feeling," he said. "I just hope it's not another one of your rock and roll confessions."

"That's not nice," she said.

"Okay, but sometimes I get the feeling you're still hooked into the mythology and idolatry of rock and roll. Everybody wants to be a rock star; even movie stars want to be rock stars. There are great alternatives. . . . You could always be a clown. Clowns are soulful."

"Oh, come on, what's bothering me has nothing to do with rock and roll."

They lay side by side on Mary's bed, sipping lingonberry tea, with Two Toes between them, and Mary told Thaddeus about how she'd met *Other Mary*.

"The Blessed Virgin, you know, Mary, beautiful Mary," she said, "the one who looks so kind in all the pictures, whose eyes were sad. All those years I saw her whenever I was singing, and I sang for her. It was as if there were two of me: the rock and roll freak, the smoking-drinking-drugging-cursing-nutcase-tantrum-throwing rocker; and then there was me, the girl who played alone in the woods and made a friend. The problem is, she never visits me anymore. Sometimes I wonder if I only imagined her. I guess I toughened up about the whole thing, walking around San Francisco like a zombie for the last bunch of years, but then when my mother called about doing this gig in my hometown, I started to think about her, to wish I could at least dream about her. But she's nowhere. And besides, what kind of a freak would think that the Blessed Mother would visit them? I don't think I can do a show without her, but is she even real? I mean, I've loved her for so long, really *loved* her . . . and I thought that she . . . loved me. Now I just feel humiliated by the whole thing. What's love, anyway?"

Thaddeus had not said a word; Mary looked over at him and saw that his eyes were closed. "Are you asleep? Goddamn it! Thaddeus!"

His eyes opened slowly, and he looked up at the ceiling for a moment before he said, calmly, "Nope. I'm right here. I was listening to you, Mary."

"Well, don't you have anything to say?"

"It's an amazing thing that happened to you. Look, kid, not everybody gets a visit from the Blessed Mother. Maybe once is enough. If I'd met her, I don't think I'd doubt her. I'd think she was real, why not? Why don't you believe what you saw? One thing you might want to ask yourself is why she came to you. Doesn't she usually have a message?"

"She told me sing, that's all, she said I should sing for her."

"Well, then, there you are. Obviously, she feels you don't need to see her anymore. Maybe she thinks you have faith."

"But I don't have faith, I don't know how," Mary said.

"Listen, Mary," Thaddeus said. "I don't know *Other Mary,* so I can't speak for her, but here's something I think you could do, and you can laugh all you want. How about on Tuesday you start coming over to band practice and play your songs with the band, and that's how you prepare for your gig?"

Mary thought about the band: the girl drummer with the sideburns, the old man with the white hair playing the electric guitar, and the sad-sack guy with the clarinet, who looked like a piece of bacon standing up.

"You're serious, Thaddeus," said Mary.

"Yeah, don't be a snob."

"My songs are important to me. It's not a joke," she said, ashamed to admit it.

"My band is important to me, and it's not a joke, either," he said.

"But my songs are strange, not typical."

"Sweetheart, are you actually saying that to me? Like my band is typical?"

They both laughed. "God, first I'm working at the Crumb Bunny," Mary said. "Now this . . ."

They lay on the bed for a moment, petting Two Toes in silence, and then Thaddeus said, "Do you think you're better than those people?"

"Oh, come on, Thaddeus, what kind of a question is that?" Mary said.

"No, I'm curious, really," he said.

Mary thought about it and said, "I don't know. I guess I'm afraid to be a loser."

"That's interesting," said Thaddeus. "I guess that makes sense, but I wonder . . . what's a loser, anyway? I've always thought a loser is somebody who has lost something."

"What?" said Mary. "Oh, God, okay."

Thirteen
....

SWALLOW, NEW YORK
January 2010

The winters in Swallow were deadening, and Jean could go for days without leaving the house. If she wanted to venture out, she'd have to spend half an hour putting on layers of shirts and sweaters, her ugly salt-stained boots, hats, scarves, and mittens over gloves. It wasn't worth it. For what—to go to ShopRite to pick up half-and-half? After Christmas, Jean settled in like a sleeping bear. The incident at Three Forks Home had left her feeling bruised, and she hadn't wanted to go back there; for one thing, she was afraid to come face-to-face with Mrs. Hollingberry. She actually had the thought of sneaking into Bub's room by way of his window. Ludicrous.

On an up note, she had received a nice Christmas card from Delores from the home; it had a painting of a Nativity scene, with chipmunks looking on as Mary and Joseph marveled over Jesus in a crib of straw sheltered by a humble manger. Inside the card it said, *Christmas is special and so are you.* Delores had handwritten *Thank you for sticking up for me. Yours in the Lord, Delores Jones.* It made Jean feel a little better about her tantrum at Three Forks; after all, Mrs. Hollingberry had needed a talking-to. But Jean was not looking forward to seeing her again, now that the cat was out of the bag about how she really felt toward the woman.

Truth was, Jean just wasn't *herself.* She was down in the dumps, chalking it up to the cold weather and the sunless days, but there was more; she was disappointed in things. For example, Father Ben. She didn't like the way that one had turned out at all. She never should have asked him to read Mary's letter, only to have him ignore her; he hadn't even called her back. At church on Sundays, it seemed to her that he avoided the slightest eye contact. When she went up to the altar to receive the host at Communion, with her cupped hands raised, it seemed to her that he'd say *The body of Christ* very quickly, then drop the host into her hands and move to the next parishioner as if she weren't even there.

Another thing that was gnawing at Jean was that, when she'd spoken to her daughter on Christmas Day, at the end of the conversation, when Mary said, "I love you, Ma, can't wait to see you in June for the concert," Jean didn't say "I love you" back, and in fact she was dreading Mary's concert. On top of that, she couldn't bring herself to mention to Mary that she'd met Vincent, *Garbagio's* father. The absurdity and accident of their meeting was confusing to her.

Secretly, she wished she could see Vincent Calabrese again, but at the same time, that possibility was another reason she avoided going back to the home. He was a nice man; she thought they could become friends, and for a moment it had looked as though she might be able to help him through the painful experience of bringing his wife into Three Forks. Jean found herself blaming Mary, as if she had interfered, but it was absurd to be angry; Mary hadn't done anything. Jean's thoughts collided around all these niggling points of darkness, leaving her feeling selfish and small, and she wished she could break free. I give up, she thought. Give up what, though? One can't just give up living.

On a snowy Monday morning in late January, Jean got a call from Betty, who sounded panicked. "Jean? It's me, dear," she said.

"Is everything okay, Betty? You sound upset."

"I'm fine, but . . . Father Ben," she said, lowering her voice, "asked me to call you and make an appointment to see you. Isn't that odd?"

"Oh, dear," said Jean.

"Is Thursday morning at ten good for you?"

"Yes, I guess so."

"Okay, I'll see you then," Betty said but added, timidly, "Are we still going to the poodle skirt dance on Saturday?"

"You know, Betty, I'm not so sure I'm up for it this year."

"Oh, Jean. It's for a real good cause, I don't have to tell you that, and this year it's a five-county effort."

"You're right, but I just don't know. I'll see how I feel," said Jean, irritated.

"I hate to pry, but is everything all right with you? You've seemed a bit down."

"Oh, for goodness' sake, Betty, I'm fine. If I don't want to go to the poodle skirt dance, it doesn't mean a thing. I think I'm just sick of the winter."

"Jean, I'm sorry, I . . . miss you."

"What?" said Jean, embarrassed.

"Have I done something to offend you?" asked Betty.

"Nonsense, Betty. No," said Jean.

"You mean a lot to me," said Betty.

"Of course," said Jean, in agony. "Listen, I'm sure the poodle skirt dance will be a smash, with me or without me, barring another snowstorm. In the meantime, I'll see you at the rectory on Thursday."

Jean fretted for the next few days about the meeting with Father Ben, and she arrived promptly at ten, having driven over the snow-dusted streets, careful not to hit an ice patch. Betty ushered her into the rectory, just as she had done a few months back, but something was different. This time Jean barely noticed the big brown furniture, the velvety drapes and thick rugs, and she wasn't overcome by the grandness of the place. She was more concerned about holding her own and wasn't worried so much about whether she had a right to be there.

Father Ben seemed different, too. When he saw her, he got right to the point. "Mrs. Saint," he said, "please, right this way, and thank you for coming on such a frigid morning."

"Of course, Father," she said, knowing exactly where she should sit. She had taken off her coat and hat, scarf and gloves and mittens in the foyer, so she was ready for business as soon as she sat down.

"I've been thinking and praying on your problem for the last few months," he said, and Jean could see that she'd been wrong about Father Ben; the problem had been weighing heavily on him, and his beautiful eyes were pained as he looked at her. "Sometimes my job is very difficult. I am supposed to be a holy man, a man of God, somehow *know* what to do about things. I want you to realize, I thought long and hard about this before I went to the monsignor, and I'm not sure, even now, that I've done the right thing."

That was not what Jean wanted to hear, and she dreaded hearing the rest. She could kick herself for bringing the letter to him in the first place. Father Ben looked down at his desk, and tapping his pen idly on his ink blotter, he began to talk. "I have to be frank, Mrs. Saint, Monsignor did not have a good reaction. In fact, he was pretty annoyed. In his opinion, there was no way this visitation could have occurred. He warned that these kinds of fraudulent reports are very much looked down upon by the Church, and he reminded me that even holy nuns had been heavily reprimanded—and in one case that he noted, excommunicated— for claiming to have had visions of the Blessed Mother. I hate to have to tell you that he went so far as to suggest you break off with your daughter. Now, between you and me, I think that's rather harsh. I'm just reporting back to you what he said." Father Ben took a moment and looked helplessly at Jean before he con- tinued. "He also asked me if I could get him a copy of the letter," he said, adjusting his collar.

Jean stared at him, her mind racing. What popped into her thoughts was the incident that had occurred years ago with the mother superior when Mary wet her pants at school; how the nun had humiliated Mary, shamed her—and Jean had done noth- ing. Mother Superior, probably now long dead—a mere mortal. What made her so *superior*? And so it was with Father Ben; it almost seemed to Jean that he was begging her to see that he was just a man, an ordinary man, a *sinner* just like she was. They were both God's children, both imperfect, both clueless about the mysteries surrounding their lives.

As devout as Jean was, there was no way that this Monsignor, whom she'd never met, was going to determine what her ties with her daughter were going to be. Jean would not turn Mary away, no matter what, and she would certainly not release the letter from her possession. She was trapped, though, and she had to think fast, so she laughed, and she laughed until she almost cried. Jean Saint, the actress, *VaVaVa Voom,* as Mary used to say, gave the performance of a lifetime.

"Goodness," she said, calming herself down, "I should have come or called sooner, Father Ben. I meant to tell you that I had a conversation with my daughter about this after we spoke last time, and she just laughed at me, saying the whole thing had been in her imagination. As I mentioned to you before, she's a poet and an artist, and you know, those types have wild imaginations, and their own way of thinking. She told me the whole story was a *metaphor.* And she couldn't have been more repentant and so forth," Jean fibbed.

"Really, I see. I'd say that's pretty good news, Mrs. Saint," Father Ben said, but Jean suspected that he knew she'd lied, and she could sense his relief.

"I'm just terribly sorry that I didn't mention it to you earlier," added Jean.

"No, no, it's perfectly fine, not to worry," said the priest. "I think that's probably the best outcome we could have hoped for. As I said, sometimes it's hard to know what to do."

"I'm sure you did the right thing, Father." Jean stood up, in a hurry to leave. She clutched her purse, and Father Ben asked her if she would like a blessing before she went. "What?" said Jean. "Yes, yes, of course." Father Ben extended his hand to her forehead, making the sign of the cross with his thumb, and afterward they shook hands and took a moment to look each other in the eye. Jean thought the priest seemed weary; maybe the winter was getting to him, too.

As she opened the door to leave his office, Father Ben said, "Mrs. Saint, the last time you were here you mentioned that your daughter was going to be giving a concert here in town. Is that coming up soon?"

"It's going to be in June. I know it's hard to believe that June will ever come, with this dreary January weather keeping us all shut in."

"Ah, well, I'm looking forward to the spring, for sure, and to your daughter's concert. I'm very curious to hear her sing."

Jean was surprised; it hadn't occurred to her that Father Ben would attend.

On her way out of the rectory, Jean poked her head into Betty's little alcove and said, "*Psst* . . . I just wanted to let you know that I've decided I will go to the poodle skirt dance after all. I don't know what got into me the other day, must have been the snowstorm. Anyway, I'll pick you up at seven on Saturday?"

"Wonderful," said Betty. "Seven is perfect." And she walked Jean to the front hallway, adding, "And bundle up, honey, stay warm."

Jean marveled at herself, she marveled at her lie. She'd

actually done something wrong—deliberately. Lying to a priest! What next? Instead of feeling guilty, though, she felt all puffed up; she shook her head, and wondered, and shook her head again. One good thing: she knew that Father Ben was a kindhearted man. And she knew that the next time Mary called, she would be able to say *I love you* back to her.

Fourteen

SAN FRANCISCO, CALIFORNIA
January 2010

Mary's first shift at the Crumb Bunny was on a dreary Sunday morning. Rain had fallen during the night, and everything outside was damp and gray, with a smell of wet garbage in the air. She and Thaddeus arrived early to open the shop. Thaddeus was carrying bags of bread, muffins, and pastries, stuffed into a big plastic bag, that they'd picked up from the wholesale bakery. Haight Street was deserted, ripe from the night before, littered with soggy trash, empty soda cans and bottles of vodka, wet newspapers mashed into the pavement, and half-eaten pieces of pizza stuck to paper plates. There was even a pink bra hanging off a bicycle, which was chained to a parking meter. Its wheels were missing.

"This street smells like cows," said Thaddeus as he took his sack of keys out of his shoulder bag. "We have to hose the sidewalk down."

"Hose the sidewalk? Shit."

Once they were inside, Thaddeus showed Mary where the lights were. The place was stuffy, smelling of stale milk; chairs were upside down on the small round café tables, and Thaddeus started pulling them off. "You look stunned. You want to help me with this, love?"

"Of course," said Mary, as if being knocked out of trance, and she took a chair off a table but said, "Yikes, this is heavy—and sticky. Disgusting."

"They're all filthy, we'll wash 'em down. You're frail, Mary, we have to get you strong. Lifting chairs is a good job for you." He hoisted one of them over his head. "You thought I was a weakling?"

Thaddeus rinsed a rag for each of them, and they started to wipe everything down—the tables, chairs, counter, and even the cash register.

"Don't people clean up at night?" asked Mary.

"Well, some do a better job than others." Thaddeus worked with speedy elegance, whipping around from cappuccino maker to coffee machine, scooping tablespoons of coffee into filters, filling the creamers with milk and half-and-half, grabbing packets of low-cal sweeteners from the cabinet under the sink and sticking them in with the regular sugars, replenishing the stirrers and straws. He had Mary set out the muffins and pastries in the case.

"Use a napkin, please. No bare hands."

"You're really good at this, Thaddeus," she said, impressed at how easy he made the job look.

"You'll get to be an expert in no time. It's not brain surgery."

The first day was rough, though. Jeff came in just as the doors were opening; he was going to wait the tables while Thaddeus and Mary stayed behind the counter. Jeff was hungover and in need of a strong cup of coffee.

"You've come to the right place, Jeffrey," said Thaddeus, handing him a double espresso. "You should try spending Saturday night with me, you'll feel better on Sunday."

When the customers started coming in, things got hairy. It was hard for Mary to remember what kind of coffee people wanted. It wasn't just the differences between mochas, lattes, and cappuccinos; it was whether they wanted them made with skim or whole milk, decaf or regular. It was her job to take the orders and relay them to Thaddeus. She made mistakes, which resulted in customers being annoyed and created extra work for Thaddeus. By three o'clock in the afternoon, she'd run out of gas.

A group of seven young women piled in; they were tourists, laden with cameras and shopping bags, a moving cloud of deodorant and cheap perfume. They ordered iced teas, lattes, hazelnut coffees, and muffins with butter, and scones without butter—just jam—orange, cranberry, and ginger-apple juices, and one of them wanted a plain glass of water. Mary got overwhelmed when one of the women, in sunglasses that made her look like a bug in a cartoon, said in a huff, "Um, miss, *hello?* I said mochaccino, not cappuccino, and I said *Grande* not *Venti*." Mary threw up her hands and turned to Thaddeus, who promptly interceded, smiling at the girl. "It's not a tragedy, kid, people are starving in other parts of the world, and by the way, this is no Starbucks. We say *small*, *medium*, and *large* at the Crumb Bunny. So just cool down, and tell me what you want."

The girl apologized. "Medium mochaccino," she said, timidly.

Thaddeus handed her the drink, and after she sat down with her friends, he whispered into Mary's ear, "Don't be so sensitive, it's only your first day."

At the end of their shift, around six o'clock, when things had calmed down considerably, Cooper came in to check up on the place. "So, Miss Wiggy, how did you do?" he said, looking past her at the condition of the counter, which Thaddeus was tidying up.

Jeff, who seemed to have recovered from his hangover, said, "She's a natural. She did great. The Crumb Bunny loves Mary," and he put both thumbs up.

"Hey, hey, Jeff actually likes something," said Cooper. "Alert the media."

Mary looked down at her dress, which was stained with coffee, jam, and peanut butter. For a moment she felt humiliated. She saw her reflection in the pastry cabinet, the silly blond wig with its pink streaks; it turned out no one had really even looked at her, much less recognized her. She felt like a dishrag, but that was when Thaddeus said, "You look alive, beautiful."

Set to rehearse for the first time two days later, Mary tumbled into an extreme state of insecurity about herself and all her songs. She had been practicing alone in her room for several months. Without *Other Mary* she felt lonely, and she missed her band. She resisted picking up her guitar; all day she'd circle around waiting for the perfect hour and a half when she could finally settle in. The calluses on her fingers had returned, her voice was getting stronger, but the process remained mysterious. Some days she would not be able to remember her own words, and she'd stumble through the chords of the songs as if she hadn't sung and played them a million times before. Other days it was easy and she'd fall effortlessly into them, enjoying the physical sensation of singing. At times, her songs embarrassed her, she thought they were awful and wondered why she had even written them. Other times, she'd think that they were the only genuine scraps of her that remained. But the worst of it was when she'd find herself in the middle of a song and hear the bass parts that Anthony used to play, or the shadowy pulse of the drums and lead guitar. Then she'd lie back on the bed, discouraged, hoping to fall asleep. When would the mourning end? She was tired of being defeated.

Sick to her stomach from nerves on her way to the church, she switched her guitar case from one hand to the other every few blocks and stopped to rest. She wondered if she was getting too involved with Thaddeus; maybe it was desperation that drove her to him. She couldn't trust herself. In fact, she didn't really know that much about him, even how old he was. She figured he was probably in his late thirties or even forty, but when was his birthday? It had never come up; he artfully avoided answering questions about himself. Her birthday was noted joyously: "November sixteenth. It's a national holiday," Thaddeus had said, holding out a half dozen cupcakes that he'd slipped past Cooper. But somehow, an invisible force field kept her from asking him even the most basic questions.

He wouldn't always say where he was going, and once in a while he'd stay out all night. She was sure he was sober; he was a regular at AA and NA meetings, not a footdragger like she was, but she assumed he had a secret, and she had no idea what it was.

She couldn't help but notice the other day at the Crumb Bunny, in the midst of the rush of coffee cups and apple turnovers, a guy had come in, looking like a picture of a very handsome man: a little too blond, weirdly tanned, and muscle-bound, in a striped T-shirt. He lingered at the cash register with Thaddeus, and he raised his finger up to Thaddeus's lip, perhaps to wipe a crumb. It was a subtle gesture, but it made her think that maybe something was going on between them. Mary had even felt a pang of jealousy. Later, when they were walking home, she'd asked Thaddeus who the guy was, and he had sighed and said, "That's Dennis—here today, gone tomorrow, probably."

"He's pretty good looking," Mary said.

"You think so? Maybe not the smartest guy on the block, but better than a poke in the eye with a sharp stick," said Thaddeus.

"You didn't tell me you were seeing someone."

"Well, I can see him, if that's what you mean."

But that was the extent of their conversation. Maybe it was none of her business. She was shy about the subject; it had been a long time since there'd been so much as a flirtatious glance between her and anyone else, except for Thaddeus. They flirted for affection, not sex.

"How does it feel to be a sex symbol?" a journalist backstage at a club in Detroit had once asked her.

"Do you think I'm sexy?" Mary had answered.

"People do," he'd said, with a hostility that surprised her.

It had made her feel bad. "I think of it as part of my job," she'd replied, pissed off, worrying that it was probably true.

Later on, when she was tired of journalists asking questions like that, she used to tell them that she thought of herself as a prostitute. Mostly, they took notes and nodded, as if they were interns on a mental ward, hurrying to finish their rounds. They must have been sick of interviewing girls like Mary—smart-ass, second-string rock stars. There was a conveyor belt of such girls, festooned in low-cut shirts and colored bras, short skirts and clunky high heels, leaving lipstick marks on the filters of their cigarettes, spewing curses and yawning—and a conveyor belt of *them*—the journalists; usually smart nerds who wished that they had rockin' girlfriends but who were really obsessed with their gurus, the men of rock and roll.

When Mary Saint was young, strutting around on the stage, it wasn't false; she had *Other Mary* to sing for. She stayed apart from any scene; she was aloof, which probably made her more appealing, but it also kept her from putting roots down or making friends. Sliced Ham, a small spinning unit, generated energy from itself, and Mary was the renegade queen. It was not unusual for her to walk out after a show and have a line of fans wanting to touch her. "Please, can I kiss your arm?" or "Aaah, yer so smart and sexy, I love you, baby," or even, whispered, "You are a goddess and I jerk off to you." It wasn't hard to walk through that line and hear those things. It wasn't hard until it was over.

She'd had that one experience, somewhere in the blurry year after Anthony's death, before the rehab. The great Flick Zeez, one of the top twenty rock stars, who had ruled the popular music roost for nearly twenty-five years by continuously reinventing himself and churning out hit recordings, had contacted her out of the blue. She had never met him before and couldn't figure out what he wanted. Everybody knew that Mary had gone down in flames, losing everything and her lover, too—she was young and in pain; perhaps he found that irresistible.

Flick's assistant had called her directly. How the woman got her number, Mary couldn't figure out. She'd rented a small flat in San Francisco and didn't realize that anyone knew where she was. She doubted that the guys in the band would give out her number. Maybe somebody at Donal Hogan's office had leaked it. After all, rock stars were like presidents; they had *access*.

"Flick would like to invite you to his home for a few days," the assistant said.

Mary was caught off guard. "Really?"

A few days later, Flick himself called. "It's Flick Zeez. Is this Mary Saint?"

"Oh, hi," she said but couldn't think of another word after that.

"You might think this is a little strange, but I was hoping you might come down to my place for a visit. You're in San Francisco, right?" He spoke slowly and softly.

"Yeah, I am, but yes, it is . . . a little . . . why . . . do you want me to . . . ?" said Mary, her voice trailing off into a whisper.

"I dunno. Just a hunch, I guess. It's near Big Sur. I have a pool. It's peaceful here. I thought you might like it. I was thinking about Friday."

"Whoa, well . . . hmmm . . . ," she said looking in the mirror and mouthing to herself "No! Say *no!*"

But Mary Saint said yes, and Flick Zeez arranged for her to be driven from San Francisco in a private car. She dressed simply, in an old pair of jeans and a prim cardigan sweater. At the last minute, she threw her leather jacket on. On the trip down she sat in the back of the black limousine with her head against the window, looking out as San Francisco dissolved into a mess of freeways, and then into the small towns along the Pacific Highway. Lazy from the wine she'd drunk the night before, and nervous at the prospect of spending time with a rock icon, she knew she had no ability to fake anything, including adoration.

Years ago, Donal had given her his definition of a rock star: "Your man that truly thinks he's better than the rest of us— is of course a genius—most often has a hottie on his arm— hip to his own tender feelings, a bit discombobulated—how could someone so brilliant be expected to be able to keep his knickers pressed?—a plonker so superiorly talented, he'll say the music business is full of useless toerags, and yet he seems to know every last one of them, making a holy show of himself, boring people to tears with the repeated telling of incidents that highlight his propensity for greatness. It's uncanny how predictable it is, Mary. Whatever you do, don't be like that."

Had she been like that? She didn't know. It was all about hierarchy, anyway. Who was the biggest rock star? Certainly not her. She had been a distant star, and one of these light-years, she might go shooting across the sky.

A while back this would have been big news in the band. *Guess whose house I'm going to?* They would have gotten a big kick out of it and teased her for weeks. She might not have gone. She and Anthony would have had a field day with it, but she had no one to tell the story to anymore. Why *was* she going? Loneliness? Curiosity? Was it just impossible to say no to somebody as famous as Flick Zeez? She didn't know what she was doing.

As it turned out, Flick's place was, as he had said so plainly, peaceful. The California hills, the color of a lion, were stretched out in the distance beyond a gated entrance, which opened, magically, on its own. A stack of huge odd-shaped boxes that seemed to be his house sat hidden at the end of a long driveway; it had slanted roofs and glass windows on its many sides. Flick was standing at the front door when Mary arrived. He held a fistful of weeds that he'd apparently just pulled from one of his flower beds. The driver, whose face, Mary realized, she hadn't even bothered to notice, simply drove away when she got out of the car.

The sight of Flick Zeez made her laugh to herself. She hadn't realized that he was so short.

"Howdy, Miss Mary Saint," he said. "Welcome to my nest."

Inside, the house was simple, sparsely decorated with very little furniture; its walls were light gray and the rugs were white. The back of the house was one gigantic window, which was open onto the patio, landscaped with pink stones, similar to the ones that Mary had been throwing down at cars the night of Anthony's death, and the sight of them spooked her. The ocean lay beyond the patio in silvery infinity, while a sunken pool shimmered off to the left. The smells of rosemary, lavender, and sage wafted from the garden, which overflowed with wildflowers—orange and red nasturtiums—brilliant in the sunlight. The sun was the only mark in the sky, like a hole in a pair of faded blue jeans. Flick's house, built on a cliff, had a view that appeared to include the entire Pacific Ocean. A thin cushion of clouds hung in the air offshore, and from the patio it was possible to see both above and below the clouds, which was something Mary had not known was possible.

Flick Zeez allowed her a moment to survey the scene, and then he said, "You're just in time for a swim before the sunset, how does that sound?" and he brought Mary onto the patio.

"Wow," she said, looking out over the ocean. "Just sitting here will be fine." They settled back onto white chairs with goldenrod pillows, he offered her a pull on a joint, and they waited for the sunset in silence. Mary wrapped her leather jacket around her, glad that she had thought to bring it, and tried to relax.

She was grateful, it was okay; it was more than okay. It was heartbreakingly beautiful. As the sun inched closer to the horizon, it threw light across the expanse of the sky, making colors that Mary couldn't have imagined. The sunset lazed along; the world slowed down, and Flick Zeez kept mercifully quiet. At one point, an older Asian woman appeared out of nowhere. She was dressed in a gray silk robe, which seemed to match the walls of the house. Her hair, every strand in place, was pulled back into a loose bun. She carried a tray onto the patio: assorted cheeses, figs, apples and grapes, walnuts and almonds and olives, a bottle of chilled wine and two glasses. She discreetly poured a glass for each of them.

"Thank you, Layla," said Flick graciously, and Layla nodded her head, smiled at Mary, and then disappeared into one of the rectangles in the house. Mary allowed herself to take a good look at her host. Flick Zeez had the typical look of an older rock star; a suntanned, chiseled face, a sheepish expression—*I used to be young and a little bit cuter, except for the nose.* His rather unusual hairdo, probably styled to cover a bald spot, blew around as night began to fall and the wind picked up. He looked personal-trainer fit in khaki slacks, a T-shirt, a well-designed tour jacket (she'd noticed right away that his name was on the back of it). He wore flip-flops and an ankle bracelet made of red and blue string.

When the sun was completely gone, the air cooled quickly, and Flick made a move toward Mary; dragging his chair next to her, he took her hand. She flinched and backed away, afraid. "Hey, I just wanted to show you the first star. There she is, Venus—actually, a planet," he said.

"Yes."

He sighed, and then, playing with a curl in her hair, he said, "I'm a huge fan of yours. You look so sad. I'm sorry."

"Thank you for being kind to me," she said, looking at her hands in her lap.

"Things will get better for you."

She looked at him closely. For a moment she wondered why she couldn't fall for him, evaporate into his lovely world. But it was the silence and the beauty that she was after. Instead of wanting him, she wanted one of his chairs, and a piece of his view, so she could curl up and gaze toward heaven whenever she pleased. Her craving for the world beyond him made her feel guilty.

"You're special," he said.

"I don't mean to be."

"No, don't apologize for who you are, you really are special," he said.

"Look, I'm not. I'm very, very ordinary, and I don't want to be otherwise," she said, wishing he would get off the subject of her.

"Maybe you can't see what you are, but I see something very unusual," he insisted.

The talk went round and round like this until she looked up at him, resigned, and said, "I think you want to have sex with me." *I consider it part of my job.*

"I want to make love to you, if that's what you mean."

"Yes, that's what I mean," she said, as if she were an actress, playing the part of herself. "I guess it's okay," she whispered.

"It's a good thing to do," he said. By then it had gotten cold, and Mary was shivering.

He took her by the hand and led her into the house, down a hall, and into a bedroom, where a simple bed with soft sheets and many pillows waited for them. Everything was white and wonderful. "Wanna take off that animal you're wearing?" he said, of her leather jacket. She did what she was told. She felt him unbutton her jeans, and off they went; then he lifted her sweater over her arms. She was wearing no bra, just cotton panties, and she lay back on the bed. Flick slipped off her panties with the skill of a man who has done it a thousand times, and before she knew it he had unzipped his pants and was out of his own clothes. Mary realized he was reaching into what must be his *rubbers* drawer. She lay motionless while he showered her with kisses; she noticed that her right hand was fingering the edges of the pillowcase. She opened herself up to him in a sort of gratitude, and she heard him moan as he entered her. He was a *professional*, she thought. His love-making was like his music, well rehearsed, recognizable, and cleverly crafted. It made sense that this was the guy who wrote "Mr. Moonlit I" and "Every Hour in the Love Shower," big hits about romantic love. She thought of one of the lines in "Mr. Moonlit I"— *Tie me to the moon.* She'd seen him perform the song on TV; his mostly female audience had howled like coyotes when he sang the line. But, far from howling, she could only wish that it would be over soon, thinking, maybe even hoping, that this would be the last word in the chapter of Anthony, although somehow she sensed the chapter would never end.

In the morning when she woke up, Flick wasn't there. As she got out of the bed, she noticed a pair of silver hoop earrings, with the clasps undone, lying on the bedside table. Obviously they belonged to someone else who had recently slept there. It was odd the way the house was so uncluttered and yet the earrings remained. They looked so perfect, as if they were part of the décor. After she dressed, she wandered out into the kitchen, and Layla greeted her with coffee and a plate of warm blueberry muffins. Layla explained that Mr. Zeez had left for an appointment and had arranged for the car to take her home whenever it was convenient for her. Mary sat alone and sipped some coffee, leaving the muffins, like the earrings, where they belonged.

She never heard from Flick Zeez again.

As she approached the church steps, in anticipation of her rehearsal with Thaddeus's band, Mary had to laugh—if Mr. Zeez could see her now. As she entered the vestibule, she could hear the band tuning up. She seriously considered leaving when she peeked into the room, but Thaddeus was on the lookout and quick to see her through the little square window in the door. He came over and swung the door open. He was suited up in his blue silk pajama top, the one he always wore for rehearsals, and he was barefoot, as usual, but he had makeup on, which was odd.

"Thaddeus, why is your face painted like that?" she whispered.

"I'm charged up, and I wanted my face to show it. And look at you; I think you're excited, too. Come on in and meet the gang."

Mary had dressed in a black lace dress, one of her old stage costumes, and she'd thrown a beaded necklace around her neck and worn her old combat boots for fun. But nothing about this seemed fun. As she entered the church and saw the band, she had the thought that if she played a song with these people her life would explode. She was afraid of them. A change was coming, but her anger and pride stood in the way. She didn't feel like herself, and Thaddeus, with his face made up, seemed like a total stranger. Being around people was just too hard.

Thaddeus introduced Nancy, the drummer, first. Close up, Mary realized that the girl was younger than she had originally seemed. Only about twenty, and quite plump, she did, in fact, have fuzzy sideburns. Her tiny eyes were buried in her face, and they darted around like a blue jay's above her small, sharp nose, while the rest of her was round, giving the impression that there was another person inside her body, trying to get out. She didn't look straight at Mary but somewhere off to her side, eventually waddling out from behind her drum kit, stepping on the cuffs of her jeans. She paused to pick up a can of diet Coke and then parked herself in front of Mary, sucking up her soda with a straw.

Mary put down her guitar and offered her hand to shake. "Hey, Nancy, good to meet you."

"Uh-huh," said Nancy. She didn't offer her own hand, and Mary couldn't tell if it was just that the girl was nervous.

Thaddeus said, "And this is Nelson, on superfunky lead guitar."

"Don't oversell me, Thaddy," he said. "I'm just an old hippie with a broken heart. You can call me Nels, it makes me sound more like an English rocker," he said, forming the peace sign with his fingers.

Mary bit her bottom lip to keep from smiling. "Cool," she said.

"And this is Miguel, on clarinet." Miguel might have been Mexican, she couldn't tell, but he was probably about fifty. His face was worn, but Mary could see he'd been handsome once. There was something frighteningly hostile about him. He was very thin, teetering on skeletal. "I'm not sure about a clarinet on your songs," he said, looking her straight in the eye. "Thaddeus played me some of your tunes. Cruel."

The use of the word hit Mary like a stone between the eyes. She took a moment, looked up to the stained glass, and then, turning back to him, said, "I never had a chance to have a clarinet on my songs. I think it will be interesting."

Thaddeus stepped in. "Shall we do it, lovelies?"

Mary got her guitar out of its case; she'd brought her very old Martin, the acoustic, not the electric guitar she normally would play. She tuned it up and put it around herself like an old coat.

"So, Mary, everybody here knows that you have a big gig coming up at your old high school, and we're all here to help you get ready and support you. Right, you nuts?" Thaddeus looked around at the band. Obviously, they'd discussed the situation; Mary could only imagine what had been said, and it was taking all her strength to keep from making a snide comment. She felt rebellious and, just like Miguel had said, cruel. But she backed herself down.

Nelson turned on his amp, played a screaming lead line, and said, "Damn right!" Nancy hit the drum, attempting a complicated fill that didn't quite work.

Mary began; there was nothing else to do. She could not

believe that she was standing in a church in a circle of weirdos, about to play a song.

"Okay, this is 'Over Daddy's Dead Body.' Here's the groove." She played the chord progression solidly and went over to Nancy, who picked up the beat with the drums, and it didn't feel half bad. After eight bars, Nelson came in with a heavy-handed lick, like something from a horror movie, and Mary threw her head back. *That's perfect,* she thought, and the song kept going. Thaddeus was dancing, his long brown arms outstretched. Miguel was silent, swaying to the beat and waiting, his eyes shut tight. Mary started to sing:

> I'll be seeing you, him, her, me, they
> Over Daddy's dead body hey-hey
> Daddy's gonna smack me down
> All around this trash can town

Thaddeus threw in a couple of high, raspy *oohs* and *aaahs*, and soon they were on their way. Mary took a break from singing for the solo to begin. Miguel had moved outside the circle, and she wondered if he didn't like the song or couldn't figure out how to fit in, but then he started to play. It was a mournful noise, and Nelson quieted down, settling into a softer guitar line. When they found themselves at the end of the song, they looked at each other, a little stunned.

"Was it any good?" asked Nancy.

Nobody said anything for a minute.

"I liked it," said Nelson.

"Maybe we don't need to evaluate it," said Thaddeus.

"It's a weird fucking song," said Nancy. "What, did your father beat you up and shit?"

"Whoa, easy, tiger," said Nelson.

"No, it's okay," said Mary. "You know what, Nancy? A lot of my songs are hard to take. They're hard to take *literally,* too." And then she said, "But, yeah, my father did beat me up."

"What? What's literally?" Nancy said, as if she'd been accused of something. "I mean—I like the song. My aunt's the one beat me up. I never heard a song that admitted it before," she said, looking around. "Big fuckin' deal. I'm cool."

Mary was relieved to have gotten to the end of one song, but she wasn't sure she could go on. She happened to catch Miguel's eye and wondered why he looked so angry. She wanted to say "What's your problem, buddy?" She wanted to pick up one of the chairs and throw it across the room, to cry, to stomp, to set a match to all her songs and watch them burn. But she did nothing. Stood still.

The band awkwardly gathered around, and Mary started playing again. They fell into the next song sheepishly, the edges of their personalities a little less sharp. The music was strange, but it worked somehow, like a newfangled machine, built by people on a forsaken island. At one point, in the middle of "Feet and Knuckles," Mary dared to open her eyes and look, really look, at the people in the band. There was Nelson, whaling away on his guitar, eyes tightly closed, teeth clenched; an old man playing rock and roll, which was probably the one thing he ever wanted to do. Nancy bopped her head to the beat, deep into the music, concentrating, understanding the language of rhythm, being appreciated, welcomed, and included. Miguel seemed worn-out in every way but one; his shirt and pants were hanging off his bones, and his fingers were pressing lightly on the keys of the clarinet. The easy sound of it was coming up from the depth of his lungs, giving a voice to whatever was left of him. Thaddeus was ridiculous and strange; dancing around, laughable, yet inspired.

Mary thought of Anthony, and she thought of *Other Mary*.

I wish you guys could see this.

Fifteen

THE POODLE SKIRT DANCE
February 2010

The poodle skirt dance was just not Jean's thing. She attended every year with Betty because Betty was on the board of the St. Vincent de Paul society's local chapter, and the dance was a fund-raiser for the society. It meant the world to Betty, but for some reason Jean couldn't be all puppies and rainbows about it. She tended to complain about the food: slabs of overdone roast beef and fish so rubbery that you had to cut it with a serrated knife.

"I prefer Birds Eye's frozen fish sticks," she'd told Betty last year, knowing that it was a mean thing to say but not being able to stop it from coming out of her mouth. The concept—a fifties-style dance—seemed silly, too. "We weren't even kids in the fifties, what do we care about it?"

Betty had said, "It's just something fun to do, I don't know, and it's for a good cause."

Jean wondered where the money actually went, but she wouldn't dare bring that up, as it would have sent Betty into a tizzy. Jean's prickliness about the event resulted in Betty tiptoeing around her in vain attempts to please her, which further irritated Jean, and so on. It was a circle of annoyance that went around like a child's choo-choo train on a small track. Sometimes Jean felt that they were like an old married couple, with all their bickering and un-spoken complaints.

If Jean could be honest about it, she'd admit she was jealous of Betty's involvement in the dance. Back when the dance was in its first year and involved only folks in the town of Swallow, Jean hadn't thought much of it, but now that it was a five-county event, it was impressive. This year, for the first time, it was going to be held at the brand-new Radisson hotel on Route 82, where the high-end shopping malls were spread out like small, glittering cities.

And then there were the outfits; Jean's poodle skirt was made of red felt. She had sewn it herself several years ago, but instead of putting a poodle on the front, which most of the women did, she decided upon a lady with a hat and umbrella. She thought it would look more sophisticated, but she'd designed the figure herself, and it didn't really come out right. The lady she made was too plump, and the hat too garish, not to mention that the um-brella was always peeling off the skirt, and each year, when she pulled it out of the closet, it needed mending.

She huffed and sighed as she took the sewing box out of the closet and threaded the needle to reattach the umbrella. There was no question about it, Betty's skirt was better than hers; it had the poodle on the front—b-o-r-i-n-g—but it actually looked store-bought, even though Betty had, in fact, sewn it herself.

The drive to the Radisson was tense. They got lost once, having made a wrong turn, which Jean felt was Betty's fault. Betty had the directions in her lap, but she said she thought that

Jean knew the way, and she was sorry. But Jean said, "Betty, it's dark out!"

When they got there and walked through the magnificent doors of the Radisson, Jean could not conceal the fact that she was wowed, and she was sorry she'd snapped at Betty. The ball-room was grand—crystal chandeliers everywhere and brocade wallpaper in yellow and red on every wall. The round tables were draped in golden cloths, adorned with candles and balloons, and a chair with a thick maroon cushion was perfectly placed in front of every plate. The settings were elaborate; on each shining white plate was a black cloth napkin trimmed with gold, and on either side of the plates were multiple forks and knives and several wine and water glasses. The tables had numbers, and the attendees were milling about looking for their seats, which had supposedly been randomly assigned in order to mix up the crowd and encourage guests to talk to people they didn't know.

Practically all the women were wearing poodle skirts, each a different color and design, and many of them were wearing saddle shoes. Some had gone so far as to attach ponytail hairpieces to their hair, like the kind Jean had seen being sold at the mall. The men, for the most part, were dressed in football sweaters and slacks, although a few wore shirts and ties; they didn't seem to take the costume part of the dance seriously.

Jean and Betty spotted some of their friends, and Betty said, "Look, there's Rachel Cummings, and that Sue—what's-her-name? And Lorraine Flotard, and oh, dear, ugh . . . there's Adele, too. Let's wait for her to move on and then say hello."

"Good idea," said Jean, glad to have an opportunity to laugh about something with Betty.

After they'd greeted the people they knew, they found their table and sat down, assessing its importance and noting that it wasn't bad. (Jean happened to notice that Adele was stuck at a back table, over by the restrooms.)

Betty and Jean went about introducing themselves.

"Hello, I'm Jean Saint," said Jean, with an exaggerated smile that she herself couldn't stand when she saw it on others. She extended her hand to the lady who was sitting beside her.

"We're the Fulsoms, Holly and John." Mrs. Fulsom had a tightly cropped head of dyed red hair. Jean thought she looked like a tiny dinosaur in a sweater and skirt.

"And this is Betty," said Jean.

"Nice to meet you," said Holly Fulsom, reaching across Jean's face with her bird-claw hands to greet Betty. John Fulsom, a man way too big for his chair, skipped the pleasantries and stuck his napkin in his collar, as if it were a cork into his rage.

"Betty is one of the main organizers of the event," Jean said.

"She's the one whose name should be *saint,* I guess!" said Holly, finding herself funny.

Jean bristled, and that was about all she could think of to say, especially since the person seated behind her at the next table kept banging into her chair. She thought that she would not make it through the dinner if the banging persisted but couldn't figure out how to be polite about asking for it to stop. It was as if every two seconds whoever it was had the urge to push up against her chair for the express purpose of driving her crazy.

The servers began to place shrimp cocktails in front of each guest, and Jean knew she'd have to stop the banging quickly in order to enjoy the dinner at all. She turned around and saw that it was a man, a large man, in a creamy white sweater. She tapped him on the shoulder, and when he turned around, her incensed face looked squarely into the kind eyes of Vincent Calabrese.

"Jean!" he said. "What a surprise!" He couldn't quite get his head around because of the thickness of his neck. The backs of their chairs were touching, and it would have been too tight a squeeze for either one of them to stand.

"Oh my, these tables are too close together," said Jean, trying to turn around herself, but she wound up pointing that remark into Betty's ear.

Betty said, "What's wrong?"

"Nothing, nothing, I know the man behind me."

"You what?"

"It's a man . . . from the home." Jean wondered if Vincent could hear her.

"A man?"

"From Three Forks," she said, raising her voice over the noise in the room.

Vincent somehow managed to inch his chair around so he could almost turn his head toward her. "You ran away," he said, but Betty thought he was talking to her.

Jean wiped her mouth with her napkin, just for something to do, as Betty said to him, "What on earth are you talking about?"

Jean said, "No, Betty, he's talking to me."

"Okay, this is not the time or place," said Vincent. "We'll have to wait until the dance begins. We'll enjoy our dinner and meet up on the dance floor." He turned back around, and the chair knocking ceased. Jean happened to notice he was with a woman; she certainly didn't appear to be ready for Three Forks Home.

Jean, who didn't usually take a drink, decided to sip on the champagne that was poured, and then, miraculously, there was a glass of white wine before her, and she sipped on that, too, until it was gone, and then the waiter filled her glass again. Soon the conversation at her table flowed; instead of roast beef, they had hanger steak this year, and she sawed through it with her knife without complaint.

Halfway through Jean's second glass of wine, the music started. A disc jockey was spinning old 45s. He played them all: The Coasters sang "Yakety Yak," and the Chordettes with their version of "Mr. Sandman" got quite a few folks on their feet. The Fontane sisters harmonized on "Hearts of Stone," and when the Platters sang "The Great Pretender," Jean felt a tap upon her shoulder. Vincent Calabrese had extricated himself from his table and was asking her to dance.

In a cloud of champagne and wine, Jean surprised herself by standing up. Betty, with her mouth full of food half-chewed, watched in disbelief as Vincent led Jean away.

Once on the floor, they danced under the mirror ball that was hanging from the ceiling, its slow rotation throwing diamonds of light about the room. Vincent put his arm around Jean's waist and held her right hand up, in the classic pose.

"Goodness, it's been years since I've danced," she said.

"Oh, good, I hope you don't mind."

"Really, I feel like a schoolgirl."

"Jean, I was worried when you ran out that day at the home." He spoke loudly into her ear.

"I see you decided against the home," said Jean.

"What? No, Vivian is there as we speak. You didn't know?

And she's doing well! Just like you said she would. You were so helpful."

"Oh . . ."

"The woman here with me tonight is Vivian's sister, Donna."

"I'm . . ."

"Jean, I'm so glad to have the opportunity to apologize to you. I realize that whatever I said to you that day in the chapel must have struck a nerve. Forgive me, I was in such a state myself."

Jean let a few moments of music go by.

"*. . . Yes, I'm the great pretender . . . adrift in a world of my own.*"

She spoke directly into his ear. "Vincent, I actually should thank you for whatever it was that you said. I can't even remember it now. But it was . . . meaningful . . . to meet you. To hear you talk about your son, and the strange coincidence . . . and the awful . . ."

"I know. It was a difficult day, but things are working out. Don't you believe in miracles?"

"It's hard to believe in anything," she said, but not into his ear.

Jean was suddenly exhausted . . . exhausted . . . exhausted, and she couldn't resist the wide-open space where his heart was beating; it lay before her like the pillow on her very own bed, and she rested her head on his chest and let him lead her all around the floor.

They finished out the song in silence, turning around and around, while Betty sat at attention, staring, and not knowing what to think.

The next morning when Jean woke up, she saw that she'd thrown her poodle skirt and blouse over the back of the chair. Her saddle shoes were strewn; one was lying on its side, the other was halfway under the dresser, and she remembered that she'd had quite a few sips at the dance, and that Betty had driven the two of them home. When she sat up in the bed, she realized she still had her bobby socks on. She and Betty had sung songs on the way home. "Five Foot Two"—and what was the other one? "You Are My Sunshine." *Now, those are real songs!* They'd laughed about the Fulsoms and marveled at the swankiness of the Radisson. Jean had said it was the best dance ever, and Betty was beaming with pride. They'd even made a wrong turn, which sent them into a fit of laughter.

When Betty said, "Now, Jean, come on, who was that man?" Jean said, "Oh, Betty, he's just someone from Three Forks. The poor fellow, I met him one day in the chapel. He was quite brokenhearted about having to bring his wife there."

"It seemed to me that he was rather fond of you."

"Nonsense," said Jean. "At our age? Don't make me laugh," and the two gals dissolved into laughter again.

Sixteen

SAN FRANCISCO, CALIFORNIA
March 2010

It didn't take long for Mary Saint to grow fond of her new band. During rehearsals there were many moments of ridiculous joy. She would leave work at the Crumb Bunny and start the long trek over to the church to play with the band three nights a week. Mary was also getting to be an acrobat behind the counter at the Bunny, able to deliver multiple orders—cappuccinos, teas, toasts, muffins; she'd even invented a new Crumb Bunny special: peanut butter and chocolate sauce on a scone. She had come up with it one afternoon when Cooper was complaining that the scones were always left uneaten at the end of the day, and he'd be damned if he was going to give them away.

After work, she'd set out for the church, and when she reached Fell Street, she would pull off her wig and stuff it into her bag, letting her black hair fall freely around her shoulders. Her guitar, which had seemed heavy just weeks ago, was not so hard to carry anymore, especially since Thaddeus had surprised her one evening with an old canvas guitar case he'd found in a thrift shop that could be worn like a backpack. So what if it was spray-painted with peace signs?

If Thaddeus had been working with her, they'd walk to rehearsal together and talk about how someday they'd rob a bank. "We'll only take enough for a down payment on the Bunny. We'll even say we're sorry on our way out and leave them some pastries," Thaddeus would say. "Then we'll head straight to the Bunny, plop the cash on the counter, and give Cooper an offer he can't refuse, put him out of his misery. He'll keel over at the sight of such a pile of money."

"We could buy some new cups," Mary would say. "Finally get rid of those chipped, cracked things he calls treasures. We could put up some local art—you know that guy, what's his name, the one with the thick glasses?"

"Oh, you mean Sanford Farkus?"

"Yeah, have you ever seen his paintings? He showed me his book of prints; they're really bluesy, in a sort of uplifting way."

"Yes, and we could paint the place. Maybe Farkus could do it. Get rid of that cream-of-vomit color Cooper insists on keeping on the walls."

"Why can't money grow on trees? I wish I had met you years ago, when I had some," she said.

"I smell money in our future."

"Thaddeus, I never heard of anyone smelling the future."

Once at the church, they'd get right down to it. When Thaddeus would emerge from the back office suited up in his blue pajama top, the band knew it was time to start. The back office was the secret sanctuary of the church. "All good things come from that room," Thaddeus would say. "It's the *heart* room."

"Yeah," said Nelson. "And the fart room, too."

When Thaddeus looked at him, Nelson said, "No! It's good to have a separate room for farting. It's a joke, jeez."

"Nelson, you scare me sometimes," said Thaddeus.

They bumbled through the rehearsals and Mary knew that the band was rough, to put it mildly, but occasionally the music seemed to jell and it worked for everyone somehow. It was uncomfortable for Mary to have her songs on the table, but she'd come to believe it was necessary. Nelson was in heaven just to be able to play rock and roll, and Nancy got a kick out of her own drumming and began to consider the possibility that she could be good at something, that she could *try*. Only Miguel remained sullen. Though he played beautifully and revealed himself to be a deep musician, he barely said a word to anyone.

Before they started to sing, Thaddeus would gather the band and invite them to hold hands while he said thank-you to an unnamed entity he believed was responsible for bringing them together. The motley band followed their leader but occasionally a sigh or comment would slip out and the group would tighten. Thaddeus would open his eyes and survey the scene. "What's up?" he'd ask, and something about the way he looked at them, like a child who didn't get the joke, would make them wish they hadn't grumbled.

Mary felt herself getting stronger. She wasn't so worried about her songs and whether she had a right to sing them, and it felt good to let her voice cry out in the church. She understood what Thaddeus was up to, and she surrendered.

One night after rehearsal, when Thaddeus had gone to the

heart room to change, Miguel approached Mary and said, "Hey, listen, uh, can I speak to you in the heart room?"

Nancy and Nelson looked around nervously, leaving Mary to deal with it, but at first she thought he was kidding and continued packing up her guitar. "You'll have to ask the boss, Miguel," she said. They all knew that the heart room was Thaddeus's sanctuary, but Thaddeus, upon returning, seemed unfazed.

"That's okay with me, a meeting in the heart room sounds like a good thing, but I have to run to pick up the flyers for the tag sale before the print shop closes," he said, kissing her on the cheek. "If you aren't here when I get back, I'll meet up with you later. Just flip the lights on your way out; the front door will lock automatically."

They watched him leave, and Mary realized how strange it was for the band to be together without Thaddeus. Without him, they had very little in common, and nothing to say to each other.

Nelson packed up his guitar and said, "Come on, Nancy, I'll walk you up to Van Ness."

As they left the room, Mary could hear Nancy say, "What are they going to do in the heart room?"

Miguel and Mary stood in the empty church together. Mary said, "Well, I guess we could just talk here, since we're all alone."

"No, I think the heart room is the place," said Miguel.

Mary began to feel uneasy, and she wished Thaddeus hadn't left.

They walked into the heart room, which was a mess. It was where the bills were paid—or unpaid—a private room, where church matters were discussed, letters got filed or stacked. A big wooden desk, overflowing with papers, took up a large portion of the room, and three framed photographs—one of Jesus Christ, one of a Buddha, and one of Farrah Fawcett—were precariously placed on top of the to-be-filed tray. Shelves lined a back wall, packed with self-help books—*You Are Rainshine* and *Call Out the Devils*—and Bibles in many translations; books in Sanskrit, Swahili, and French; there were coloring books and comic books; a few novels, including *Lolita;* assorted pamphlets—"How to Cure Your Hemorrhoids in Three Days" and "If Your Parent Is in Jail." A ripped American flag, hung with thumbtacks, sagged on the wall, and up against a statue of St. Francis leaned a half-shriveled blow-up doll. A poster of Martin Luther King Jr. with the lyrics "Ain't gonna study war no more" wallpapered a closet door, and rolled in the corner, behind the chair that Thaddeus used to sleep in, stood a yoga mat. Taped on the wall above it was a picture of a waterfall with the quotation, "Love is everywhere." Someone had put a Post-it on it that read "even in your underwear."

Miguel closed the door.

"So?" said Mary, feeling her heart speed up.

"So?" said Miguel.

Shit, shit, shit, thought Mary.

"What's the matter, you're afraid of me?" asked Miguel, nervously.

"No, I'm not afraid of you," she said, looking straight at him.

"How come?" He stared back.

"Look, Miguel, what was it you wanted to say to me?"

"Don't laugh," he said, coldly.

"I'm not laughing, do I look like I'm laughing?" she said.

"I think you look like you're . . . beautiful," he said, plainly, never taking his eyes off of hers.

"Uh . . . ," she said.

"You look like something I want to kiss," he said, moving toward her.

"No," she said, putting up her hands.

He stopped. "You *are* afraid of me," he said. "I knew it, I just knew it."

"Miguel, you're like a loaded gun."

"I recognize you."

"No, I don't think so. You have no idea who I am," she said. "You think I'm cruel, as if being cruel is a game, but I'm not cruel, and you have no idea who I am. You and I are just two nutjobs who should keep to ourselves."

"I'm not violent," he said.

"I didn't say you were."

Miguel moved in closer.

"I think you should just back up and let me leave now," she said, shaking a little.

He backed away slightly, and Mary stood by the desk, motionless, not knowing what to do.

"What, you think you're some fancy rock star? I can play rings around you," he said.

Mary's heart was beating so fast that she could hardly catch her breath. She couldn't calm down; her hands and legs were shaking now, the fear and rage mixing up into a bad concoction.

"Oh, great," she said. "That's perfect. I've been waiting for the shoe to drop with this whole situation. You say something like that and then you think you want to kiss me? You have no idea about my music and what it means. And I'm not about to talk to you about it. We are really lost here. You and I are a bad combination, Miguel. I get that you're pissed off, but I can't help you, not in any way."

"You *are* helping me," he said in a desperate voice.

"No, Thaddeus is helping you, not me. I'm not going to be your girlfriend, Miguel, if that's what you think, and you're not going to touch me, either. Just let me pass." They stared at each other, and neither one of them would give in. There was a faint knocking at the door. Mary rushed to open it, relieved to see Thaddeus, who came into the room and immediately sensed something was off.

"Hey, Miguel, what are you doing?" He saw that Miguel was about to ignite. "What's going on in here?"

"We freaked each other out is all," said Miguel, calming down.

"Miguel and I were getting a few things straight," said Mary.

"You guys are too much," said Thaddeus. "I told you that this room was a powerful place. I guess it's a good thing I was wrong about the flyers being ready tonight, or else you two might have given each other a heart attack."

They filed out of the heart room and into the church. When they walked out onto the street, Miguel turned to Mary and said, "I'm sorry if I spooked you."

"I wasn't spooked," she said, somehow feeling that he would like it if she had been. She wasn't going to let on that she'd been scared shitless.

Miguel turned toward Thaddeus, and Thaddeus reached for Miguel's hand, shook it with both of his, and said, "You take care of yourself, my friend, stay out of trouble."

"Yeah, thanks, Thaddeus." Before he turned to go, Miguel

said, "I didn't do nothing wrong, Thaddeus." Mary watched Miguel walk away; he was carrying his clarinet like a baby in his arms.

After Miguel was halfway down the block, Thaddeus turned to Mary and said, "Everything is going to be all right, just relax."

"I don't know about that," said Mary. "If you hadn't come back . . ."

"You would have figured it out," he said. "Miguel is not a bad guy."

"You trust people too much; he's fucking nuts," said Mary.

"Everybody's nuts, that's what I think. I wonder about myself sometimes," Thaddeus said.

Mary could feel herself getting angry. "Everything and every-body is not okay, Thaddeus. You're perfect, you have no idea what people are like. That guy is creepy," she said. "Everything's all love and peace with you—horseshit! It's not real, Thaddeus."

"What's real?"

"You're above it all, and the rest of us are crawling around like rats. You're perfect, and I hate it," she said, deliberately try-ing to hurt him.

"You're wrong," said Thaddeus. "Don't put me on a pedestal, Mary; seriously, I've got my stuff."

"Oh, yeah, like what . . . you got drunk a few times? Oooo, fucking scary," she said, mocking him.

"I don't think you can handle knowing about me."

"Why not? Why don't you ever say anything about yourself? What makes you so goddamn special? It's like you're on this weird ego trip."

Thaddeus turned away from her and sat down on the steps of

the church. "Look, Mary, there's a reason why I keep my mouth shut. There is something really bad about me that you don't know."

"Come on, Thaddeus, you're always telling me not to think that I'm so unique; now you're the big bad guy of all bad guys? I find that hard to believe. I'm sick of it."

Thaddeus took a deep breath. "Okay, Mary, but you have to pull back, I can't take your hostility right now. This is serious. You can't be mean to me; you have to stop."

Mary folded her arms, trying to hold back her temper, but it was lit. "Okay, okay," she said, and she moved away a few feet, looking at Thaddeus as he sat on the steps with his hands in his lap.

"I don't know how else to say this, Mary." A young couple walked by in between them on the sidewalk, and Thaddeus waited until they passed. When they were halfway down the block, he said, "I murdered my father."

"What are you talking about?" said Mary.

He looked up at her and said, "I killed him. With his own gun. You know, he couldn't stop kicking me around, and he'd do it to my mother, too. Maybe I just got sick of it, I really don't know. But you didn't kill your father, and Nancy didn't kill her aunt. Little boys don't usually kill people. Why did I do it?

"What's weird is that it was the most beautiful day—Easter Sunday. I was eleven years old. He went into a rage because I gave him a pink Easter egg that said 'Daddy' on it. He couldn't stand having a little gay boy. He accused my mother of ruining me. She tried to get between us, but he punched her in the face, can you believe that? He was a tough motherfucker. His life was one conniption after another. That day she fell, and he kicked her. Who does that? Who kicks a woman who is lying on the floor?

"So, I got his big, ugly gun out of the closet and I shot him. She took the blame. She told me it was her fault. She convinced me to lie. She died in the Louisiana Correctional Center for Women, Mary. And I'm a murderer. That's the kind of perfect I am."

"Fuck," said Mary, turning away, afraid.

"I guess that's about as good a reaction as any," said Thaddeus.

"I'm sorry. How could you not have told me?"

"Really? Why would I?" he asked. "What do you do with someone who tells you something like that? My whole life is about how sorry I am; there's nothing else for me to do but try to make up for it. Bad things happen and people change. They need help. So that's what I do. For all the things Miguel has done he never killed anyone." Mary took her guitar off her back and sat down beside him on the church steps. After a while, Thaddeus said, "You see?"

"Yes, I see. But what your father did was wrong," said Mary.

"Mary, what I did was wrong," said Thaddeus.

They sat there for a long time, in silence, as the fog crept in and the night air turned colder. They huddled close together, with their arms and legs touching. Finally, Mary looked at Thaddeus; she put her hand on his arm and said, "Shall we go home?"

"Yep, let's," he replied, realizing that he actually had a home.

Mary picked up her guitar, and Thaddeus helped her put it on her shoulders. "I'm sorry I was yelling," she said.

"It's all right," said Thaddeus, but Mary could tell that he was shaken up. "Do you like your guitar case?" he said, trying to change the subject.

"Yeah, a lot, of course I do," she said.

"You don't mind the peace signs?"

"Love the peace signs," she said.

"Good, because I was worried about that."

Mary and Thaddeus walked home together without saying much, both lost in their own worlds. Mary felt ashamed, worried that she had hurt her friend; her mind was racing, wondering if something between them would be forever changed.

Thaddeus was reliving the scene of his father's death; the thing he most remembered—the look in his mother's eyes when she'd realized what her son had done—came back at him vividly. That moment had played over and over again in his memory. It was as if she were surprised that he had any strength at all, as if she saw, in that instant, that all those years it had been he who had been protecting her, and not the other way around.

Thinking of it now, Thaddeus only wished that he could see his mother again; hear her laugh the way she used to laugh when she gossiped on the phone with her sister, or when he sat curled up on the couch with his head in her lap, sharing a bag of pretzels, while the two of them watched *The Mary Tyler Moore Show*.

PART

Three

Seventeen

SWALLOW, NEW YORK
May 2010

Bill De Sockie was psyched; the ticket sales for Mary Saint were booming, and the concert loomed in the future, still a month away. The daffodils and pansies had exploded all over Swallow, and the kids in his classes had spring fever, which made teaching nearly impossible. He didn't fight it. Let them smell the lilacs; that was his theory. His affair with Sarah Spalding had petered out, and she had moved on to snag the valedictorian of the senior class, Henry Harms, the only student from Swallow ever to be accepted to Harvard. He was a *dick*, as far as De Sockie was concerned, a self-important bullshit artist whom De Sockie could imagine, years from now, as a young professor at some second-rate college, or even at a high school, banging his own students, just like—*ha-ha*—himself. It occurred to De Sockie that Sarah had a tragic flaw—bad taste in men—and as smart as she was, she might wind up flip-flopped and pregnant with some windbag of a nuclear physicist or, worse, a *successful* popular poet—her brains leaking out of her ears into a washing machine in the basement of her lovely suburban home. Oh, well, at least I was the first, he thought, disgusted with himself.

With his classes in disintegrated chaos, he had more time to concentrate on writing his final exams and also on finishing the arrangements for the concert. He'd had to call Mrs. Saint to get direct contact information for her daughter, because up until now he'd communicated with her only through her mother, but he really needed to talk about the technical requirements for the sound, and about anything else she might need for the concert. It had taken a few tries before he got an e-mail address out of Mrs. Saint. It was obviously not Mary Saint's personal address but some weird church thing: Godskindness@sflink.com. When he first saw the address, he thought it said God Skind Ness, assuming it was some kind of poetic lyric of hers, but then he realized it was a religious, New Agey name, God's Kindness, and wondered if Mary Saint had gone soft. He really hoped not. It would be a drag if she were singing Christian music now.

Their correspondence was bizarre. Before he sent the initial e-mail, De Sockie had called Eliot Bemblatt down in Nashville to see about the wording and tone of it, so he wouldn't sound like a complete jerk. Bemblatt had suggested something like this:

Dear Mary Saint, We're so jazzed you're coming. Can you send a stage plot and any sound requirements and a rider for the backstage, etc.? Thanks, Bill De Sockie. (I'm the high school teacher who's running this shindig.)

The reply was

Mr. D., One vocal mic, one direct box, one monitor, professional speakers, a sound check at 4:00 PM and a sound guy who KNOWS WHAT HE'S DOING and some fresh organic fruit in a dressing room with a mirror and a bathroom. Thank you. —From Mary Saint's Person

The next e-mail exchange was the last one:

Dear Mary Saint's Person, (Funny!) That's all cool (by the way, I can get you some liquor, etc., if you keep it in a paper cup, since it's the high school and all, I have to be a little bit discreet. ☺) I'd be happy to pick you up at the airport, take you out for a meal after the sound check, put you up at my place (I have a spare room) so you don't have to stay with your mother, I know how that is. (There are still no hotels in Swallow!) Just let me know. I'm at your service. —Bill De Sockie

The reply was

No, none of the above, thank you —Mary Saint's Person

When De Sockie forwarded these exchanges to Bemblatt, he got a call immediately.

"De Sockie, this is going to be interesting. It's *weird*! No contract? Nothing but these e-mails? I love it. I'm definitely coming up—I wouldn't miss this. The Twinsters are going to drive, I'm going to fly, and we're going to need more mics and stuff, so I'll send you the list," he said. "By the way, you've got to get their contract back to me, signed."

"Listen, Bemblatt, I don't want to have to rent a whole bunch of extra crap for the opening act," said De Sockie.

"It won't be that much, De Sockie, don't cheap me," said Bemblatt.

"Me cheap you? That's a riot, Bemblatt," said De Sockie.

"I'm already forking over for a plane ticket. Oh, by the way, I can stay at your place, right?"

"Well, I guess so, sure," said De Sockie. As long as Mary Saint wasn't going to, what did he care?

"And how about the Twinsters, can you squeeze them in, too?"

"Aw, shit, Bemblatt, you are something else."

"What's it to you? It'll be fun, and besides, they're going to be big stars someday, bigger than Mary Saint, you'll see."

"Mary Saint was always alternative, too good for the mainstream, Bemblatt. They'll have to be a lot bigger than she was to be considered big stars. Remember, we're talking about a shitty small-town concert here. You're acting like this is . . . I don't know what."

"Hey, De Sockie, you're the one who's putting this thing on . . . What's the matter, is it making you feel old? None of the high school kids think you're cool?"

"Ouch," he said. "Maybe I'm not on the cutting edge, but I'm a fan of hers, she means a lot to me."

"Come on, De Sockie, don't get your feelings hurt. I know she means a lot to you. I'm just saying, she's not part of the *now*."

"The now?"

"Yeah, the now."

"Okay, I'll work on that. I'm forty years old, Bemblatt, and so are you."

"Big fucking deal how old I am."

"All right, all right."

De Sockie got off the phone as fast as he could. Why was everyone so snide? His students were snide, Bemblatt was snide, even he himself was snide. It seemed to him that everything had gone down the same drain. He'd spend hours thinking about what his students should read, poring over the poetry of Yeats, of Browning—he always tried to find the perfect Shakespearean sonnet, something that would capture their imaginations. He let himself get caught up in his choices, and then all of it seemed meaningless when he put it before the class. Most of the time it seemed like they didn't bother to read the stuff. Even Sarah Spalding—after all the kissing and the fucking, all the music he'd played her, it ended up nowhere. The whole idea of having the Mary Saint concert had popped into the part of his brain that was still sincere, still alive; it had seemed like a *creative* idea, and he was excited about it, but the concept was clouded by resistance, like everything else. The e-mails from Mary Saint seemed closed off and harsh— why? He was just trying to be friendly. And on top of it, Mary Saint's mother seemed to think he was a snake. Why was the world such a concrete slab? There was no other choice but to carry on. For all he knew the concert would be inspiring, if nothing else. He hoped that it would mean something to some young kid, and maybe somebody would think he was a better guy.

Eighteen

SWALLOW, NEW YORK

May 2010

Jean had been meaning to clean the spare bedroom, and the advent of Mary's visit was as good a reason as any. When she first moved into "the Meadow" as they all called it, Jean had stored whatever she couldn't bring herself to throw away in the second bedroom. She'd come to think of it as a closet, except a closet shouldn't be the size of an entire room. The room had such a presence that she was beginning to feel like she had a housemate. So much was on Jean's mind lately, what with the concert coming up; she figured it would do her good to tackle a big job.

The first thing she did was throw open the windows and let the spring breeze blow in. The room was stuffy, as if it had been vacuum-packed, stale with the smells of old cardboard boxes and mothballs. It occurred to her that she'd gone overboard with the mothballs, and she began tossing fistfuls of them into a garbage bag. As Jean went through the boxes stacked beside the dresser, she got caught up looking over the contents. She had saved some of Mary's sketches and homemade birthday cards, and she found a few homework assignments. One was a picture of Thomas Jefferson that Mary had drawn, his face colored blue. The teacher

had marked the page with a big D and a scribbled note that said,
"Nobody's face is blue." Jean looked closely at the picture and had
to admit there was something disturbing about it. Mary's Thomas
Jefferson looked like a thug or a criminal, but still, Jean thought
the teacher's comment was unnecessarily blunt. Who knows
what Thomas Jefferson was really like, anyway? Mary had always
seen things differently: she saw blue faces, she saw frightening
ghosts in her bedroom at night, and she saw . . . Blessed Marys.
So what?

In another box, Jean came across some of Bub's old clothes.
She had taken most of his things over to the Goodwill when she
moved him into the home, but a few items proved harder to part
with. Everyday clothes he had worn for years were threadbare;
no one else would wear them, and she hadn't had the heart to
throw them away or tear them up for dustcloths. She took some
old shirts out of the box and considered whether the time had
come to let them go. As she refolded them and felt the softness of
the cotton flannel, it was as if Bub were right there in the room
with her, and she was gripped with a sense of longing. What a
strange man he was. He'd come up from nothing, for the most
part, uneducated. His parents were British, from Dorchester,
and Jean remembered when he'd introduced her to them, how
embarrassed he'd been by their thick country accents. His father
and mother both worked in a dog food factory near Suffern, New
York, and Bub's father later claimed it was the factory that had
provided the horse's head for the famous scene in *The Godfather*.
The father told that story over and over, maybe never knowing
how much it irritated his son.

Jean sensed that her husband had always thought of himself

as less than other men, and perhaps that was at the root of all his rage. She'd never understood what haunted him, and these days she wondered if it was possible to really know someone else. The life they had shared seemed like a dreary movie to her now, and yet she suspected she was still mulling it over somewhere in the back of her mind.

Lately she'd been a different person, meeting up at Three Forks with Vincent, the two of them pushing Bub and Vivian around in their wheelchairs as if they were their children, walking past Mrs. Hollingberry and her raised eyebrows. It seemed the most natural thing in the world for Jean and Vincent to be good friends, and they'd managed to find each other in the middle of a nursing home; who could have guessed it?

Jean piled the stack of clothes on the bed and was about to dump the mothballs out of the box and into the trash when she noticed an old wallet of Bub's, flattened at the bottom of the box. She picked it up and ran her fingers over the soft leather, and when she examined it further she discovered a five-dollar bill and a piece of paper folded into a small square. Jean fished out the paper, immediately recognizing it. Bub had always kept a yellow legal pad by his chair; it seemed to Jean that the pad was always blank and just lay there day after day with a ballpoint pen on top of it.

She held the paper in her hands, feeling its delicate age, and was careful as she unfolded it.

My Dears Jean and Mary,

How does someone say their sorry. What made me so stiff and ugly I don't know. I failed you both. You were my tresures my angels and I did you wrong. I didn't mean it. Too late now. I sit here and stare out the window. I don't deserve the ground you walk on. I never should of hit you. It's wrong to hit and yell like the way I always did.

Whatever was wrong with me I'll fix myself in hell.

This is from your husband and your father who did wrong but somebody who loved you both in his own way. I hope your lives will be better without me someday. I'll probably die before you and don't bother crying over me or feel pity. ——Bub Saint (Daddy)

Jean set the paper down beside her. Closing her eyes, she took a long, deep breath, imagining that Bub might have written the note a hundred times and ripped it up, only to sit down and write it again. She thought of Bub's hands and how shaky they were of late; he couldn't even hold a pencil if he tried. He used to be powerful, but now he was skeletal in almost every way. It had been a lonely, bitter marriage; she could finally admit it. And Mary, caught in the middle of their private mess, had suffered, too, but they were free now, as free as they could be. Sitting alone on her bed, Jean understood how much she had loved them, but she had lost them, too. How terribly sad, but Jean could blame herself no more.

She opened her eyes and looked out the window to her patch of blue sky, and then she glanced around at her things: the single bed, perfectly made, the white lace lampshades, the delicate twin vases painted with swirls of sapphire blue. Her precious, breakable things. She couldn't have been more the opposite of Bub, who had little interest in things, whose attention had been fixed in a landscape of shame and discontent, in a world that Jean would never understand, and wanted no part of.

Jean's feelings, like old rubber bands, had lost their elasticity. They were not able to hold anything in place; no longer did anyone require them to, and she wasn't sure what use they had anymore. She allowed her feelings to collide, merge, and dissipate. In the end, she guessed she felt *okay,* prepared to carry on. She picked up Bub's shirts and stacked them back in the box, and she put the letter into the pocket of her apron, thinking that if the right moment rolled around she would share it with Mary. For the rest of the day Jean stopped from time to time between chores to reread the letter, until the letter lost its charge.

The quiet of her dusting and her sweeping soothed her as she entertained thoughts of what might happen from now on. The truth was, no one really cared what had become of Jean Saint, and she had the fleeting sense that even she was not that concerned. For a moment, she saw herself as a dust mote floating through a ray of sunlight—weightless—freefalling and unencumbered, like all the other nonspecific particles; a tiny piece of anything. But as she passed by the mirror in the front hall, she came eye to eye with herself. Oh come on, she thought, I've never seen a speck of dust with a face like that.

Nineteen
···

SAN FRANCISCO, CALIFORNIA
June 2010

The night before Mary Saint would set out on her long trip across the country she sat on her bed, unable to pack. In the old days, she'd hop on a plane and zigzag from state to state, even crisscross oceans without thinking twice. Her suitcase was always on the floor, open and ready to go. But this trip was different. She hadn't traveled through an airport in years, and she was anxious about how she would actually accomplish the little things, like getting through security with her guitar.

The fact that passengers had to take off their jackets, shoes, belts, and watches, to wait in stocking feet for a machine to scan their bodies—their bones? their hearts?—seemed bizarre and too intimate. Security guards with wands could fiddle around in people's crotches and underneath their shirts as if it were the most natural thing in the world. She worried that she might make a mistake, lose something, like her license or her boarding pass, her temper, or, secretly, her mind. Even being on a plane would be a challenge; she never used to wonder about what kept airplanes in the air, and now she couldn't help thinking they were too heavy to fly. She felt dangerously out of it, wary of it, whatever it was—the big *it*—the mainstream, perhaps.

Her ideas about planets farther away, stars that burned in a far-off galaxy, other expanded worlds of wonder and insight, were not going to help her navigate her way across the country, at a rental car counter, through an airport, or through the modern culture of America that had left her in the dust. She once had an entourage that bounced along in its merry bubble, but now she was going to be alone and expected to comply with the rules of a world that she'd almost entirely dropped out of.

Thaddeus had helped set up an itinerary for her, he'd spelled out every detail. He planned to go with her to the airport; flights, rental car confirmation number, and MapQuest directions were typed up clearly and stapled together. Mary hadn't driven in years, so they borrowed a car from one of Nelson's friends who owned a used-car dealership and went on a test run. She did well. She even enjoyed driving, which surprised both Thaddeus and Mary. They turned the radio up and sang along to the Beach Boys' "California Girls," with the windows rolled down, as they sailed across the Bay Bridge. She wished that Thaddeus could go with her, she even asked him, almost begged him, but she knew he couldn't: Cooper would never give the two of them time off together because at this point they were practically running the Crumb Bunny by themselves.

"Besides, Mary," Thaddeus said, "it's not like there's extra money floating around for a plane ticket. We never did rob that bank. And who would take care of Two Toes? I'm not sure we could really trust anyone." She knew that he was right, but she felt herself clinging to him.

What was secretly eating at her, though, was the Blessed Mother. She'd come to feel ashamed of her visit with *Other Mary,* as if she'd made the whole thing up, as if her experience were a child's fantasy or, worse, an encounter with a disturbed woman. She pondered the phrase *Blessed Mother.* What did it mean to her? She had started going to the library to look at books about religious art, hoping she might see her *Other Mary* in the faces of the Blessed Mother that artists had painted. She floated through the pages of the books in her way, not sure what she could recognize, but the faces were beautiful and strange, and sometimes she would spot them in her dreams. While meandering home one night, she'd wandered into a secondhand junk store and seen a set of rosary beads, made of blue plastic, like the ones she used to have when she was a girl. The woman behind the counter, who was slurping soup from a ceramic bowl, looked up at Mary, who asked her, "How much?"

"Ten dolla," said the woman.

"That's a lot," said Mary. "How about five dollars?"

"These very special, very old, magic," said the woman, not willing to bargain.

Mary bought them. She tried to say the rosary, to remember how, to finger the beads the way she used to do. She said the prayers slowly and wondered what they meant:

Hail, Mary, full of grace . . . Blessed art thou . . . Mother of God . . . pray for us sinners . . .

She kept the rosary beads by her bed, asking nothing of them.

The night before Mary left for the concert, she and Thad-
deus and, to an extent, Two Toes had what Thaddeus called a
costume party in Mary's bedroom. Thaddeus had cleaned and
pressed his blue silk pajama top, the one he always wore at rehearsal, and presented it to Mary as a possible piece to build her
outfit around, and she loved the idea. Using the pajama dress as
a base, they went through her entire closet and his bag of clothes,
trying to assemble something for her to wear onstage at the high
school in Swallow. They tried every set of beads, different scarves,
hats, and even wigs. Mary had long since stopped wearing the
blond wig to the Crumb Bunny after someone recognized her
even when she had it on. She'd survived the incident and decided
she couldn't care less. After that, there were a dozen other
times that she'd been spotted.

Once two guys came up to her at the counter and asked her
if she was Mary Saint from Sliced Ham, and she said yes, and
they could not contain themselves. It was more than they could
bear to see Mary Saint from Sliced Ham behind the counter in a
coffee shop, handing muffins to people—and they had to run
out in hysterics, not waiting for their order. Even that didn't faze
Mary, as she'd begun to dismantle her identity, and if she didn't
know who she was, how could anybody recognize her?

"No wig for the concert," she said. "I think I can go without."

She and Thaddeus concocted an outfit that pleased them. In
the end, after starting out with way too many boas and scarves,
they pared down.

"You look elegant, classic," said Thaddeus. "What a beauty
you are."

"Oh, come on. But actually, I like this outfit, I feel okay, but I can't calm down." She sat down on the bed next to Two Toes. "I just wish I was easier to take," she said.

"Your songs are deep, Mary. They may not be for everyone, but you'll be fine. Think of *Other Mary,* how she told you to sing for her."

"I'm sick of being a baby. I owe you big time, Thaddeus."

"Mary, you forget that I was sleeping in the chair in the heart room before you invited me into your home. I think we've done a lot for each other, we're a good combo." Thaddeus jumped up off the bed and said, "Oh, I almost forgot. I have something for you, and I don't want any arguments." He went into the other room, brought back a small brown bag, and put it next to her.

Mary looked inside and said, "Thaddeus. Are you crazy? A cell phone!"

"I know, you hate them. But I really want to be able to be in touch with you. I'm going to miss you, too, you know," he said. "It's all hooked up, and the phone number is on your itinerary." He showed her how it worked; they went through it step by step. He suggested she call him on his cell phone, and they spoke into their phones while sitting side by side on the bed, laughing at the absurdity of it all. He also showed her how to text.

"This thing is amazing, but it's so expensive," she said, knowing how hard it must have been for Thaddeus to scrape together the cost of the phone.

"Well, it's about time you had one anyway. So, just remember to text me when you get there. Two Toes and I will be waiting. Just type in L-A-N-D-E-D, and don't lose the darn thing."

The security line snaked around, a slow-moving maze of travelers, and Mary kept looking back and waving. Thaddeus waved, too, until she had made it through the metal detector and he saw her retrieve her guitar, disappear into the crowd. He knew that he would cry; after all, the airport was alive with partings and reunions, a place of great emotion, where tears flowed in abundance and without embarrassment. It seemed to him that, in the ordinary mechanics of a day, there were plenty of reasons to cry. It could be a fleeting look in a stranger's eye, a simple act of someone holding open a door, or a rudeness, like the way the woman at the ticket counter had snapped at Mary because she couldn't find her license fast enough.

Right before Mary turned to go she'd said, "Please come with me," and he could see how frightened she was. He laughed and lied, "I'm busy, Mary, you remember my friend Dennis? I have a date with him: big plans, big plans." The truth was he hadn't heard from Dennis in weeks, but he didn't want Mary to think he was worried about her. In fact, Thaddeus was worried, and as soon as Mary was out of sight, for reasons that he didn't question, he sat on a bench and wept, watching as travelers lifted and surrendered their enormous suitcases and turned to their loved ones to say good-bye. Each parting set off a fresh round of sobs, and as tears rolled down his cheeks, he laughed at himself, glad to be alone and far from anyone's concern. He blew his nose into a pile of napkins that he'd stuffed into his pocket days earlier, just in case something like this should happen.

Twenty

SWALLOW, NEW YORK

June 2010

Jean Saint nearly knocked Bill De Sockie down on the sidewalk outside the Silver Tray as she rushed in to place an order for the gathering Betty planned to have after the concert. Even though, after her run-in with Adele, she'd been determined not to set foot in the place again, she couldn't resist going back to the Silver Tray to order a lemon cake; it was touted to be the best cake for miles around. Let bygones be bygones. Jean could not contain herself; the worry and anticipation were almost over, and finally Mary was coming home.

"The article in *The Woodside* has pushed this thing right over the edge," said De Sockie once they were in the shop. "I think we're close to a sellout."

"Isn't that just great," said Jean, and she hoped that Adele had heard him.

"I couldn't be happier. Tell Mary, when she gets here, we're all set for her sound check," he said after he'd gotten his coffee and was on his way out the door.

"Will do," said Jean, as if she knew what a sound check was.

Jean had arranged to meet Vincent at Three Forks that afternoon, and it was a beautiful day. Red and yellow tulips stood at attention at the entrance to the home, and the leaves on the trees were light green and fragrant. She figured they'd be able to sit out in the garden with Vivian and Bub. When she arrived, she saw Delores behind the desk.

"Hello, Delores, what a day!"

"Hi, doll, yes, it's glorious," said Delores. "Mr. Calabrese is in Vivian's room. She's a little under the weather today."

"Oh, really?" said Jean.

She walked quickly to the room and found Vincent sitting by the bed, holding his wife's hand. Vivian was half asleep.

"What's wrong?" asked Jean.

"Jean, come in, come in," he said, letting go of Vivian's hand and pulling up a chair. "I think she'll be fine. She was agitated earlier and of course it's hard to tell what's bothering her, but she's calmed down a bit."

Vincent and Jean had become close friends. Not only was Vincent relieved to have Jean's companionship but it had changed Jean's whole outlook. Her heart had opened; she found she had more patience with Bub, and her problems with Mrs. Hollingberry eased because, of course, the director would never be rude to the aides in front of Mr. Calabrese. Lateisha, Rowena, and Alvin were always glad to see them, and Jean had the feeling that everyone was charmed by the relationship between her and Vincent, and the way the two couples all sat together on their visits.

"It's a fantastic day. I think we should sit out in the garden," said Vincent. "Why don't you get Bub and I'll see if we can convince Mrs. C to get up and we'll meet out there."

That was how they passed the afternoon, with the sun warming them on the patio, overlooking the great lawn behind the home. The birch trees around the pond had sprouted leaves, and the one big dogwood tree was in bloom. The two in the wheelchairs sat quietly, occasionally making a motion with a hand or turning a head. The couples watched the blue jays swoop, they even saw a hummingbird, and they ate bologna sandwiches on kaiser rolls that Vivian's sister, Donna, had made for them.

Jean and Vincent talked about the concert and how surprised Mary would be to hear of their meeting. Jean expressed her concerns about Betty Dunster hosting a get-together afterward. Vincent said he thought that it would all work out somehow. When they finished their picnic, they wheeled their spouses back to their rooms and saw to it that they were tucked in for the evening. As they were saying good-bye, Vincent almost succeeded in placing a kiss on Jean's cheek though she turned her face away at the last minute, embarrassed. Vincent said he'd meet her in the lobby before the concert, and Jean said that was a nice idea but she'd be selling CDs for Mary and so she'd probably be busy and he should find a seat without her.

"I didn't know you'd be selling CDs. A family act," he said. "I'm impressed."

"Well, Mary asked me to. She sent me a few box loads that she had stored in a warehouse in New Jersey, and I thought it might be helpful, and I certainly hope sales will be brisk."

"I'm sure you'll be swamped with takers," said Vincent.

They got into their cars, and the two vehicles wound their way down the long driveway from Three Forks. Once they reached Gazely Highway, they pulled their cars side by side and honked at each other before they drove off in opposite directions.

Twenty-one

BIG SUR, CALIFORNIA
June 2010

On the other side of the country, completely unaware of— and not the slightest bit interested in—Mary Saint's concert at Swallow High, Flick Zeez stood, exhausted and disturbed, on his patio overlooking the Pacific Ocean. It was reminding him of the inside of his brain: a blanket of blue nothing, slowly rippling out into oblivion. He'd been experimenting lately with an exotic medicinal plant found in the depths of the rain forest. The drug was called ayahuasca, and Flick had recently returned from Peru, where a private guide had taken him and a few select others through a series of experiences with the magic plant. The adventure had rattled him, and cracked him open, like the nut he'd always suspected he was, but he was having a hell of a time putting himself back together.

He'd gone down to Peru at the urging of John Strand, the prominent Hollywood movie director, whom he'd met at the presidential inauguration; they had been seated together at one of the balls. Strand had a string of blockbusters under his belt, known for their "otherworldliness." Flick and Strand had hit it off big time and couldn't believe that they hadn't met before, especially since Strand was a big fan of Flick's. They vowed to keep in touch and said they'd both wrack their brains to come up with a project to collaborate on soon.

It was Strand's idea to mess around with ayahuasca, which had become somewhat trendy, not only among celebrities and artists but among scholars, psychiatrists, and scientists as well. Strand called Flick and explained that he'd found the right people, who really knew what they were doing with the drug, and he'd finally gotten the whole trip hooked up. It would be a small, discreet group, and all Flick had to do was show up at LAX; Strand had arranged for a private jet to take them down. Flick had his doubts but said, "What the hell."

On the plane ride, over Iranian caviar and champagne, their last indulgence before they started a strict cleansing fast at the lodge in the rain forest (Strand had warned Flick it would be "very basic"), Strand told Flick about his new project, a mystery thriller about a teenage serial killer who terrorizes a small suburban town by cutting the heads off his victims and stuffing them into school lockers and local flower beds. It gets revealed that the killer is the quarterback of the football team, and the heroes of the piece are two nerdy girls who figure the whole thing out and wind up being embraced by the town. Strand was looking for ways to deepen the somewhat cheesy plot and wanted the music to be a big part of the film, a sort of road map to the thoughts of all the teenagers.

Flick found that he had a lot of ideas about what kind of music might be good, and Strand seemed genuinely open to his suggestions. They had a ball, like two hip teenagers, batting songs back and forth on each other's iPods, trying to come up with a direction for the songs that Flick would write. By the time they landed in Peru with champagne headaches, they'd pretty much agreed on going with a retro grunge-type feel for the whole movie.

Once they got to their thatched hut deep in the jungle, the movie was the least of their concerns, and the schemes and themes of Hollywood fell quickly to the back of their minds, replaced by a sticky, uncomfortable, and alarming new reality called ayahuasca. It was clear to everyone in the small group that they were in for a rough time; this was not just any old celebrity joyride. Flick found the heat and rain claustrophobic, and discovered that he had an inordinate fear of bugs. He was particularly shocked to learn that he had to share a hut with John Strand, who had a disturbing preference for being naked whenever possible, most especially while doing yoga. More than once he opened his eyes to see his friend ass-up in a downward dog or, worse, standing on his head with Big Al and the Twins hanging upside down.

Their guide for the week was a soulful, brainy guy in his early thirties who went by the name Truth, and he gave them the straight dope on the drug. "This is no party," he said as they all sat like nervous freshmen, cross-legged in a circle. "We're here to search, to go deep into the mystery. Everyone has a different response, and I won't lie to you, these experiences can be frightening and downright torturous. You will go into a place where there is access to a deeper understanding of the universe. The bottom line is suffering, and the *through* line is mystical wonder."

Flick looked around nervously at the group, which in addition to himself and Strand included two hedge fund managers from New York; a prominent psychiatrist from the University of Michigan at Ann Arbor; and his wife, a yoga teacher.

After taking a moment to make eye contact with each member of the group, Truth said, "And you might shit yourself or puke."

Flick was having second thoughts; he was all for depth and searching, but he enjoyed the comforts of home; he preferred vacationing in exclusive resorts; and he realized, too late, that he'd let himself get caught up in John Strand's kooky idea. Now that they were in the rain forest, there was obviously no way out. After the initiations and rituals, they all drank the brew—no one balked—and at first it was incredible. Flick journeyed to a place of great sorrow and openness; he wept uncontrollably, a good kind of weeping, a weeping for the world, a weeping *of* the world. He saw way beyond himself, into the enormity of all beings, concepts, and possibilities, just as Truth had said he would. Finally out of my own bullshit, he thought. But then the trip boomeranged and turned him against himself with the most vicious self-hatred he'd ever experienced. He saw visions he couldn't bear—like his sister hanging from one of the trees with a rope around her neck—and the forest rose up before him in blame and hostility. He thought he was going to die, and he thought he *should* die. Trees posed as monsters and bushes as rabid dogs. His impulse was to chop off his fingers and toes and eat them, and when he looked at John Strand, he saw that his friend's head had turned into a gorilla's head; sweat was rolling down his chest, dissolving into blood that dripped onto the dirt and created little streams of red worms. Flick thought he screamed but couldn't hear his voice. He thought he saw his mother, but it might have just been the yoga teacher. The last image he could remember of his trip on ayahuasca was the gorilla head baring sharp teeth and spewing undigested food. He eventually came down from the drug, covered in his own excrement, crying for his high school sweetheart.

Truth was there when Flick's eyes opened, wiping a cool cloth on his forehead, whispering that nothing was wrong. "It's all good," he said, one of those annoying sayings that Flick hated. "You're a real trouper—of the soul," Truth added. Flick whimpered and curled himself into a ball. The rest of the group stood around in solidarity, looking at him with a mixture of relief and suspicion, having fared a little bit better on their own journeys. And though they all talked about their experiences in an atmosphere of openness and "love," as Truth described it, Flick felt terrified and a little bit resentful. He still could not look at John Strand without seeing the gorilla's head, and he wished he wasn't sharing a private plane with the man on the way home. He actually considered trying to switch to a commercial flight, but his head was so far up his ass that he couldn't deal with making the arrangements, or even calling someone to help him.

When Flick finally returned to L.A., after an awkward good-bye—a strange kiss on the lips from Strand—he decided to go up to Big Sur for a while. As he explained it to his manager, Tom Easterly, he had to heal from the healing, and he also had to get to work on the songs for John Strand's movie; he'd committed to it, and it promised to be a big movie with a gargantuan budget. The problem was that since his experience with ayahuasca, not only was he confused about life in general, but nothing seemed to matter much. In particular the grunge bands they'd listened to on the plane just didn't seem right for the sound track. Flick found he longed for something that rang true, something that would bring him more into the head of the magic brew. Showbiz was a tough landscape for him right now, and though he was sure he'd wind himself back eventually, in the meantime, if he was going to *create,* it would have to be something that was important to him. He stared at the ocean for hours without a clue as to what to do, or even the slightest desire to pick up his guitar.

He decided to take a nap, and when he went into his bedroom, which was clean and silent, he lay down on the fresh white sheets and soft doughy pillows, feeling immensely grateful that he was not in the damp, mosquito-infested lodge in the rain forest. It was there, in his comfortable bedroom, that he found the answer. He happened to notice the hoop earrings on the bedside table, the ones he kept replacing; he had a box of them in his closet, and he always set a pair out when a girl was coming to spend the night, just to see whether she would be able to resist the temptation to take them. It had started as a fluke, a joke, but then it became a tradition, and in every case, the earrings were gone the next day. Every case but one—the time Mary Saint had been there. Of course, Mary Saint. How could he not have thought of her music for the film? Suddenly, it seemed so clear to him that the songs should be written by a girl—and not just any girl, but a girl whose music was deep, tragic, and provocative.

He spent the rest of the day, and several days thereafter, blaring her music throughout the house, searching for the perfect song, but there were so many that seemed perfect, and not just for the movie. Old songs like "Anklebone of Love Dust" or "I Can't Stop Eating" would be excellent:

> *. . . chewed my muscles*
> *sucked my fingers*
> *gnawed my bones*
> *my half a heart string lingers . . .*

He marveled at the songs, hearing a depth in them that he'd never heard before, and he realized the attraction to Mary and her music that he'd had years ago was just a taste of what he was experiencing now. Her profanity, her sorrow, her comedy, her nerve, and her willingness to go as far as she could into the darkness, were things he would never have been able to realize fully back then.

He sent the songs to John Strand, who was blown away.

Donal Hogan was notorious for getting top dollar in all his negotiations, and people dreaded dealing with him for precisely that reason. So when Flick Zeez decided that he wanted to use four of Mary Saint's songs in the movie he was scoring, Tom Easterly tried to talk him out of it. "You'll pay through the nose," Tom told him.

"I need those songs, Tom," said Flick, thinking that "Pay Through the Nose" could be another song.

"I'm going to have to go through Donal Hogan; I looked into this. He's the gatekeeper of her publishing, and I assure you he will bleed us," Tom said, shaking his head.

"Look, the budget is there, and I intend to score the movie

around these songs, and I might even want her to sing them, or else use the original recordings."

"Oh, nuts, Flick, we'll have to buy the original masters? Come on. At least rerecord them."

"I don't know. Those original versions are raw, I've already played them for John Strand and he creamed in his pants, and he agrees with me that they'd be bad," said Flick.

Tom knew that when Flick said *bad*, he meant *great,* and that, in itself, was annoying, but he also knew that once Flick had his head wrapped around an idea, he wouldn't budge.

Donal Hogan would suck up every penny he could, and in Mary Saint's case, he owned a piece of everything she'd ever done. Everybody knew she'd pretty much put him on the map. Tom figured that even though Mary Saint was an *old shoe,* Donal Hogan would go to bat for her. Tom knew they'd be broke before they knew what hit them.

"Mornin' to yeh," said Donal when he finally returned Tom's call.

"I guess you've been out of town, Donal," said Tom, trying to make his point.

"No, not at all," said Donal. "What's up with yeh?"

"Remember Mary Saint?" asked Tom.

"Of course, yes, Mary Saint, brilliant," said Donal, which made Tom wince.

"Flick Zeez wants to use four of her tracks in the new movie he's scoring; it's a John Strand movie starring Hedda Grimes and Paul Mason."

"Hedda Grimes, she's not too hard on the eyes, eh?" said Donal.

"I'm sure Mary Saint could use a break right about now. She'll probably be delighted," said Tom. "I just want to warn you, Hogan, the budget is tight."

"What a load of tosh, Tom," said Donal, and Tom knew he was sunk.

"Look, they might go with some other songs if the price is too stiff; Mary Saint's not exactly, you know, happening right now," said Tom, trying a different approach. "She's been yesterday's party for quite some time."

"Yep, yep, you're right. Maybe they should get some other songs, easy to do," said Donal.

"Look, I'm sure you'd like to get a deal for Mary. After all, you worked a long time with her," said Tom.

"She's a survivor, she'll be fine if you pass, she's the real deal, Easterly," said Donal.

"Come on, Hogan, she's fuckin' lucky that somebody like Flick even knows her music." Tom knew that he had misfired.

"You're right, Tom, Mary Saint is lucky . . . I know her, she's fooking brilliant, we'll pass."

Tom was then forced to go crawling back. They went round and round until the agreement was made, and Tom had to admit that Donal was almost fair; he didn't demand an exorbitant amount up front, although it was more than Tom thought the songs were worth. If it had been anybody else, Tom would have been able to get them for next to nothing. He couldn't figure out whether he despised Donal Hogan or admired him. At one point, Donal asked Tom why Flick couldn't write the songs himself. "That way you'd make yerself a bundle, Tom."

At the end of the negotiations, which took a few phone calls, only one of which involved Donal hanging up on Tom, they made their peace and Donal said, "Nice doing business with yeh, my best to Flick. Cheers." In a matter of several days, Donal had ensured that Mary Saint, regardless of how well the film did, would make a small fortune, and if it was a hit—and chances were it would be—she would be in for a windfall. All of this occurred without the slightest bit of worry on Donal's part; he sipped cups of tea throughout the phone calls, made his notes, and just kept saying nope until he got what he wanted, all the while thinking about what route he would take on his bike ride through Manhattan when the weekend rolled around, chuffed that his wife's family was coming down from the country for Sunday dinner, and that his kids and their cousins would make a racket until they were taken for a carousel ride in Central Park.

But Donal wanted to call Mary personally. He was sure she'd probably run out of money by now; he hadn't even consulted her about this deal, worried that she might be in rough shape. He'd seen enough talented people to know that once a person went down the rehab road, there was a chance they'd relapsed if they stopped putting out new work, and no one had heard a new song from Mary Saint in years. As far as he could tell, Mary's career was over; she never did make it big enough to have the lifetime span that the heavy hitters have. It would be practically impossible for her to make a comeback. Still, Donal Hogan had tender feelings for his friend. They'd been all over the block together.

He had an old number for her in San Francisco and took a moment to look over the skyline of Manhattan before he made the call. There was a time when he would have followed her to

the ends of her despair; she was hugely talented, and she could be a sweet pile of gold; besides, in an odd way, he loved her. He actually did. She hadn't even gotten mad at him when he had to sever ties. Most of the time it got nasty when the run was over. He could never understand why Mary couldn't really succeed beyond a certain point, though. They'd had great times together, many laughs; sure, he'd thought he was *in* love with her, but that wasn't really it; he simply saw who she was and understood her value, the way an art dealer can appraise a painting. They'd been young once, another era. Ah, life.

He dialed the number, and a machine picked up. Somehow he wasn't surprised that she was still at the same number; he recognized her voice immediately, and it made him smile.

"Hello, this is Mary, you can leave a message after the beep."

It was a simple message, dignified and clear. He hung up the phone, figuring he'd try her again later, but every time he called, he got the machine, so he finally left a message:

"Cheers, my dear, it's Donal Hogan, it's been ages. Hope you're well, eh? Good news. Your man Flick Zeez is set to use four of your songs in the new John Strand movie he's scoring. I made yeh a deal, and you'll be gittin' a nice sum of money fer it. Yeh could stand to make a huge chunk in royalties as well. Call me when yeh have a chance, and I'll let yeh know what I've worked out. Yeh know where to find me, Mary luv."

When Thaddeus came home after pacing around all day in Golden Gate Park, he'd already gotten a text from Mary saying "L-A-N-D-E-D." There were two messages on her machine: the

first one was from Nelson, wondering where the hell Thaddeus been all day, and the second was the one from Donal Hogan. Not knowing what else to do, Thaddeus raised his hands in gratitude and made up a song on the spot, and the song had one word— *hallelujah!*—at which point he heard the familiar *thwack* of Two Toes jumping off the bed. She wandered in with her tail wagging lazily and her head swinging from side to side, to see what the commotion was all about. Thaddeus picked up her front legs, and the two of them danced for a few seconds like a couple of awkward teenagers at a prom. Thaddeus couldn't resist calling Mary's cell phone, even though they'd promised not to spend the extra money. But all he heard was his own voice saying, "This is the cell phone of Mary Saint, the famous rock and roll singer. Leave a message and she'll quack like a duck."

He didn't leave a message; he wanted to hear her voice.

Twenty-two

SAN FRANCISCO TO SWALLOW

June 2010

It hadn't been so bad going through the security line at the airport after all. Mary managed to get her shoes off and still keep track of her bag, and she didn't have any altercations with people in uniforms, one of the things she used to have a knack for. She remembered a time when she'd gotten into a scrape with a flight attendant because the woman wouldn't let her carry her guitar onto the plane, even though she'd bought a seat for it. The flight attendant had looked at the ticket, which had the name Guitar Saint on it, and she'd said, "There's no such name as Guitar." Mary made the mistake of saying, "Bullshit," and the next thing she knew she was on the tarmac, face-to-face with the pilot, telling him that if the neck on her guitar got broken on the flight, she would break *his* neck. The police were called, and the band was thrown off the plane.

This time, Mary was fully prepared to surrender her guitar, but no one suggested it. An older flight attendant with a weary, no-nonsense look greeted her at the door of the plane and said, "Can I help you with that, ma'am?" The woman took the guitar and put it in the first-class closet, which, Mary knew, was a major favor. The attendant winked at her as she passed to find her seat.

Mary sailed across the country through a cloudless blue sky; she kept her head against the window for most of the flight, which was hardly full; entire rows were empty. First, as the plane lifted itself up and out over San Francisco Bay, she watched her city fade, thinking that Thaddeus must be almost home by now. Then the ground show began. The mountains went by, looking like the surface of the moon, and they gave way to the brown, tan, and green squares of farmland. The cities, some large, some small, all passed below her as the plane, with the sun gleaming against its silver wing, went serenely on its way, as if it were the most natural thing in the world for a hundred thousand pounds of aluminum to fly. She was amazed. Had she ever really bothered to look out the window of a plane before without being wrapped up in her own confusion, wrecked from a hangover, or groggy on a Xanax? It was thrilling, and she felt like a kid and an adult at the same time. She was calm but excited, thinking *this must be what it feels like to be alive.*

When she arrived in Detroit, she had to make a connection to a commuter airline, and she hurried through the airport to the gate, caught her plane to Albany in plenty of time, and ate her peanut butter sandwich on whole wheat bread while flying over Pennsylvania. After the plane touched down, Mary took a moment to get her cell phone out, turn it on, and type the word L-A-N-D-E-D. For a moment she felt like part of the *Mission: Impossible* team.

It wasn't until Mary drove past the ENTERING SWALLOW sign that she felt the old familiar choke hold of despair. The streets of her hometown seemed narrow and broken, as if they hadn't been paved in years, and as she passed the police station her heart began to beat faster. She slowed the car, careful not to speed, and turned down Cherry Street, where some kids were smoking by a dumpster out behind the Tiffany diner. The very sight of the ShopRite filled her with angst; she felt afraid of the town itself. She had hated living in Swallow, where small-mindedness was built into the architecture, and the ideal of conformity was glorified in row after row of dull-colored houses, now worn and weathered, meant to give the impression of happiness, a sense of an *us* that agreed about everything.

Times had changed, though, and the suburbs weren't the suburbs of her childhood anymore, she knew that. The new citizens of Swallow were strangers to her; their world had been expanded by the Internet, by technology, by the current pop culture. Still, she couldn't help feeling trapped. Driving back into Swallow seemed like defeat. She remembered the day she had left. Her friends had sped her out of town, they were laughing, and the radio was blaring. It was a song she'd never heard before or since:

> *I am everywhere; the sun is my heart and the stars are my*
> *eyes . . .*

"Fuck you, Daddy!" she'd yelled into the streets of Swallow, sticking her middle finger in the air while hanging out the window of the car before her friend Teddy Masters yanked her by her T-shirt back inside and handed her a joint. She'd smoked and drunk herself into a dispassionate stupor for several days in a row before it really hit her that there was no going back to Swallow, and she had proclaimed it to be the beginning of her life. Yet here she was, almost twenty years later, driving into town, tamed, with her manners in line, her confidence shaken, and her ass kicked, like someone who'd been given shock therapy at a loony bin and was coming home to Mama.

She drove right past the high school, where the concert would be taking place, and was surprised to see that the big red-brick building looked exactly the same, as if it had been preserved in formaldehyde, like the frogs in the biology lab. The two enormous white columns stood strong and wide on either side of the steps that led up to the front doors. She never used those doors, because right past them was the principal's office and she always tried to avoid Mr. McCarthy—or Mr. McFarty, as she and her friends used to call him—at all costs.

She thought about a math teacher she'd had in her sophomore year whose name was Mr. Volpe. He had had no control over the class, which was a metropolis of flying paper airplanes and soaring pens. Teenagers would slouch around the room, sitting on windowsills and desktops drinking bottles of Snapple and snacking on bags of Doritos as if it were a party, while the poor man stood in front of an obsolete contraption that projected images of equations he'd sloppily scribbled on a piece of paper up onto the blackboard. He'd solve the problems in an audible drone with only one or two of the nerdiest kids in the school, sitting in the front row, just barely paying attention, even they looked bored.

Mary had heckled him relentlessly through most of the year, making jokes to her buddies in the back of the classroom. She'd raise her hand, and when he called on her she'd say, "I just wanted to let you know your fly is down again, Mr. Volpe." And everybody in the back half of the room would curl around their desks in convulsive laughter. Or there was the time she stood up in the middle of one of his long-winded lectures on something like common denominators and said, "Mr. Volpe, I have my period, do you have any tampons in your desk?" Even her cohorts thought that was going a little too far, and instead of laughter her comment elicited a disgusted groan, but Mary Saint was never afraid to go too far, and most of the time it felt to her that she never went far enough.

One day when she had come into school with a black eye, compliments of her father, she'd wandered, humiliated, through the hallways; everybody could see it, and even her friends kept their distance. This was back in the days before parents were reported for such offenses; what went on inside the little houses of Swallow was nobody's business. When Mary went into her math class after lunch, she sat in the back of the room and tried to pretend she was reading the math book (of all things) in order to hide her face. Mr. Volpe had come over to her desk, crouched down, and put his hand on her shoulder. "Mary, what's happened to you?" he whispered.

"Nothing," she said with a sneer. "A doorknob, a door closed on my face."

"Are you sure no one did this to you?" he said. "Is there anything I can do?"

There was a split second when she looked into his eyes and

thought she might dissolve into tears because he actually seemed to care. But she couldn't afford to dissolve into anything, and she said, "Yeah, I'd like a Budweiser, got one?"

Mary's drive through the streets of Swallow was getting the better of her, and she couldn't bring herself to arrive at her mother's house in such a state. She had to find a way to pull herself together. In a panic, she decided to go to the woods, the place where she'd originally met *Other Mary*. She drove down the back streets of West Swallow until she came to the dead end, Trudy Lane, where she pulled over and got out of the car. She looked around, worried that she was doing something wrong, breaking an obscure rule. In Swallow, there were rules, and she had a way of coming up against them.

An overgrown path led into the woods, and she followed it, stepping over the rocks and through the branches. The smells of the dirt and trees touched off something deep within her, and she was surprised by her appetite for it. As she wandered farther in, she arrived at the stream, and she stopped to feel the skunk cabbage leaves and run her fingers across the mossy rocks. She came upon the ruins of the Boy Scout camp, which had worn away to just a few ragged boards, and continued on, hoping to find the circle of trees, all the while checking behind her to see if anyone was there.

When she came upon the trees, she was shocked to discover that a steel chain-link fence had been built; it passed right through the middle of the circle, and on the other side of the fence the trees had been cut down and in their place was a pristine lawn, which led to a corporate building. She put her fingers through the links of the fence and pressed her face against it, trying without success to see what the building was. She turned back to what remained of the trees—a family cut in half—and leaning on the fence, she said aloud, "Hello? Are you here?" The sound of her voice in the woods embarrassed her, and again she glanced around to make sure she was alone.

She looked to the sky, to the birds, the roots and rocks, branches, logs, and wildflowers, as if they could help her out. It was a perfect day. Perfect.

"Hello? Are you here?" She said it again, but what did she expect? A visit from the Blessed Virgin? Really? How pathetic, and yet, maybe it was what she had hoped for. *Other Mary* was nowhere to be seen, and she felt bad for the little believer, the kid who she once was.

"I let you down," Mary called out. "I didn't mean to, I'm sorry," she said. She couldn't help but try again. "I was screwed up, I made a mess of things. Can't you forgive me?"

She lingered awhile longer. It was peaceful there, and she didn't want to leave. "Hail, Mary, full of grace . . . Blessed art thou," she said. "I hope that you—" But with that, she turned to go. Thaddeus had said something to her months ago that popped into her head as she glanced back one more time—*Look, kid, not everybody gets a visit from the Blessed Mother. Maybe once is enough.*

As Mary wound her way back through the Boy Scout camp, she came upon a boy and girl, playing. They looked to be eight or nine, and deeply involved in a game of their own imagining.

She startled them, and they abruptly stopped what they were doing and stood side by side with their arms touching, obviously afraid of her.

"Hi," she said. The girl had long brown hair, and her stomach was sticking out of her shirt above her shorts. The boy was thinner, dirty blond; Mary thought he must be her younger brother, the way he seemed to defer to her. They eyed her suspiciously. "Don't mind me, I'm just taking a walk," she said. But the two kids just stared at her. "Really, I was looking for a friend of mine. You haven't seen anybody in here, have you?"

The little girl shook her head no.

"Okay, well, if you do, you can say hello to her for me," said Mary.

The little boy spoke up. "What does she look like?"

Mary thought for a moment and said, "She looks a little bit like me, but she'd probably be wearing a dress made out of rags."

The kids considered this.

"Okay," said the girl, relaxing a bit.

Mary said good-bye and starting walking away, but she turned to look at them again. They had already gone back to their game, and she watched them dance around in their invisible world before making her way back to her car.

When she was almost out of the woods, she stopped to gather wildflowers; there were many to choose from—chokeberry, trout lilies, ragged robin, and yellow hawkweed. She picked a big bouquet of as many different flowers as she could find, so she'd have something special to bring home to her mother.

Twenty-three
....

THE CONCERT

The high school looked regal, all lit up on the evening of Mary Saint's concert, and Jean had dressed for the occasion, feeling somewhat like the mother of the bride and looking particularly lovely in a dusty blue sweater with a dolphin pin and a floor-length navy skirt. All her friends were coming: of course, Vincent and her best friend, Betty; several neighbors from down the street at East Swallow Meadows whom she hardly knew; members of the church choir; and a few of her fellow volunteers from the hospital. Even Father Ben had a ticket, and she had a sneaking suspicion that Adele, from the Silver Tray, wouldn't be able to stay away.

Bill De Sockie had set up a table in the vestibule for Mary's CDs, and Jean had come early to lay them out. To her chagrin, it turned out there was an opening act whose merchandise table had many more items, such as T-shirts and a mailing list, as well as pens and buttons stamped with the logo of the duo, which was called the Tennessee Twinsters. A clever name, Jean thought. They also had lovely display stands for their CDs, the sort that would be in a record store, while Jean had no choice but to lay her CDs flat. Their table was across the lobby, being arranged by a pushy guy who was introduced to her as Eliot Bemblatt, the group's manager. He was ordering Bill De Sockie around, demanding a tablecloth for their table and asking for special vegetarian food to be brought in, as if it was even possible to find vegetarian food in Swallow. The way Bill De Sockie was running around trying to please their manager, it seemed as if the Tennessee Twinsters was the main act. De Sockie had barely said a word to Jean, which she thought was rude, considering none of this would be happening if it hadn't been for her. Not to mention the fact that he'd imposed upon her to ask Betty if he could bring a group of his students to the gathering after the show, claiming it would be *educational*. Great, a bunch of teenagers eating all the food. Oh, phooey, what did she care? She wished she didn't have to be so petty.

A glossy photo of the Twinsters stood on an easel beside their table; they were all smiles, posing under one giant cowboy hat. Jean thought it was a cute picture and had to admit she felt a twinge of embarrassment about Mary's appearance.

Mary had shown up at the house two days before the concert in a rented car and a beat-up leather jacket; she seemed thin, and Jean was surprised to see a few strands of gray spiraling up out of her thick black hair, which was crazy with curls and falling over her face. Mary was loving and affectionate, and she'd even brought wildflowers that she'd picked on her way into town; Jean was moved. Mary carried the flowers through the living room, letting the dirt trail onto the rug and into the kitchen.

Jean had to restrain herself from getting the vacuum out, but when Mary kissed her four or five times on each cheek, and held her tightly with genuine feeling, Jean felt years of lost joy rising up; her girl was home, even though Mary smelled odd to her, like a mixture of sweat and something she'd once sniffed while walking past an Indian restaurant on a visit to Albany.

They spent an awkward time together, during which they tried so hard to be nice to each other that Jean found herself exhausted. She fed Mary fish sticks, which Jean remembered as one of her daughter's favorite meals, but Mary left them on the plate, eating only the cucumber salad, and they both seemed ready for bed by nine o'clock. But they stayed up to watch an episode of *Law & Order,* which Mary looked at intently, her mouth ajar, as if there were an actual crime investigation going on in Jean's living room. The second day, when Jean asked Mary if there was anything she'd like to do in town, Mary suggested they go to the dog pound, which was the last place Jean wanted to go, but off they went, and once they were there, Mary seemed delighted just to look in the cages at the mangy old hounds and talk about how cute they were, while the scent of the place was enough to make Jean gag.

When they got home, both of them took naps, and then Jean made hamburgers for dinner, figuring that everybody loved those, but Mary said outright that she was sorry but she couldn't eat the meat, and Jean remembered that Garbagio had been a vegetarian—perhaps that was why—and why hadn't she thought of that?

Jean had many things she longed to say to Mary; for months

she'd remembered a tidbit here and there that she wanted to be sure to tell her. She was dying to reveal the incredible story of Vincent Calabrese and how they'd met, and she wanted to show Mary the letter from Bub that she'd found, but once her daughter was sitting across the table from her, Jean's mind went blank. It was all she could do to keep from putting her arms around her. Now that Mary was home, Jean didn't want to let her go. But she never did feel comfortable enough to do that. It was just the way she was. Jean wanted to say *I'm sorry, so awfully sorry* for what went wrong, if only this, if only that . . . but she found herself distracted by the person Mary actually was. Struck by the fact that she hadn't really looked at her daughter for years and years, now she could see how she'd aged, the little lines around her eyes; well, it was only natural. If only they could go on a typical mother-daughter shopping trip to the mall, or trot down to Karen's Nails to get a manicure and an upper lip wax— what would be so wrong with that? But Jean would sooner set the house on fire than dare suggest any of those things. Mary had been on her own at such an early age, so much of her life had been lived in the danger zone, and Jean knew that Mary had been through some very big traumas. She was reminded, yet again, that her daughter was *different,* and that would never change, which was hard for Jean—very, very hard—and she figured that Mary had suffered enough because of it.

At one point, Mary broke a silence by asking about her father, and though Jean had wanted desperately to share his letter with her, she couldn't bring herself to. It was the perfect opportunity, and yet she let it pass. Her secret hope to visit Bub at Three

Forks with Mary seemed far out of the question, for she sensed that Mary could not forgive her father. It was Jean's fault, she knew; she should have put a stop to the abuse. But how? Divorce? As the past crumbled away, its structures seemed more and more absurd, but it couldn't be undone. Lately, Jean had a hard time remembering what had kept them all so tightly pulled into Bub's orbit.

There were moments when Mary looked as if she might cry, and sometimes she seemed spooked just to be in Jean's house. The one thing Mary did seem interested in was hearing Jean talk about her life. She wanted to know the details about who her friends were, and Jean mentioned Betty Dunster and Adele Graham, and Mary laughed out loud at her descriptions of the characters who lived in East Swallow Meadows and the ridiculous rules about which flowers could be planted and what colors the houses could be. But whenever Jean asked what her life was like in San Francisco, Mary would become quiet and change the subject. Jean worried that it was because she had no friends.

Late that night, after Mary had turned in, Jean did something that she wasn't sure she should have done. She put Bub's letter in an envelope and wrote Mary's name on it, tiptoed into her own living room, and slowly unzipped Mary's bag, hoping not to make a sound. She felt like a thief as she reached down and put the envelope underneath Mary's clothes. How could she feel that she was taking something from Mary when, in fact, she was giving her an apology from her father? Would that be something that she'd want? Jean honestly didn't know, there was so much about her daughter that she didn't understand. When she had carefully rezipped the bag, she was gripped by sadness. Just having her hand in Mary's things filled her with sorrow. Everything about her daughter was foreign to her.

At a quarter to eight, Jean stood in the lobby of the high school, in front of the theater, greeting the citizens of Swallow. There were many people she didn't recognize: students, young couples, old folks, and she noticed that there were *outsiders,* too. A few large groups of younger people arrived together, clad in dark, dirty denim; the girls were scantily dressed, some of them with different shades of dyed hair—orange and pink—not the usual Swallow clientele. These people worried Jean, but she hoped that she was greeting everyone politely; anyone who approached her would get the same welcome: "Hello, I'm Mary's mother," as if she were hosting an exceptionally large party.

Vincent walked into the lobby, and the sight of him in a crisp checkered dress shirt and brown slacks sent a wave of relief over Jean, but she shooed him off, warning him to find a seat before the theater filled up. The same thing with Betty, who was nervous about the after party. Jean could not take on another burden at the moment; her hands were full, and she had a bad case of the jitters.

Finally, the lights flashed on and off, signaling that the show was about to begin. Bill De Sockie could be seen running around frantically, and folks who were lingering in the lobby started to move quickly into the auditorium. The show began, and Jean could hear the laughter and applause from the audience, relieved that the concert was finally under way. She slipped in and watched as the Tennessee Twinsters gave a rousing show; Jean thought their in-between-song patter was charming, and they were both clean-cut, like characters out of the musical *Oklahoma!* The girl was gay and lively in a square-dancing dress, and her brother was handsome in a white starched shirt and bolo tie. It turned out that they were, in fact, twins, and they delighted the audience with anecdotes about their childhood in Tennessee. *"My sister, Rose, was the favorite, she could do no wrong. Believe me, folks, I spent my share of time in the doghouse, and I mean . . . the doghouse."* Their show closed with a hand-clapping sing-along, and at the end the crowd stood up and cheered, calling for more, but the duo had played longer than their allotted time and so they couldn't do an encore, which caused some people to boo. But Bill De Sockie hopped up onto the stage and said that Mary Saint would soon be up and they were in for a real treat.

The audience poured out of the auditorium during the intermission; there was much lively conversation as many of them stepped up to the Twinsters' table to buy CDs from Eliot Bemblatt. Jean stood by, a little bit jealous, and concerned that Mary might not go over as well as the opening act had. She busied herself by rearranging the CDs on her table while trying to ignore their covers, which only reminded her that much could go wrong. Betty rushed over, and soon Vincent appeared as well.

"They're adorable!" said Betty, to Jean's annoyance.

"Yes, I thought so, too, very cute," said Jean, trying to be big about it.

"I'd say they were a great warm-up for the show," said Vincent.

Jean couldn't bear the small talk. "Now, you two should

wander back in before it starts," she said. The whole thing was proving to be too much.

Mary was "backstage" in a classroom, getting ready to go on. Bill De Sockie had provided the mirror that she'd asked for and he'd put a bowl of green apples on the teacher's desk, but the nearest bathroom was down the hall. She wound up getting dressed in the classroom, hoping that no one was peering into the windows or else about to bust through the door without knocking. Nervously, she kept tuning her guitar, but eventually couldn't resist fishing her cell phone out of her purse. If she could touch base with Thaddeus, it might straighten her up; she was losing her footing, getting confused. She figured out how to turn the phone on, called her home number, hoping he would be there, but the machine kicked in and she heard her own voice on the message. "Thaddeus? Are you there?" she said. "I'm back-stage, shaking. You must be on your date with Dennis. Okay, don't worry. I'll call you later."

Utterly alone, she considered the phrase *climbing the walls.* There was no escape; she simply had to do the show. She thought she might die. What if she fainted or collapsed onstage? What in the world had she been thinking to agree to do a concert in Swallow? If she'd wanted to see her mother, she should have just come for a visit. These thoughts raced around her head, making her dizzy—crazy—but she stopped herself. *No craziness.* She ap-proached the big blank blackboard at the front of the classroom and picked up a piece of chalk that was on its ledge. The feeling of the chalk in her hands brought her back to when she was sixteen. Everything at Swallow High seemed frozen in time; hadn't they gotten new blackboards in twenty years? In huge letters that spread across the expanse of the board, she wrote, I AM OKAY.

Stepping back, she admired her creation, realizing that a part of her wanted to do the show; in fact, she was lucky to have a chance to stand up and say her piece. It had been a long time since she had spoken out, and she had to believe that she knew what she was doing. *Sing,* she said to herself. Just *sing.* She put her guitar on and sang into the mirror, peering at her image. Who *is* that person? In Thaddeus's blue silk pajamas, a white tank top, and red satin boxer shorts, she was all-American, wrinkled in red, white, and blue. The fishnet stockings bagged at the knees, and her beads, like the contents of a dead lady's jewelry box, hung weightily around her neck. Her soldier's boots were big black mounds around her skinny calves; she lifted one and then the other to inspect them from every angle and laughed aloud, taking another moment to check herself closely. She'd given herself red lips, lined her eyelids in black kohl, and brushed her cheeks with pink, even remembering to glue a shiny paper star under her eye, for old times' sake. But who was she supposed to be now? She looked like a clown—*a clown?*—but of course.

"*I'll sing it for you . . . ,*" Mary said aloud, and she understood, with great relief, that it was all she had to do.

When Mary's portion of the concert was about to begin, Jean waited until everyone was seated before she entered the auditorium and stood by the door, just under an exit sign that shed a soft glow, as if a spotlight had been focused just for her. A soundman, carrying Mary's guitar, scurried across the stage, plugged it in, and set it securely in its stand; then he tapped the microphone to check that it was on and returned to the monitor board. As the house lights went down, Bill De Sockie came bounding out from behind the red velvet curtain, nearly tripping over his untied shoelace. He stood at the microphone with a crumpled sheet of paper, somber as a nervous child.

"Oh, man, this is a dream come true for me." Wiping sweat off his forehead, he said, "I'm Bill De Sockie." He paused, waiting for applause, but there was none, so he continued. "Ladies and gentlemen, tonight we are in the presence of a great artist who grew up right here in our little town." He tried to follow the words on his paper while his hands shook. "I think this is a proud moment for Swallow High. It's not every day . . ." He trailed off, losing his spot on his notes and his train of thought. "The heck with it . . ." He crushed his paper into a ball and shoved it in his pocket. "Look, I prepared an introduction, but I'm just going to speak from my heart. I hope you don't mind."

"Mr. De Sockie, whatever you do, don't cry," yelled Hazel Froelich from the balcony.

"Okay, Miss Froelich, very funny." A ripple of laughter spread through the auditorium, and Bill De Sockie thought better of speaking from his heart. "All right, okay," he said. "Ladies and gentlemen, please welcome Mary Saint." With that he jumped off the stage, disappeared up the aisle into the black of the auditorium, and ducked into a seat in the back that he'd saved for himself.

Mary came onto the stage to eager applause, whistles, and

yelps from her die-hard fans. She stood in silence before the microphone and looked across the audience with concern, as if surveying whitecaps on a sea that was about to storm. She was breathing hard, dressed in what looked to Jean like a wrinkled blue slip and a scuffed-up pair of soldier's boots, with several strings of gaudy beads hanging from her neck. Her hair was a wild tangle that flew around her head and covered half her face. Mary said nothing; she took her time. Jean thought that her daughter looked confused—*why hadn't she combed her hair?* Jean had the sudden maternal urge to call the whole thing off, to rescue her.

Someone yelled, "You're beautiful!"

Mary turned ever so slightly toward whomever it was and stared, expressionless, as if she didn't understand the meaning of the word. Finally, she went for her electric guitar, which was leaning in its stand; she strapped it on and strummed down hard. A loud ugly scraping noise filled the space, and she stopped the sound abruptly by putting her hand on the strings. She grabbed the microphone and spoke slowly, savoring every word. "Helloooo, Swalloooo. Glad to be here. This song is called 'The Back of My Ass.'"

Somebody shouted, "Yes!" but Jean's heart thumped. She froze, wishing she'd heard wrong.

The song began. Jean had no idea what it was about; the words flowed inexplicably into one another. Mary's voice was pure, strong but heartbreaking, and the guitar screeched along like a churning garbage truck. The song's obscure meaning hung in the air; it had a sorrowful sentiment that Jean could not imagine anyone wanting to comprehend. But when the chorus rolled around, the meaning became clear enough, too clear, for Jean.

> *Put your horsey boner in your pants*
> *And all your little sicko bad boy rants*
> *'Cause the back of my ass is all you'll see*
> *And the back of my ass belongs to me . . .*

Jean thought she was dreaming—this couldn't be—and when the song was over, the audience clapped, because what else could they do? One rude young man in the front row yelled out, "Fuckin' A," while others whooped, which only made matters worse.

Mary threw her head back and stomped on the stage with her big old boots; she penetrated the darkness of the auditorium; her eyes darted around as if there were things she saw that no one else could see. Then she closed her eyes, and reaching down into a private pool of power, she started to wail again. Jean was amazed by her strength—*who is this person?*—her daughter seemed like a wild tiger hooked to a chain. How cruel, Jean thought; something so wild should be set free.

The songs kept coming. There was "Tom's Dick and Harry," a horrifying rant that appeared to be about a gay man's murder; Jean thought she heard something about someone being dumped into a river with his hands cut off, and the refrain "*why, why, why*" was repeated so often that Jean wished she could answer the question herself, just to stop her daughter from singing it again. There was "Over Daddy's Dead Body," "I Can't Stop Eating," and "Lay Down upon My Smarmy Liver," a bitter dirge obviously alluding to Mary's alcohol and drug use, a diatribe of self-hatred and anger, which ended with the unlikely relentless chant: *I desire you, desire you . . .* , sending her small core group of fans into a tizzy of delight but leaving the rest of the audience confused. Mary sang "Feet and Knuckles," dedicated it to Garbagio, and her followers raggedly cheered her on, but the song was, for Jean, only a reminder that Vincent was sitting somewhere in the auditorium listening to all of this.

For Mary, up onstage, there was no way out. Something simple was driving her, and she was sure of what she was doing. Each song was a reminder of everywhere she'd ever been, of all that had gone wrong, of the choices she'd made, the public exposure of her glorious mistakes; and what she had going for her now was the audacity to carry on. She wasn't about to abandon herself on the stage. She wanted to say, "Hey, folks, don't mind me, I'm what's left of a girl who, years ago, curled up behind one of the seats in this auditorium and hid all night, afraid of my father, and scared to death of all of you. But that's okay, 'cause look how good I turned out." But she didn't say anything; she sang. Mary would stand there with that girl until the last song was sung. She heard the tunes go by. They were angry, violent, painful—maybe even *stoopid*. But they were hers, she'd created them, and she was going to let them fly away into the dark air of the auditorium at Swallow High.

But during "Bored by My Own Big Mouth," she inexplicably forgot the words and stopped. Her mind raced around, searching. It was as if an airplane had suddenly lost power while flying over the middle of the ocean.

. . . my mouth . . . where all the words are stored . . .

The audience stared, and she stared back at them. A minute passed, but nothing came, not a sound. It seemed an eternity; the silence dragged on and on, and a teenager who was squirming in her seat yelled out, "Oh, God, come on, sing something."

But Mary wasn't willing to give up the song; she waited at attention for the words to come. Finally she said, as if to someone who wasn't even there, "I forgot the words . . . no, no, no . . . what are the words?" She continued to play the chords on the guitar, banging with her boots on the stage, chanting . . . "the words, the words, the words."

Jean felt sick, watching her daughter struggle. A half row of fans stood, and the ridiculous army of five chanted along with her . . . "the words, the words, the words!" until Bill De Sockie rose and yelled out over the chant, "Mary, the words are *they're lying at the bottom of the C-sharp chord!*"

"Yes," said Mary, looking over at De Sockie. "That's them. Thank you, my friend. That's your teacher, folks, give the guy a hand." It was the first time that Mary had really acknowledged Bill De Sockie all day, and he felt light-headed and proud, as if he'd just been inducted into the Rock and Roll Hall of Fame. He listened in shock as Mary Saint sailed on through the song, and then barreled right into "Please Don't Punch Me Anymore," which segued into "Bend Over Bob."

An overwhelming sense of unease gripped the auditorium, differences of opinion, uncomfortable silences. It was as if the audience was at war with itself, split evenly between two small factions: the ones who loved Mary and the ones who most definitely did not, leaving the bulk of them to seesaw on the fence and wonder what to think. No one quite knew what to do.

Jean stood through all of this, watching her daughter's slender body sway. How could Mary bear it? Jean thought she seemed superhuman, with her eyes scrunched shut, and her face looked about to break from pain. Though the words made little sense, they somehow threatened to tell the ugly story that Jean had been so careful to keep to herself all these years. Jean heard the echoes of Mary's refrain reverberating through her mind—*why, why, why.*

The set seemed to climax during her song about her old hometown, "I Can't Swallow You No More":

> *I'm in you like a padded cell*
> *your brick wall wishing well*
> *whatever it is you're hollow for*
> *I can't swallow you no more . . .*

A few of Mary's fans stood up at the end of the song and raised their fists in solidarity. One of them yelled, "You are the shit!"

Mary turned around in a full circle and let her silk pajamas swirl about her, and when she looked at the audience, she almost seemed surprised that they were there. She put her hand up to her eyes in an effort to see through the darkness into the crowd, and with her lips up against the microphone, she said, "Listen, folks, it was hard to grow up in Swallow, so I had to move away. But my songs are all about this town, in a way. I'd like to take a moment to thank my mother for sticking with me through the tough times, and I'm sorry if I've caused you any pain, Ma. Ma? *Ma?* Are you there? You are my favorite song," she said, peering around the auditorium.

Jean heard the words, and felt the town's eyes upon her, but she kept her gaze fixed on her daughter; she could hardly breathe. Somehow, of all the words that Mary had spewed forth, these were the hardest to handle, and among the few she understood.

Jean's mouth opened; she felt herself try but fail to speak. She tried again. "I'm here," she said, but it was just a little squeak that no one seemed to hear.

"I guess she's . . . Well, wherever you are, Ma, this one's for you."

Mercifully, Mary began her final song, which Jean could not believe was one she actually recognized. It was "Sewer Flower."

> *. . . she grew out of cow dung and a dirty little song was sung . . .*

Just as Jean felt that she could not take one more moment, the door beside her opened slightly and in slipped a tall woman in a long blue veil; she wore a dress made out of what appeared to be scarves. When Jean turned to look at her, she noticed that the woman was holding rosary beads, and her face was delicate and beautiful; it was hard to look away from her. Jean thought that she might faint as it crossed her mind that this was the Blessed Mother, the *Other Mary* her daughter had seen in the woods, but she knew that was preposterous.

From the stage, Mary saw the woman, too, and she stopped in the middle of the song, which caused the audience to look around nervously. Mary had thought that the show was over, that every corner had been swept, all the garbage burned away, that she was utterly empty, and her job was done.

But it turned out that for Mary there was one last frontier, the most elusive inner space, so tiny and frozen, it was hard to feel. Now, in an instant, it melted like a snowflake on a windowpane. Mary felt it as it happened; it was the answered prayer that she'd never even prayed. *Somebody loves you, Mary,* and for the first time in so many years, she realized that she'd been seen and understood.

The audience watched as Mary opened her arms toward the woman, who was walking slowly down the aisle and up the stairs to the stage. The woman moved with elegance, her hands folded in prayer, rosary beads dangling. Mary beamed as she waited for the woman to come close to her. The audience sat in confused silence and watched the two join together in a long embrace.

Mary whispered, "Holy crap, where did you get the money?" but of course every word was picked up by the microphone. Then the murmuring began; people in the crowd wanted to know who the woman was.

Finally, the veiled lady stepped up and addressed the audience; in a raspy voice just barely above a whisper, she said, "You've already met Mary, I am *Other Mary.* And we're going to perform a song for you now."

The woman turned and spoke into Mary's ear. "Cooper gave me the money, and by the way, nice show, looks like you're finally graduating from high school," she said, and Mary kissed her best friend on the mouth.

The audience was unsettled. A little girl yelled out, "Are you the Blessed Mother?"

Someone else shouted, "Who's Cooper? What the heck is this?" and the man got up to leave.

An entire row of fans stood and chanted, "We love you!"

Mary said, "This song is called 'I Sing for You,' and it's a love song." As she started into the chord progression, all eyes followed the graceful lady who danced while Mary sang. She was wonderful and strange as she twirled around the stage with her rosary beads, in her flowing veil and gown. Mary closed her eyes and sang the song.

> *. . . who loves the ones who come undone . . . I sing for*
> *you . . .*

At the end of the song, the two Marys held hands and bowed to their audience with great humility. Some of the people hurried from the hall, and some stood up and raised their hands above their heads in wild applause and admiration. Several opened their cell phones and swayed, but most didn't know what to do and offered a polite round of clapping, because that's what's done at the end of a show. Bill De Sockie, who could not contain himself, hid his face in his sleeve in a desperate attempt to keep his students from seeing him cry. Jean hurried out to her CD table as if it were a place to hide, and as the audience filed out of the auditorium, she furiously rearranged the CDs and eyed the crowd that was gathering again around the Tennessee Twinsters, who had come out for a "shake and howdy." Betty rushed over to Jean, her arms extended.

"Mary's quite the poet!" Betty said, a little too loudly, and, looking to Jean for some kind of sign, whispered, "Are we still on for the party?" Before Jean had a chance to answer, Betty grabbed her elbow, having spotted Father Ben, who was on his way over. Father Ben approached cautiously with a Twinster CD in his hand and said, "What a wild ride. Mary put on quite a show. Fascinating." And then he turned to Betty and said, "Is there still a gathering at your place? I'm looking forward to meeting Mary."

"Yes, Father," said Betty, looking anxiously toward Jean. "I'd better get over to the house, then."

Jean noted with disgust that Adele from the Silver Tray was at the Twinsters' table getting an autograph, and the words *my son, tuba,* and *the St. Louis Philharmonic Orchestra* rose like crescendos above the crowd. Meanwhile, a bearded fan with a small glass bone in his nose came up to Jean and grabbed her hand. "Your daughter is *awesome,* man," he said solemnly and bought a CD with fifteen crumpled dollars that Jean was afraid to touch. It was the only one sold.

As the lobby thinned out, Jean wondered what had happened to Vincent and feared that he had left the concert without saying anything in order to spare her any embarrassment, which was probably just as well. She didn't think she could face him.

The high school was empty now, and Jean waited alone on the sidewalk, leaning against a parking meter, barely able to stand, wishing Mary would come quickly out the side door. Bill De Sockie had pulled himself together and helped Jean pack the CDs, and before he said good night he shook his head and commented that he didn't think much of the audience understood Mary.

"Some of those people were out of it. They didn't get it. And I'll probably take some heat from Dick Dworkin about this, judging from the long faces I saw on Mrs. Perble and some of my other colleagues, who shall remain nameless. Just between you and me, a bunch of them were huddled together in the lobby after the show, most likely trashing me. But I think Mary's a genius; she hasn't lost an ounce of integrity. Mrs. Saint, I'll never forget this night. And heck, we made some money," he said. Jean didn't know how to respond, but she supposed he was right about one thing; she'd never forget this night, either. She sneezed into a tissue, blew her nose, and watched him get into his car and drive away, presumably to Betty Dunster's house.

By that point Jean knew that she'd have to call Betty and wriggle out of going to the party. There was no way that she could face a crowd, especially if Father Ben was going to be there. Exhausted and confused, she couldn't figure out what had happened; the night had been like a fever dream, inexplicable and frightening, and who, she wondered, was the woman in the long blue veil? She gazed up at the sky and saw that the moon was out. It cast a hazy glow on the crab apple trees that lined the main street of Swallow. If only she could just go home and sleep forever.

Finally, the side door opened, and Mary came out, lugging her guitar, but she was not alone. Jean immediately realized that Vincent was with her and someone else, too. As they got closer, Jean saw that the other person was the woman who'd danced with Mary on the stage. She had taken off her veil and had it draped across her arm now. Her hair was cropped short, like a boy's.

"Are you okay, Ma?"

"Am I okay? Well, yes, of course," said Jean. "I'm just confused,

I'm a little bit confused. And you, Mary?" Jean said, eyeing Vincent.

"Yes, I'm good, Ma," said Mary, and Jean was surprised to see that she meant it.

"Well, then," said Jean, relieved.

Vincent put his arm around Jean, and then Mary said excitedly, "How could you not tell me about Mr. Calabrese? I can't believe it! It's a wonderful thing that's happened! And, Ma, this is my friend Thaddeus. He lives with me in San Francisco. He surprised me tonight."

"I think he surprised us all," Jean said, confounded.

"It's such an honor to meet you, Mrs. Saint," said Thaddeus, reaching out his hand toward her. "Everybody loves Mary, she's such a dear, lovely person; you must be very proud."

"Proud? Yes, proud. I'm very proud."

Twenty-four

AFTER THE SHOW

What Thaddeus noticed when he entered the party at Betty Dunster's house were the crucifixes—she must have had thirty of them, different sizes and shapes, hanging all over the walls. He heard a loudmouthed guy and spotted him in the corner sipping a glass of wine, spouting off to a man who kept adjusting his hearing aid. As Thaddeus looked around further he saw that the lamplit room was filled with elderly people sitting on soft chairs or just standing around holding napkins and cocktails, and except for the one loudmouth, they were all speaking in low tones and seemed rather unshaken about the concert as far as he could tell. He hadn't known what to expect. Mary had convinced him to put his veil back on for the party, which he did only after asking Jean if she would mind, and Jean said, "What the heck, I think I've seen it all by now." The fact that the Blessed Mother appeared to have walked into Betty's house did not seem to be a problem for the older folks; it could have been that they were being unduly polite, but perhaps they, too, had seen it all in movies and on TV, and nothing could faze them anymore, not even a Blessed Mother—not even a *chocolate tranny.*

Jean nudged Mary to tell her that the man in the corner who was making the racket was the manager of the Tennessee Twinsters—Eliot Bemblatt—and Jean made a face. Mary said, "Oh, are the Twinsters here? I wanted to say hello."

Betty rushed over to them as they entered the living room, and the guests erupted into a modest round of applause. Mary and Thaddeus walked arm in arm into the center of the room, and Bill De Sockie ran up and handed them each a glass of wine, which they declined, saying they'd prefer cups of tea if that were possible. Vincent intervened and said he'd take the wine off Bill De Sockie's hands; Jean took a couple of swift sips, and everybody raised their glasses with a cheer.

Beyond the living room, on the table in the dining room, was an enormous yellow sheet cake with white frosting that said WEL-COME HOME MARY in pink letters. Thaddeus saw that there was a priest across the room. Their eyes met, and the priest smiled and walked over to introduce himself.

"Hello there, I'm Father Ben," said the priest, who held a snifter of whiskey.

Thaddeus offered his hand warily and said, "Nice to meet you Father Ben, I'm—"

"I know who you are, you're *Other Mary*," said the priest, chuckling. "I guess we're both in our costumes."

"They do come in handy," said Thaddeus.

"You did a wonderful thing tonight," said Father Ben.

Thaddeus was surprised. "Well, thank you, I'm glad you understood."

"Would you introduce me to Mary?"

Mary had wandered off, and Thaddeus called her over and let

the two shake hands. He noticed that Jean was watching them out of the corner of her eye. Betty, too, seemed to pay close attention. Thaddeus was intrigued by the scene, but at the same time he felt on edge; he hadn't been anywhere near a Catholic priest in years, and the forsaken town of Swallow was hardly his turf. He was waiting for a misstep, an insult to be hurled, or a gun to go off.

"Mary, I was quite taken by your music this evening. You made me think very deeply," said Father Ben.

"Really? I don't mean to doubt you, but I never thought a priest would be able to take me in," said Mary.

"Perhaps you underestimate us; besides, each one of us is different."

"Yes, of course you're right," said Mary. "It's a big mistake to assume anything."

"I see what you're up against, though, and I hope you find an easier way to . . . well . . . it just seems like you've had to carry a lot of pain," said Father Ben.

Thaddeus stepped in and said, "But, Father, you must bear a load of heartache yourself, a priest has so much to shoulder . . . the sorrows and joys of an entire parish. It's hard to fathom. Just thinking of it makes me tired."

"True enough. I have a hunch that you might have something of the priest in you. It takes one to know one, doesn't it?" said Father Ben, looking directly at him. "I guess there's no escaping pain."

"I think you got that right," Thaddeus said. "I've had a rough time with the Catholic Church, or shall I say it's had a rough time with me. I've always loved the symbolism and the music, but . . . well, you know . . ."

"Yes, I do know . . . it's a tough terrain," said Father Ben.

Vincent had ambled over to their circle, and he put his two cents in. "Interesting observations, Father. I think you hit the nail on the head, though; there's enough pain to go around. I'll drink to that. If you ask me, it's empathy that's missing nowadays." The four of them clinked their glasses.

The doorbell rang, and about ten teenagers filed into the party, looking like a pack of lost dogs, and Thaddeus thought he detected a slight wince come across De Sockie's smile as he went over to them.

"Well, well, guys, you made it, come on in," said De Sockie. Under his breath, he added, "Hello, Sarah, nice to see you."

"Hi, Mr. De Sockie," said Sarah, grabbing her boyfriend's arm. "You know Henry Harms, don't you?"

"Oh, yeah, you're a senior, right?"

"Yep," said Henry.

"Where are you headed next year?" said De Sockie, as if he didn't know.

"Harvard," said Henry Harms, displaying a wide grin of perfect teeth.

"Well, been there, done that," said De Sockie, immediately regretting it.

"Really? You went to Harvard?" said Henry.

"No, no. I meant I know how it feels to be going to college; it's exciting," De Sockie said.

Sarah said, "Didn't you say you went somewhere in Ohio?"

"Yeah, that's right, Columbus," said De Sockie, and then,

pretending to hear his name being called, he said, "Listen, gang, come on in and have some food," and he walked into the living room.

Thaddeus was afraid of teenagers, since he'd had several bad scenes on the streets with them, including one incident recently that had almost exploded into a fight. Luckily no one had been harmed, but teenagers were volatile, especially around Thaddeus, and sure enough, he heard one of De Sockie's students whisper, "Oh, my God, that weirdo is here."

Mary, sensing her friend's discomfort, pulled him by the arm into the dining room, where they stood and admired the cake as if it were a Picasso, and that was how they met Adele, who had somehow managed to get herself invited to the party. Thaddeus and Mary listened with great interest as she took credit for making the cake—even though it was really made by the all-night baker, old Joe Stringer. She told them all about her son who was in the St. Louis Philharmonic. They seemed charmed by her story, and Mary told Adele that the tuba was one of her favorite instruments, a remark that managed to leave the older woman with nothing more to say.

The Tennessee Twinsters came barreling out of the kitchen with plates full of beef stew, which was simmering on the stove, and Mary reached out her hand, saying, "Hi, I'm Mary Saint. I missed your set because I was trembling in a classroom down the hall while you were onstage. I heard that it was really great."

Rose said, "Thank you. We watched your show from the

wings; it was inspiring, I have to say. I never saw anything like it, and I dig your outfits, too," she said, eyeing Thaddeus.

Ned rushed in, in an effort to go deeper. "I loved that song "Anklebone of Love Dust" with the line 'the dungeons of my feet,'" he said. "It's such a wicked image." He looked at Thaddeus and said, "And you coming up at the end, marvelous; it seemed completely impromptu. Genius."

One of the teenagers, a boy with thick glasses and a mouthful of braces, who looked young for his age, had wandered into the dining room, and he added, "I didn't know what you meant by that or by most of the things you said; honestly, your songs kind of creeped me out, and some of them were a little bit disgusting."

Bill De Sockie, sensing that a real discussion was about to begin, brought the whole group of kids into the dining room and said, "Mary, I'd like to introduce you to some of my students. They were all at the concert tonight. All year, we've been discussing poetry in our class. Oh, and don't mind Pete, he's always pretty frank." De Sockie felt bad for Pete, who couldn't seem to get a handle on how to talk to people. "Pete, isn't there another way for you to communicate what you're trying to say?"

Pete continued, "No, I'm not trying to make you feel bad, Miss Saint, it's just that I thought your whole presentation was too edgy. For me, I mean. I liked the Tennessee Twinsters a whole heck of a lot more."

Henry Harms spoke up with fierce confidence. "Actually, I didn't find Mary Saint's set edgy enough; it seemed dated."

De Sockie couldn't mask his disdain for the kid. It was bad enough that Sarah Spalding was attached to him like a pocketbook, but the sheer *cockiness* of the guy, especially in relation to Mary Saint; he had no understanding of her work. De Sockie was offended; having gone deeply into her music, he couldn't help but take it all personally. He said, "Uh, Mary is standing right in front of you, you're talking as if she's not even here."

Mary seemed calm and unaffected. "It's interesting," she said, amused. "I could see how you might say that I'm not edgy. I'd describe myself as 'over the edge,' as in *I'm over it*, the edge, if you get my drift. You're a young person, your job is to be on the edge, and I wish you luck with that. You're going to need it, the edge is a sharp and painful place to hang out on."

Nice one, thought Bill De Sockie, although Henry Harms looked right through Mary. He had no use for her, his sights were set way beyond her, and he had no intention of dwelling on the edge, or any such uncomfortable place.

"Does anyone else have any thoughts?" said De Sockie. "I mean, here we've had two completely different acts performing in one evening. On the one hand, you had the Tennessee Twinsters, an up-and-coming country-type band, and then you had Mary Saint, a legendary poet and alternative rocker. Wasn't it a crazy journey, inspiring, just to see the different forms of expression?"

Henry Harms spoke up again. "Yes, yes, but is it art?" he asked, and Bill De Sockie thought he could detect a slight English accent in the kid's remark. Henry added, "I don't know, anybody can get up and sing a bunch of songs."

Eliot Bemblatt had come into the room in search of another glass of wine and was lurking in the corner by the coffeepot when he set his glass down on the table with emphasis, in order to grab the floor. "Is it art?" He laughed. "What the hell . . . are you kidding? The question is: can you sell it? Who cares if it's art? I get a real kick out of that. You'll get over that art crap once you have rent to pay, kid." For some reason, Bemblatt's remark cut through Henry Harms's wall of confidence; it was as if Henry had recognized a kindred spirit in Bemblatt, and he shook his head in something like agreement as he considered the logic of what Bemblatt was saying.

Fred, from Fred's Papers and Mags, adjusted his earpiece and said, "Will somebody tell me what the heck this guy is talking about? He's been yabbering all night and I can't understand a word he's saying." He patted Eliot Bemblatt on the back to indicate he was only kidding.

One of the students, whose long brown hair reached past the hem of her dress, piped up, speaking to Mary. "I thought you were out of this world—magical—and I was so caught up that, when the Blessed Virgin came on the stage, well, I know it's silly, but for a minute I believed it was *her*." She looked at Thaddeus and added timidly, "Don't be mad, but are you a man or a woman?" Thaddeus's eyes darted around nervously. Mary had never seen him this uncomfortable before, but it made perfect sense to her that a group of suburban teenagers would be a lot more threatening to him than a bunch of downtrodden *Tenderloiners*.

Luckily, Jean had slipped into the room to get herself a cup of coffee, having had enough wine after one glass, and happened to overhear the question about Thaddeus. She said, nonchalantly, "Oh, don't worry about him, he's a chocolate tranny," trying out the phrase, which pleased her to no end.

Some of the kids looked at each other, with no idea what that meant. "What?" said Pete with the big glasses and braced teeth. Some of the others rolled their eyes, and the older people, who had been only halfway interested in the conversation, started to filter into the room on the hunt for coffee and cake.

Thaddeus turned to Mary and whispered in her ear, "Sweetie, do you think we could go soon?"

"Of course we can. Let's get the hell out of here."

Later on, back at Jean's house, Jean, Mary, Thaddeus, and Vincent sat exhausted around the kitchen table over cups of lingonberry tea and a small plate of Oreos.

"This is interesting," said Jean, as she tasted the tea.

"It's our drink of choice. We go through gallons of the stuff each week," said Thaddeus. "You know, you two should really come out for a visit sometime."

"There's a thought," said Vincent, popping a cookie in his mouth. "I've never been to San Francisco."

Jean was embarrassed by the notion that she and Vincent might be traveling as a couple and said, "Well, no, I doubt it, we could never leave the home for that long."

"Sure we could," said Vincent.

"That would be fab. We could show you around. It's a beautiful city, and besides, we have an announcement to make," said Mary, nudging Thaddeus and alarming Jean, for it occurred to her at that moment that, on top of everything else, there was a possibility Mary and Thaddeus were somehow getting married, or having a baby, or some unthinkable thing like that, and while she didn't quite know how she would handle that, she braced herself for the next frontier.

"You tell," said Mary.

Jean noticed how strangely beautiful Thaddeus was, how perfectly formed his lips were, and how his cheekbones stood high on his face. She looked at her daughter, and she, too, was beautiful, with so much affection in her eyes as she gazed at Thaddeus. These two are best friends, Jean thought, and it occurred to her, as she glanced over at Vincent sitting in her kitchen, looking like a stuffed teddy bear that was too big for the chair, that they were two pairs of best friends, the four of them.

"Why do you look so worried?" said Mary, reaching to lay her hand on top of her mother's.

"Oh, don't mind me," Jean said. "Let's hear the news."

Thaddeus told Vincent and Jean about the message from Donal Hogan, Mary's old manager from Planet of the Stars, about how the famous rock star Flick Zeez was going to use her songs, but Jean didn't quite understand what it meant. "Who is Flick Zeez?" she asked. "That sounds like a cartoon superhero. I've never heard of him, but I suppose that doesn't mean a thing."

"What it means is, I'm going to get quite a bit of money . . . a bundle. It's very good news, especially because Thaddeus and I have been dreaming about buying a café in San Francisco," Mary explained.

Thaddeus told them about how the Crumb Bunny was on its last legs, having been run into the ground by their boss, Cooper, and how they'd often wished they could buy the place but never figured they'd have the money to do it. Now they could make an offer and see what happened.

"That seems like a great idea," said Vincent. "A sound investment."

Jean was just relieved that they weren't getting married or having a baby, and she said, "That's very nice, very nice."

"Ma, I know it was a rough night for you," said Mary. "I hope you survived the concert without too many bumps and bruises."

Jean looked at her daughter for a moment; she didn't want to lie. "Mary, what can I say? It was a real doozy," she finally admitted. "The concert was way over my head, honey, but so what? The question is, did *you* survive it?"

"You know, oddly, I loved doing the concert. It rang true, you know? Who knows, maybe I'll even do some more, maybe an annual concert at Swallow High," Mary joked.

"Oh, Mary," Jean said and laughed.

"Here's to the holy Saints of Swallow," said Thaddeus, raising his teacup. Vincent put his fat finger and thumb around the fragile handle of his cup and raised it up, too. The men clinked in a spirited toast, and Jean watched as the two antique teacups with the painted blue lilies and rims of gold shattered all over the table and onto the floor.

"Mary and Joseph," she said. "Everyone out of the kitchen, don't touch a thing, you'll all get cuts on your fingers. I'll clean this mess up later."

*Once Thaddeus and Vincent sat on the couch in Jean's liv-*ing room, they fell off to sleep quickly. Thaddeus curled up around a pillow, and Vincent just let his head fall back and allowed himself to snore.

Mary asked Jean to go out on the front steps with her for a moment to get a breath of air.

"Mary, it's late to go outside," said Jean.

"But come and see the moon and stars, they're so pretty, Ma."

Jean had already put her slippers on by then, but she agreed to go out anyway, and when they got outside, they sat down together on the steps. Off in the distance, as if in a conversation, two dogs were barking.

"I have a gift for you," Mary said. "I've had it for years, and I always wanted to give it to you in person. It's been so long since we've seen each other, the years have flown by us, it's hard to believe."

"Yes, I know. It's been lonely sometimes, hasn't it?"

"Yeah, it sure has, but I feel pretty good right now." Mary put her arm around her mother and kissed her on the cheek. "Here's your gift, Ma. But I have to warn you, it's not exactly from me," she said, pulling a small box from her pocket. Jean couldn't imagine what it could be, and she was sorry she didn't have a gift to give back.

When she opened it up, she saw that it was a small, unmarked bottle filled with liquid. Jean wondered if it was some kind of perfume, and she twisted the top off, lifting it to her nose. But it had no smell.

"Mary, what is it?" she asked.

"Well, when I was traveling in Europe years ago, I went to many places. And once, when I was in France, I was close enough to visit the town of Lourdes. It was a real strange place, Ma. A tourist trap, you could say. But I spent the whole day there and I thought of you. I wished that you'd been there with me. This is a bottle of holy water from the grotto where the Blessed Mother visited Saint Bernadette."

Jean was surprised, and Mary could tell that she was moved. "Mary, what a treasure this is," she said quietly. She thought for a moment about her daughter taking the trip to Lourdes in the midst of all her wild travels.

"I knew you would like it. Read the card."

Jean opened the card; on the front of it was the face of a dog that Mary had drawn, and Mary told Jean it was Two Toes. "You'll meet her when you come to San Francisco." Jean read what Mary had written:

From one blessed mother to another . . .

"I'm not sure I understand," said Jean. She could feel her hands shaking just the slightest bit.

"I don't know, Ma. Don't be a coo-coo head. It means you're a blessed mother . . . to me," Mary said.

"Oh dear," said Jean, embarrassed. "I don't know what to say." But she was pleased as punch and knew that, first thing in the morning, she would call Betty to tell her about the holy water that Mary had brought her. "All the way from the town of Lourdes," she'd say. She was sure that Betty would be impressed.

They sat quietly for a while, until Jean started to think that maybe they should go back into the house. But Mary pointed at the moon and said, "Look how bright it is tonight."

"It looks like a giant pearl," said Jean.

"It does," said Mary. "Isn't it great to be outside?"

Jean had to admit, it was. The streets of Swallow were peaceful and quiet. The dogs had stopped their barking. The night air smelled of grass and dirt, and a warm breeze was rustling through the maple trees. The two women sat looking up at the moon and stars. Mary pointed out the different constellations to her mother, and although Jean couldn't really see the shapes, she told Mary that she could.

Special Thanks

To Meg Wolitzer, Gail Hochman, Elisabeth Dyssegaard and the Hyperion team, Susan Brown, Stuey Kohler, and Claudia Lament.
To Family, Friends, and Strangers whose kindness and courage have been inspirational.